The Axiom of Choice

Godfrey Powell

Copyright © 2012 Godfrey Powell
All rights reserved.

ISBN-13: 9871477654507
ISBN-10: 147765450X

For Polly, who deserved better.

I wish to thank Tim Anderson, Frances Joyce, Carl Murray, Patricia Martin, Neil Croally, Kathleen Boyle, David Burns, all my family, and several good friends who prefer to remain anonymous, for all their generous help and encouragement.

Front cover image: The Hourglass Nebula, courtesy of Raghvendra Sahai and John Trauger (JPL), the WFPC2 science team, and NASA/ESA

Preface

I need to assure the reader that all the characters and events depicted in this story are entirely fictitious, as are all the so-called scientific breakthroughs. In particular, the notion of a large-scale quantum anomaly is a complete and utter work of fiction, wholly inconsistent with the foundations of modern Quantum Theory. This has to be of course. The truth is always very much stranger.

Prologue

It had to happen one day. That much at least, the ancients understood. What was less obvious was *when*. But with time, humans learned to forget and dismiss the slow silent evidence of their science. Thus does the inevitable become inconceivable. Such is the human psyche.

Chapter 1

It was a good day to die. Professor Ernst Flaubert rose early, the eastern sky already a deep salmon pink, with high wisps of cirrus cloud heralding a fine warm day. Yesterday, he had paid his bills and posted a few amiable letters to good friends. He felt calm and relieved, relaxed almost, after weeks of tortured doubt. A sudden stab of guilt checked him as he thought once more of René. Slowly, he calmed himself, relief softening his guilt.

Showering briskly, he finished with a scalding purge over his head and back, before roughly towelling himself dry. He stood naked with the cold mountain air sinking gently through the skylight as he studied his face in the mirror. His hair was still thick and dark, and he kept it slicked back, preferring the coolness and simplicity of a clear brow.

The cool breeze soothed his body and calmed his thoughts as he shaved. Ernst had a theory about shaving, as he had on most aspects of life. The razor needs a very particular speed for the best shave; too slow the bristles snag, too fast and they pluck. He set about deriving the equations and calculating the optimum speed, a mental ritual he performed every day. Having arrived at the usual result, he found he had finished his shave. Tomorrow, he would write up his …

Tomorrow? he scolded himself, brushing his teeth noisily. Rinsing his mouth, he reached for the glass shelf above, his hand hovering awkwardly over the little brown bottle, unsure of its authority. He watched it shaking gently, fingers tensed to grip and became vaguely annoyed with himself. He had suffered from rheumatism the last few years after an awkward fall on the ski slopes. Though he doubted the pills had any real effect, he swallowed them dutifully. Only not today, he decided. Nor yesterday, he recalled. Not for over a week perhaps, to judge from the bottle's contents. He stared at the small brown bottle in his hand, delicately groping for the elusive thought that had brushed his mind. It hardly mattered now.

Packing a few things for the climb, his eyes rested on a rugged aluminium case stowed neatly in the corner of his study. Its contents, three small electronic detectors carefully entombed in black anti-static sponge, represented the pinnacle of his life's work. Now when it came to it, he was unable to destroy them as planned – and repeatedly postponed. All the same, he could hardly leave them behind. He thought for a moment and made a decision. Burning his laboratory notebook in the grate, he stirred the embers carefully until the hot turbulent ash crumbled to a fine dust, then spent a final hour checking the home he was about to leave had every expectation of welcoming its owner back by dusk.

The sun was beginning to warm his neck and paint the valley floor a rich buttercup gold, as he walked briskly up the slow incline from the village. Leaving the narrow road at the first hairpin, he took the winding footpath through the trees, a route which in winter months good skiers terrorised with their final schuss into the village. Now in late spring, wild crocus decked the meadows and purple primrose lined the wood's edge.

Once more in the open, he picked his way along the stony path, trekked annually by the docile Swiss Browns as they quit their winter stables for the brief summer months of foraging on the sun-drenched alpine pastures. He envied their simple existence and innocent toil, free from worry and regret. No shame or guilt to cloud their gaze on the world. For a moment he wondered about that; perhaps they too felt hapless and exploited creatures, waiting in resigned fear of an early unfair death.

He tried to shake off the thought, but it caught somewhere within him – early unfair death. He stopped abruptly and turned to survey his progress, his eyes following the road as it meandered its way back to the village. From here the view was stunning and as he gazed, his mood lifted. Over the steeply sloping meadow a pair of red kites probed the early morning air for thermals that would carry them effortlessly up to the high pastures and their first meal of the day.

* * *

Ernst had climbed this hill since his schooldays and even now, thirty years on, it still enchanted him. Its angry streams as the last snows thawed; the first wild flowers of spring, impatient at the snows retreat; his scrambling adventures through the dense pungent forests and steep grounds crisscrossed in a tangle of roots still treacherous after a summer's storm. The pure clean light and ever-changing skyline never failed to revive him and as he climbed steadily higher he felt a familiar sense of peace and certainty engulf him like a great soft blanket and his anxieties melt away. He wondered idly if he could capture the magic somehow with technology. There would be a ready market for the hapless crowds struggling in the big cities around the world.

His goal was now in sight. Not the summit itself, but a small ledge teetering two hundred metres above the glacier below. His eyes followed the sheer plunge down the granite wall, long ago worn smooth by glaciers many times more impressive than the present occupant. Though he had scaled the summit many times before, only twice had he dared venture onto the ledge. Once as a child, in wilful spite of his mother, who had scolded him over some long-forgotten misdemeanour. And once again, four years ago with René.

He sat down on a smooth boulder to study the view and reached into his backpack for something to eat. His sudden appetite surprised him as he bit hungrily into a crusty roll, thick with unsalted butter, schwarzbrot and salami. Leaning back against the rock he started to think. At this altitude, a two hundred metre fall takes about seven seconds, followed by a high velocity impact at something like two hundred kilometres per hour. While soft and fluffy on holiday postcards, glacial ice is as hard as rock on impact. Nevertheless, at that speed, momentum ensured his mangled body would neatly bury itself, reappearing only thousands of years later at the foot of the glacier. He hoped this would not inconvenience the canton authorities too much.

He laughed gently at his own black humour and choked abruptly on a breadcrumb. Visions of prematurely asphyxiating himself set him off again until he laughed so hard his belly retched and his ribs ached. Wiping away the tears he tried to recall when he laughed with such abandon. The sudden recollection sobered him and he fell to a quiet stillness. Waves of joy and sadness lapped over him in quick succession. Something was coming out, slackening its suffocating grip and releasing his mind. Long-lost childhood memories welled up inside him and a deep longing filled his chest. For the first time in months he felt utterly at peace and fearless.

* * *

He woke with a start at some unresolved sound. Sitting up, he looked about but could see nothing to alarm. He glanced at his watch and was surprised to learn he had slept only briefly, twenty minutes at most, but a lifetime of comfort and solace today. Gathering his things he set off again. Thin ice and frost remained where sunlight had not penetrated. The punctuated views from here were breathtaking but he paid them scant attention, for now his mind was alive with urgent thoughts and memories as he relived the last six months. Little coincidences flirted briefly then parted. Why had he got so bogged down?

The quantum blister problem, obviously. A batch of detectors his group had spent the best part of three years perfecting for a CERN experiment, had been returned unusable. It was a major setback for the group but disastrous for his personal standing. Close examination revealed minute electronic blisters on the main detector surface, a sliver of pure quartz crystal. While tiny, measuring only a few hundred atoms across, the blisters rendered the device useless for CERN's purposes and the group had lost the contract.

Then an unexpected internal report criticising the quality of his leadership, closely followed by another loss of funding, sent him reeling and before he realised, he suffered a mild nervous breakdown. At least, that was what the doctor had written – six months complete rest. As far as Ernst was concerned, it was little more than an untimely viral infection and the doctor was a fool. Nevertheless, he had gone begging to the Dean for two weeks sick leave. To his surprise, he was told to take as long as necessary and not to worry about his work. Professor Rheinhalter would look after everything in his absence. And there it was. Herr

Professor Doctor Doctor Gerhard Rheinhalter, as his nameplate carefully informed.

Slimeball, René called him. An unsavoury piece of work for sure, but every large organisation has one. But in the end, his group had simply run out of time and money, and it was the university who abandoned him. That very afternoon he was called for interview with the Dean and Faculty. No notice, no agenda, no neutral witness. Just coffee and cake they said.

He arrived dishevelled and unshaven. A last minute attempt to smooth his hair with distilled water only made him appear quietly deranged and a little dangerous. A cadaver out of formaldehyde, he heard one cruel whisper. How was Ernst, these days? Well, thank you. Any news of funds? No, not yet, but very hopeful. They seemed unimpressed. And the ... crystal anomaly (they avoided his more prosaic term, quantum blister). Any progress there? He hesitated, drawing a deep breath. Slimeball was studying him intently. No, no real breakthrough yet. But many useful and extremely interesting results which, given a little ...

You realise Ernst, we do not call you away from your experiments just for coffee. We wish to help you, get you restarted. We would like to offer you an exciting new post. Ernst was genuinely taken aback. A deep sense of relief and guilt suffused his features as he acknowledged a sceptical trait within himself to think the worst of his colleagues.

Ernst, the university recognises your unique administrative skills. You will be responsible for the international collaboration of a large number of leading research groups. Your salary is of course suitably enhanced. Think about it Ernst, gifted and ambitious young scientists, all working at the cutting edge of high-energy physics. Ernst, we need someone like you with your knowledge, experience and energy to drive the project to success. A big responsibility Ernst, but we have absolute confidence in you. It's a fast moving world Ernst, and we need your decision quickly – today, in fact.

He watched them nodding encouragingly. Somewhat to one side of the group, Slimeball kept his eyes trained on him like a predator, reading his every thought, interpreting every gesture and shrug. He felt layers of guarded vagueness peel away under the intense gaze. In his mind he heard friends and colleagues urging him to accept. Give up the unequal struggle Ernst, proudly taken to the wire. Admit for once your obstinacy has failed you. Give up the unholy mess and settle down to a long secure sunset behind a desk.

And then, just when he thought he could hold out no longer, they ran out of steam. Only the Dean continued droning on about the wonderful opportunities at the hub of European research. Obviously Ernst, there is much work to be done, and very little time. Groups need to be assembled and of course, your laboratory will require a complete refit ...

He had taken them completely by surprise, so for an instant they were silent and transfixed, like a grotesque family photo stolen at the wrong moment. The Dean sat frozen in mid flow, mouth half open, lips twisted in an ugly purple pout. His timing was impeccable, though Ernst was completely unaware of his actions. He shot out of his seat with an explosive anger, the chair cart-wheeling backwards into the coffee trolley, shattering a flask in an explosion of steam across the hot plate. At the same time his long abandoned coffee recoiled in the opposite direction along a graceful parabola that Newton himself would have admired, coffee, cup and saucer appearing to part company at the apex of their flight as if seeking independent targets, as they plunged in formation towards their stunned victims.

By now the less turgid members of the panel were beginning to recover from their slumbers with a slow backing-off manoeuvre, disbelief etched across their faces and arms outstretched at peculiar angles. Only the Dean remained resolutely at his station, shouting, determined to finish his piece. We therefore need your decision by 5pm, after that we reserve the right to ...

He heard no more, having stormed into the door which burst open on its hinges with an explosive crump, then rebounded shut behind him, leaving some witnesses with the impression of gun shots. A numbed silence fell over the building, as it waited breathlessly for the next sound. Nothing stirred, not until Ernst found himself trembling in front of his laboratory door. *Bastards!* he shouted, causing a passing student to jump and burst into tears.

* * *

Then a strange thing happened. Far from haunting him, the blister phenomenon began to intrigue him. Now, with the group disbanded and working alone in the peace of his own home, he set about reviewing everything they had discovered during the last few frantic months, when they had fought against time to repair the detectors. He compiled a large chart mapping every result, every unexplained observation and inconsistency. Like a detective searching for a breakthrough, he judged no clue insignificant. He colour coded the data: red for his group's results, blue for everyone else's, green for where theory and observation agreed. Where one result depended on another, he drew a connecting line, weighted with the degree of uncertainty. Thick meant fairly definite, thin tentative. Dashed meant dubious or possibly even wrong.

He assembled the spare equipment he kept at home and began checking wherever he could, grunting with satisfaction at each new confirmation and insight. He whooped wildly one day when repeated checks proved a particularly ugly part of the chart was wrong, taking a childish delight in pasting over a corrected version. Would CERN reconsider their decision, he enquired discreetly. They declined again, politely. The word was the good professor had lost it. He let them believe what they wanted. The truth was, he was captivated with the blister phenomenon and CERN no longer seduced him.

Long hours and snatched meals caused him to lose weight. His face grew gaunt and grey, his eyes rimmed with orange hollows, his dress a far cry from the sharp professional air he once fostered. He took to spending all day in his slippers, or trainers, on the rare occasions he ventured out for supplies. But none of it mattered. He was working harder and more effectively than ever before, reliving the single-minded determination of his student days. He felt twenty years younger.

After a week of meticulous checking, he lay the finished chart on the floor of his hallway and bounded upstairs to survey it, leaning over the banister railing. The detail was not evident from here but now other aspects became apparent. Some areas seemed oddly sparse, others annoyingly choked with detail. In one area a suspiciously large number of results hung precariously by a single thread, like a ... the analogy alluded him. Absurdly, he fetched his binoculars and was startled to find the single point of support formed one of the least corroborated results on the chart. The whole effect lent an ugly lop-sidedness to the picture, as if God had mucked up somewhere with one of the equations.

When he slept that night he dreamt of the chart, and in a moment of cosmic insight solved the entire problem. He phoned René excitedly with the news, the key breakthrough that tied the whole edifice together in perfect symmetry and elegance. Suddenly René was there with him, sitting on the bed, breathlessly discussing the implications of his discovery with childlike enthusiasm. But when he woke excitedly the next morning his insight turned to slushy illusion, and René was nowhere to be seen.

And then, only yesterday, he heard through a distant relative she had quit her cottage and transferred to another university. Suddenly the whole adventure collapsed around him like the cardboard camps of his childhood. He saw what everyone else had seen all along, the sad desperate cry for help of an old man whose talent was fading. He painfully recalled the poster Slimeball had hung in the student's lobby with a knowing malice. *Respect is to be earned – not assumed.*

Nobody, least of all René, had the slightest interest in his lonely struggle. He spent the afternoon tidying up, dismantling the equipment and stowing it carefully away. He folded the chart neatly and laid it on top of his wardrobe. Then he wrote a few grateful letters to long neglected friends and another to René, care of her parents, thanking her for her valued friendship and collaboration over the years, assuring her he understood completely and that it was indeed the sensible and responsible thing to do. And then he went to bed.

* * *

Resuming now his climb, he saw with the clarity of defeat, how a basic tenet of experimental science had dogged their progress every step of the way. His recent theoretical investigation had convinced him the blister phenomenon was critically dependent on two coincident events. As good experimentalists, they had varied just one factor at a time, whereas forsaking orthodox science, they ought to have checked the effect of varying two factors simultaneously. He marvelled how obvious it seemed now and wondered idly why none of them had thought of it.

Well, it would be easy enough to check. It wasn't his idea of course, but a famous experiment that had changed the course of scientific history: a beautiful definitive experiment with a beautiful, definitive result. And now, either through good fortune or insight, he was in a position to set the whole thing going. He was happy their ledge would be part of the story. It was certainly no Pic du Midi, but definitely high enough to show a measurable effect.

He reached his destination, as usual recalling little of the climb, not even the last few spine-tingling steps onto the ledge itself, acute awareness returning only when he found himself crouching over his backpack, staring down through two hundred metres of thin mountain air onto the dazzling white ice sheet below. For a moment he froze, fearing his balance might desert him, before slowly easing himself back against the hard rock face, weak and trembling.

After a long silent moment he sighed loudly, eventually recalling the purpose of his climb. He lifted his head slowly and gazed across the valley; it was a scene he wished to remember the rest of his life. Come on Ernst, he said to himself finally, there are things to do, and with that he began to unpack. The Ferryman, he decided, would just have to wait.

Chapter 2

"Hello David, come in," said Professor Bennet, nodding to one of the plastic chairs. "How are we getting on?"

"Good. I've had a new idea on the blister formation, but I need a better laser. I rang Julian Peters in nuclear engineering and he's looking through their old stock."

"Yes, I know. I've just had his boss bellowing down the phone at me. David, we're in the process of pulling all this together now, not starting out on another open-ended enquiry. Have you forgotten I am presenting a review paper next month?"

"We have plenty of results, they just don't make much sense at the moment. That's allowed in science."

"It may be good science David, but this is the real world. We need answers."

"We're missing something, a key piece in the jigsaw. The more bits we have, the more chance we have of putting it all together. It's an evolving process. It's good science."

"I'm afraid the evolving process has reached the end of its gene line, David. Extinction."

"What do you mean? We still have ten months funding left. That's all I need."

"No, David, I'm sorry. To be exact, we have fourteen months funding to *explain*. You've been spending someone else's money, a two year research grant for studying the neutrino deficiency problem."

"Well, so what? And who cares? It's just an admin game, groups do it all the time. The airheads on the grant allocation committee wouldn't know a positron from a potato … What do you mean, *explain*?"

"Those airheads as you put it, do seem to know the difference, only too well in fact. I have been asked to report our progress on neutrino deficiency, you know, the problem we've just spent fourteen months researching. Now they have decided to poke around in other areas. The entire faculty of Physical Science is to be externally audited, going back over five years. It may be just an administrative game to you David, but it's a game we are about to lose."

"David, the blister work is dead and your results will show it died fourteen months ago. You have four weeks to complete fourteen months of experiments on your delinquent fucking neutrinos. Now is that clear enough for you?"

"That's unfair, you can't lay all this on me. I'm just a postgraduate."

"Look David, I like you tremendously. You're a gifted student with a wonderfully original mind. One day you may become a great scientist and discover something truly amazing. I gave you your head on the blister work because you were such a good student and because you went about it with tremendous energy and enthusiasm. I made a mistake – the problem was simply too fierce for you. You didn't stand a chance, for all sorts of reasons. But right now you are, as you put it, just a postgraduate – a postgraduate with an unfinished and long overdue thesis, to be brutally frank."

"That's so unfair. Science doesn't happen like that, you know it doesn't. You can't plan breakthroughs. Faraday washed up test tubes for a living, doing his experiments in a cupboard after hours. His great work wasn't on anyone's budget. Newton didn't write a business plan on gravity, he figured it out whilst hiding from the plague. Einstein did his best work doubling as a second grade filing clerk. No one knows how or when breakthroughs will happen, if they did you could program a bloody committee to do it, instead of sitting around on their fannies all day long, wasting money set aside for real science."

"Well thank you, David, for the lecture on how real science is done, I guess we never knew that. And when you figure out how to do real science in the real world, perhaps you would be so kind as to lecture us on that too. In the meantime, I have some serious arse-licking to do. In the real world that is. Now get out."

* * *

He had decided to take the boat-train, at least, that's what his mother always called it. A strange decision really, since he could probably have wangled a plane ticket out of bloody Bennet. Anyway, it gave him time to think. Losing your career and girlfriend on the same day was generally considered something to think about.

As the train pulled out of Victoria station he gazed down river towards Big Ben. The tourist season was in full swing, with boat tours plying up and down the muddy Thames and fast food outlets selling awful food at unbelievable prices. He stared at the dilapidated power station and its surrounding scrap yards and wondered what on earth the tourists made of it all, their first glimpse of a great capital city. Perhaps it was just as well they flew everywhere these days. A glam girl tottered past with a ludicrously large suitcase on tiny wheels and after a pantomime of ineffectual patting, managed to manoeuvre it into the luggage space between the seats. She sat down opposite him, flushed and smiling. He ignored her, staring morosely out the window.

Long before the train pulled into Dover, he jumped up abruptly, unable to take a further three rounds in the suitcase challenge. Pulling his holdall from the overhead rack, he started towards the front of the train. One of the first passengers off, he made his way across the crumbling concrete apron towards a line of improvised barriers.

"May I see your passport sir?" someone called out brightly, as he passed what seemed a large plastic wheelie bin. He fished out his papers and laid them on the shelf, running his finger absently along its flaking edge while the official examined his passport from cover to cover.

For some reason the 'sir' thing always bothered him, sounding hollow and vaguely provocative. He wondered if it came naturally with the job, or whether they had to practise it in training. The young customs officer was warming to his task now, at one point even turning the passport upside down, apparently willing something incriminating to fall out. David imagined at any moment he would hear the words ' … and what do we have here, sir?'

"And what is the nature of your journey sir?" The man seemed hell bent on remaining polite and interested, officially at least.

"Seeing a friend," he replied at last, retrieving his passport and moving off.

"Just one moment, sir," the official called after him. David turned and marched back to the kiosk. The officer handed him his travel documents. "You may find these useful sir."

"Thank you," David offered, grudgingly. The two considered each other for a moment, leaving David with the distinct impression he had been found guilty of harbouring illegal thoughts.

"Enjoy your stay in Zürich, Mr King."

* * *

At Calais he boarded a train and seated himself across from a humourless old man who looked like he could be trusted not to be pleasant. He'd have to change at Paris, but at least now the train was clean and quiet, and he could start to relax.

He pulled out a paperback, but quickly gave up after two attempts, glancing irritably at the back cover. It was all he could find in the rush – one of Christine's. One she said he *needed* to read, as if you could do much else with a book. It hardly looked inspiring, one flower and a half-finished coffee on the front cover. Idly, he wondered if she'd actually read it herself. He couldn't remember her ever reading very much. Come to think of it, he couldn't remember her doing very much either.

Apart from sex. She certainly did that, though never at his place. She had a small flat in Kensington, something her father had bought to help her find herself. It was all a bit of a trek, which made things awkward when it got late. In fact, the only time he ever saw her angry, was when he mentioned starting back before the tubes shut, in order to be at the lab first thing in the morning. She flared up so violently he had difficulty recalling what he could possibly have done to upset her. Anyway, she calmed down after a while, and in the end he did stay, though it was never quite the same.

Whether that still rankled with her, he had no idea. But the fact was only yesterday, when he talked about living with her, she purposefully held up her hand and waggled her fingers. He had wondered once or twice about her boyfriends of course, and even thought of raising the subject on occasion, but when he finally managed a lame 'wasn't that a bit sudden' she shouted angrily at him.

She had worn the engagement ring for three months apparently. Obviously he must have seen it, but just thought it one of her *things*. Anyway, she quietened down after a bit and became quite friendly again, even cooking him a pork chop, though cooking wasn't her greatest assets. Then inexplicably, she took him to bed, just for old time's sake she said.

* * *

At Paris there was time for a leisurely stroll around the station, but it seemed in a worse state than Victoria, so he settled himself into a quiet bistro for another stab at the book. By the third page he felt a definite sense of progress but then stumbled into a long intimate narrative of somebody's scarf.

He patiently scanned the previous page for clues. Evidently the scarf was destined to play a key role in the plot, perhaps saving the president's life or something. A young mother feeding her toddler at a nearby table, smiled when she saw his book. I mean, it's not like it adds to the plot. What was the point, he wondered. Just then, he snorted loudly and slapped the book down, this time for good. He glanced around, absently fingering the table edge. The child had evidently decided to play tennis with its food, causing the young mother to morph into freight plane ferrying mashed chips to the child's mouth. He studied the little domestic scene while his fingers investigated a small bubble in the table's trim.

"Don't forget your book," she called after him as he strolled off. He turned bemused, retracing his steps to the abandoned paperback. "Wonderfully sensitive writer," she breathed, looking knowingly into his eyes.

* * *

The intercom buzzed angrily. "Simon, have you got a moment?" It was a not really a question, and as the circuit died instantly, it scarcely expected an answer. Besides, being private secretary to the right honourable Hugh Mallison, Home Secretary to Her Majesty's Government, Simon Hamilton-Jenkins possessed an unlimited supply of moments for his boss. Such muted code, such clipped and understated command of the English language, so quintessentially middle England, was exactly what Simon adored about his job. As was the total lack of sincerity with which such powerful men held sway over their subjects.

The home secretary was on the phone and dismissed Simon to a distant sofa. A tall, broad shouldered man, invariably dark suited, he had been hewn in tender years from the sadness and restraint of his nanny's threadbare carpet. Boarding from an early age, he emerged a finely-honed loveless teenager, toughened on the muddy flints of England's most exclusive playing fields. Thin sandy hair, washed blue eyes and a soft girlish complexion, conspired numbingly with a forbidding presence, perfected with years of careful mimicry.

With the essential political niceties had come other skills; shameless flattery, obscurantism and a startling rudeness, which admiring subordinates obligingly dismissed as a mild form of Aspergers syndrome, a condition he could effect effortlessly whenever charm and logic failed his purpose. As the political climate shifted about him, he aligned himself with the greater public good as he saw it, even if the greater public did not. Sad distant memories of a small boy, lost in a hateful world and crying silently for his mother, faded over the years and rarely disturbed him now, surfacing only when his wife demanded some assurance of his humanity.

"Yes, Zürich. Some zealous passport official. New boy, apparently. Keen. Suspects everyone, I shouldn't wonder. Drive down to Dover and crucify him. Everything he remembers or suspects. Then give him a nice pat on the back." The minister slammed down the phone.

"What do you make of this?" he barked at Simon. "Sit down and read, and don't be all day." A thin buff file spun through the air towards him. Simon glanced at the file's title and protocol and skipped through its contents – a few crudely typed sheets and a handwritten note on faded blue cartridge, signed one C. J. Peterson. As he read the letter he tried to gauge the minister's mood. No lengthy waffle Simon, thank you very much. No flippant remarks either, he decided.

"Where's the distribution sheet, minister?"

"Mind your own damned business. Some crank at Aldermaston, with nothing better to do, finds a chip in his crystal. Presumably just after eating his lunch." The minister smiled at his lame joke. Simon smiled also.

"He's due for retirement, riddled with cancer, but wants us to set him up with a nest egg. In return he'll show us how to dig up the crown jewels wherever we damn well care to look." The minister was evidently very upset.

"So what did we do?" persisted Simon cautiously.

"DO!" barked the minister. "Do what we always bloody do, I shouldn't wonder. Bugger all! Come on Simon, it's fifteen years ago, how should I know? Pat him on the back, I imagine, then slap him in the face with the official secrets act. He dies soon after."

"Not a lot to go on, sir."

"Well there is now! Read this lot. American of course, so don't go flashing it to your Russian boyfriend. That's what they want us to know, of course. How far are they really with these confounded blisters?"

Evidently he was dismissed. Simon stood up and picked up the bundle of shiny plastic files. The minister stabbed a button on his console.

"Ms Carrington, kindly ask Mrs Peterson to step this way."

* * *

"Will someone kindly inform me, in plain English, what a Lagrangian point is?" The prime minister's direct question brought a timely silence to the room, rapidly extinguishing all conversation and eye contact. It was a little game he chose to play occasionally to keep his ministers alert and flush out the shirkers. It also rather conveniently set the tone of the meeting.

He carefully surveyed his assembled ministers, most of whom were now fully occupied arranging their papers, the more experienced among them effecting an air that perhaps someone more junior might adequately field the blatantly factual enquiry. The prime minister smiled his faintest of smirks. He knew them so well, as from time to time, he cared to remind them.

"Apparently, prime minister," his PA offered eventually, "it is a point in space where a satellite can hover indefinitely over the planet." There was a general murmur of consensus, as weighty ministerial heads rose fractionally in formation.

"And will somebody please tell me whose damn satellite it is then, hovering indefinitely over us?"

"We don't know, prime minister. The Americans believe it to be Chinese, but only because they know we could never have put it there. Presumably they checked first to make sure it wasn't one of their own." There was a desultory snort around the table.

"Then do we perhaps know how long it's been there," the prime minister continued icily.

"No sir. It is too small and distant to have been detected before, even with radar. It was found six months ago by research student, transiting a faint star that was being studied for some obscure reason. Even then it was assumed to be an electronic glitch, but when it happened again, someone decided to check."

"Perhaps Tompkins, you should tell us what they found."

"At first it was thought to be just a rock, which happened to find itself in this peculiar orbit."

"I thought you said it was hovering, not orbiting?"

"Well, yes sir. Seen from the Earth, it is orbiting, just like the Moon. But viewed from space, prime minister, it maintains perfect formation with us and the Moon, like the three points of an equilateral triangle." He hurried on before the prime minister could make some personal joke of his own eternal triangle.

"There are five altogether, Lagrangian points that is. This one is designated L4. There's another, L5, also occupying the same orbit as the Moon, but sixty degrees behind. The other three occur at various points along the Earth-Moon line. They were predicted by the French mathematician Joseph Louis Lagrange, who in seventeen ..."

"That's quite enough, thank you," cut in the prime minister, well aware Tompkins might go on a good hour reciting the long but factually meagre report. "So has anyone checked to see if there are another four satellites, all peering down at us from these god-given vantage points?"

"Er, no prime minister!"

"Then I suggest that is something we might be usefully doing. Now, what do we know about L4, besides its highly imaginative name?"

Tompkins was well aware that by confusing the object's name with its orbit, the prime minister was probably making history at that very moment, but thought better than to remark on it. Later the French, predictably, would strongly object to the muddled reference, but by then it would be too late; L4 would already be an immutable part of the planet's history.

"There are two known facts, prime minister. In a last minute change of plan, NASA obtained some close-up photographs by rerouting one of its Mars probes. It turns out the object is the size of a bus and the shape of an irregular potato. It's so small and dim that even at closest approach the pictures reveal very little detail, just a few small craters. So they decided to take a pot shot."

"They did what!"

"Yes Sir! They fired a lump of copper at it, hoping to analyse the impact flash using spec ... spectroscopy."

"Do tell me they missed, Tompkins," urged the prime minister, hardly able to contain himself.

"Well, no sir, scored a direct hit. They're still analysing the results of course, but first indications are that it is ... just a lump of rock."

"And now our Chinese friends seem intent on blowing it to smithereens. Has everyone gone completely mad?"

"The odd thing about the flyby sir, was the probe found itself slightly off-course after the encounter, as if it had been gravitationally nudged by an object of far greater mass, something like a small asteroid."

"A haemorrhoid?" bawled the secretary for defence, not picking up on the more ominous tone of the discussion.

Tompkins ploughed dutifully on. "Someone has done a calculation sir, and it seems the deflection is consistent with a total mass of over nine thousand tons. It ought to be substantially larger, if it were made from ordinary rock." There was a pause around the table, as ministers struggled to absorb the significance of this fact.

"And now it seems the object is only too visible, flashing hypnotically in red and green for all and sundry to see."

"Red to port, green to starboard?" asked the defence minister, facetiously.

"Hardly visible sir, it's still a telescopic object and you need to know exactly where to look. It's also flashing on and off in radar," Tompkins added quietly, "the military people seem quite upset about it." The flippant mood of the meeting had vanished for good. Even the defence minister looked thoughtful.

* * *

Exactly a week after his climb, Ernst woke eagerly and slipped contentedly into his early morning routine. As he shaved he considered the theory that people develop routines to save themselves from thinking too much. But Ernst loved his routines, freeing his mind from the daily chores of existence and allowing his thoughts to wander freely.

Undirected time, the young professors pretentiously called it, though for Ernst it was more like dreaming. And while he had little control over the direction of his thoughts, his wide-awake mind was free to follow its meanderings, sometimes delighting in the most unexpected questions and insights. As a young boy he recalled being greatly troubled by the process, believing he could intercept telepathic messages and wondering what to do with the knowledge. His mother told him he was a bit of a dreamer and not to worry so much.

As a youngster too, he would invariably run everywhere. These days he contented himself with brisk walks and hill climbing. He might walk half the morning engrossed in thought, unconscious to the passage of time. It frightened him sometimes, but today he was happy to give his mind free rein. It had been a gruelling week, testing his thesis and checking its conclusions. Now he knew for certain he understood the blister formation. Soon he would have the definitive evidence and then it would just be a matter of writing it up and telling the world of his discovery. He turned abruptly to survey his progress.

Down the valley a bright red speck detached itself from a bend in the road and moved nimbly up the hill, disappearing behind a small clump of larch. He waited with detachment, absently counting off the paces before the figure appeared, but after a full minute there was still no sign of her. Perhaps he had missed it, or just imagined the whole thing? He dismissed his doubts almost immediately. Whatever else was happening, his powers of observation were still excellent. The girl had evidently stopped for a reason. And why not? So had he.

Continuing his climb, he wondered at what point in his train of thought he had decided the hiker was a young woman. The relaxed and easy progress suggested someone fit perhaps, and the bright red jacket possibly female, but at this distance it was pure speculation. Perhaps something at the subconscious level had stirred within him.

Or perhaps it was all wishful thinking, pure and simple. Good god, he was turning into a randy old goat. The thought brought a wry smile to his lips and lightness to his step. He happily accepted it as yet another encouraging sign of recovery. Besides, if she was heading for the top he would give her a run for her money. The old goat knew a few shortcuts to the usual tourist tracks.

He mused lightly on his climb the previous week. His interview with the Dean had been a disaster of course. And though it seemed anything but a turning point at the time, something had clicked, some innocuous part of the human jigsaw had slipped discreetly into place. The Dean clearly found him an embarrassment and had precipitated him into resigning. But Slimeball kept his own agenda and for reasons known only to himself, was out to stop him.

Rheinhalter was known to play hard ball, cultivating substantial links with powerful multinationals. But if Slimeball was out to stop him, there had to be a reason and inevitably the reason had to be expensive. But by inference, that meant he was suddenly worth stopping, which begged an interesting question. A question for which Ernst could find no interesting answer.

Anyway, soon it would all be irrelevant. By good fortune and a little insight, he had stumbled upon a train of thought which led him to formulate a decisive experiment. Though barely a glimmer in his mind's eye at the time, after six days of calculation he had arrived at an incredible conclusion. A complete and definite theory which fitted all the available facts and which could be tested by a simple definitive experiment, the key element of which he was now rapidly approaching.

His discovery would have immense repercussions for the world of science and humanity as a whole. Having written up his discovery he would offer it freely to the world, first over the internet, then through the more sombre deliberations of the *Journal of Condensed Matter*. And then he would make his peace with René.

Reaching the ledge and rummaging through his knapsack he came upon his mobile phone, and declaring it a fine day for impulse, decided to ring her with the news. All the same, he was quite relieved to merely leave a message, fearing even now his courage might fail him on hearing her wounded tones. He spoke briskly, hinting he had discovered something important. One more definitive test and everything would be fine.

Realising almost immediately the insensitivity of his call after weeks of not hearing a word from him, but no doubt fully informed of the embarrassing scenes at work, he dialled again. After an awkward pause, he said simply that he loved her, always had done, since the very first day they met. And for the first time in his life, he knew exactly what to do. He was repacking when his eyes slowly focussed on something which rooted him to the spot.

* * *

She stood smiling and motionless, completely at ease. Lean and tanned, she wore a small black top tucked neatly into tight jeans. Her face showed no trace of makeup but her deep chestnut hair was short and lightly waxed back.

"My name is Pheona Curtis. I study at the *Poly*," she offered at last, her arm outstretched as if attending a cocktail party. Ernst carefully straightened, staring at her. He tried to take in the scene, an attractive young English girl with soft brown smiling eyes, two hundred metres up a precipitous cliff. She stood upright, knees slightly bent, a bright red jacket casually draped over her shoulder.

"You are Professor Ernst Flaubert, from the science faculty? You gave a seminar on solidstate physics. I was utterly captivated."

"I never forget a face," she offered by way of explanation, still motionless with her arm extended.

"I thought perhaps you needed some help." She smiled again, wondering how long she might have to keep this going. At last he began to move towards her, shuffling slowly around his knapsack, his right hand high and flat against the wall.

"You certainly get a marvellous view from here," she added breezily, gazing around. She smiled again, her perfect white teeth parted slightly in open friendship. He had nearly reached her and could smell her light scent on the breeze.

"Forgive me," he said. "Yes. I am Professor Flaubert," and slowly extended his hand. She leant forward demurely to take it, bending a little more at the knees. As she leant forward, her jacket slipped from her shoulder.

"Oops," she giggled, as they both lurched instinctively to catch it. The professor reached out, slightly over-balancing, the smooth material slipping through his outstretched fingers. The girl also reacted, her hand missing the jacket but catching instead his elbow then slipping down his forearm until her long fingers clamped securely round his wrist.

"Oh my God," she screamed, tipping forwards and shooting out a foot to steady herself, bringing it heavily down on his boot. She opened her mouth to apologise but no sound came out, or if it did, the professor didn't hear it. Instead he strained backwards against the wall. But now the silly girl was panicking, pulling him forwards until his weight transferred to his trapped foot. Desperately, he struck out with his free boot against the wall to halt his forward tip, yelling frantically for the girl to relax and let go of his wrist. Instead, she grew more hysterical, arching her back powerfully. He felt his boot about to slip as he looked pleadingly into her eyes.

A pair of cold brown eyes stared menacingly back, then softened as she lowered her gaze. He was on the point of tipping, unable to lean back and unwilling to lean any further forwards. Every fibre of his body strained back towards the safety of the wall, causing the tendons of his neck to stand out and his eyes to narrow.

The girl's gaze came to rest on his undefended crotch. Already, her left boot was slicing through the air, tensing her thigh muscles to power the blow, her eyes directing one last careful adjustment. Her boot connected with a sickening thud, as following through with her leg locked rigidly from the hip, she sank her last remaining momentum into him.

Tipping slowly forwards, his knee buckled as his mouth worked frantically around a soundless scream. His right foot, still locked against the wall, now served only to roll him out over the edge. She gazed steadily into his dumbfounded eyes, her fingers gently releasing their grip on his departing company.

Chapter 3

The next day's meeting was much more businesslike as ministers vied unashamedly for greater responsibility. Attention centred on how best to handle the press and public opinion once the story broke. What the discussion may have lacked in scientific integrity it more than made up for in massaged egos and astute political manoeuvring.

The whole affair was turning out far more manageable than previously feared. It was decided that the British, American, Russian and Chinese governments should, as a matter of urgency, discuss and agree a treaty of mutual cooperation for the exploration of space in and around the L4 object, so that in the event of the news becoming public knowledge, the four superpowers could announce a new era in international cooperation. Peace, collaboration and international investment were the bywords for everyone concerned.

The prime minister in particular was very pleased with himself. He was very much a behind the scenes man. Frequently portrayed in the press as an amiable old fool, he was content to let his cabinet have their way, gently nudging his ministers as events unfolded. Amiable he certainly was, though only in the public gaze. And a trifle old perhaps in looks, a characteristic he deployed shamelessly to detract from his encyclopaedic and devious mind. But he was certainly nobody's fool and by the time the meeting wound up he had decided on what to do and who to do it.

He liked to believe he made decisions instinctively, at the subconscious level. He was rarely proved wrong in his judgements and was quietly proud of his ability, but had the wisdom not to probe its workings too closely. He was mindful of other great leaders whose air of vague disinterest was often mistaken for the aura remote calm and authority at moments of crisis. Lately, he had begun to sense the tug of destiny.

The home secretary cleared his throat, rudely interrupting the prime minister's reveries. "Prime minister, has everyone forgotten this object is anything but a simple lump of rock? For one thing it's as heavy as the largest destroyer afloat, which means that if it ever did fall to earth it could take out a major city. At the same time, it's a whole lot more than just a lump of rock. Rocks do not flash on and off in mesmerising colour and they certainly do not disappear off our radar screens at will."

There was a discernable shift in the mood of the meeting once more, as the prime minister, inwardly grimacing, made a mental note to shift the home secretary himself at the earliest opportunity. Euro minister for Fisheries and Food seemed about right. "An excellent point, Hugh. Thank you. The home secretary reminds us, ladies and gentlemen, that we must retain an open mind on this phenomenon. Indeed, I am appointing Hugh to head a select committee to urgently pursue such questions. It needs to be thorough, leave no stone – or rock – unturned. Preliminary report to cabinet please Hugh, Tuesday morning. Clearly, such an undertaking will permit scant time for your cabinet duties: I might well have to allocate further assistance as your task grows," the prime minister beamed, looking meaningfully round the table. Now, are there any *important* points?"

Apparently there were none, for he continued without discernable pause. "May I then suggest we adjourn? Good day, ladies and gentlemen."

* * *

At Zürich Hauptbahnhof, David caught the first available bus to the *Poly* and headed straight for the physics faculty, slipstreaming behind a group of bored students ambling along to their next lecture. Tucking his small bundle of books and papers tightly under his arm, he followed their slow ambling progress up the steps and across the wide marble foyer towards the stair well.

"Einen moment, bitte!" a woman called out abruptly from behind. He continued steadily on, fearing a hesitation now might prove awkward. There was a scurry of footsteps and a hand grabbed at his elbow. He swung round, pulling on his most indignant face, and was surprised to find a young student peering up at him.

"I think maybe you drop something?" she said, smiling sweetly and holding out Christine's decidedly unscientific novel. "Perhaps the lecture is more interesting with this?" she mused, with delicately arched eyebrows. Smiling in relief, he muttered her a thanks, and jammed the book back amongst his papers, wondering whether it had developed some dark malignant power over him. Sensing she was about to discuss its powerful and sensitive writing, he began to excuse himself.

But she was having none of it. "Quick, or we are late," she said impenetrably, taking his arm, and marching towards a set of swing doors. She led him to the rear of a large lecture theatre packed with hundreds of students who, having arrived late and rowdy, were stunned into silence on finding their lecturer absent.

After a while it became apparent that a small dapper man had appeared, standing directly before them and gazing intensely at nobody in particular. To those who knew him better he seemed utterly devoid of human mannerism, the kind of man who listened for human weakness in every syllable. Somehow in his silent stillness he managed to extract all sound and emotion from the room.

In his teaching he functioned much as a textbook. Were an unwary student to ask a question, or God forbid proffer an opinion, he could recite a standard work in such careful monotones as might benefit a damaged child, all the while gazing with absorbed fascination at the featureless wall. Whether this impressive act of recall ever profited the troubled student, few could recall. Certainly very few students bothered him with further questions, and few of his colleagues ever sought his formidable knowledge, two outcomes which suited the professor admirably.

"This is Professor Rheinhalter, Head of Faculty. Why is he here?" she asked David. The professor proceeded to tell her.

"It would appear Professor Flaubert is unavailable today. We suspect he labours for CERN, nobly advancing the frontiers of scientific knowledge. It falls to me to present today's lecture, which is on the Magnetohydrodynamics of the upper atmosphere." There was a faint but audible groan from the students.

"In many ways the upper atmosphere behaves very much like a charged fluid moving through a strong magnetic field. Maxwell's equations ..."

"Follow me. Now we drink strong coffee," she whispered loudly, tugging at his wrist, as the professor proceeded to cover the whiteboard in mathematical symbols. David edged along embarrassedly behind her as she barged her way down the row of seats and out through the swing doors.

"You just can't sneak out in the middle of a lecture," he whispered as she held the door for him.

"It is not the middle. And anyway, we are invisible. Slimeball never looks at his students. Also we hear this lecture many times before. I wonder where is Professor Flaubert?" she asked again, leading him across the bright courtyard and onto the street.

"He's at CERN, the high-energy particle accelerator at Genève. Didn't you hear the professor?"

She glanced at him with a knowing smile as they walked along the bustling high street. "I do not think so. Ernst always tells us when he is away." She led him to a small café tucked behind a quiet courtyard, and promptly sat down at a sunny table. When the waitress arrived, she ordered something, for both of them it seemed, for the girl walked off smartly as David began muttering in his bad German.

"So I know only you are a handsome English knight searching for Professor Flaubert." It was probably a question.

"My name is David King. I'm here in Switzerland on a short holiday to look up some old friends," he explained, trying to sound relaxed.

"A king! But that is even so much better! Perhaps you find here your queen?" she laughed shrilly. I am Helga Tischner."

"No, I'm just here visiting old friends," he repeated. Not to mention look for a job, he thought more soberly.

"So you also have friends?" she enquired, amused. "I think that is rare for a king." David sighed mentally and glanced away, wondering why every encounter with the opposite sex always ended with a struggle. First they smile and flatter, then tease him like a small child. In no time at all it seemed, there would either be sex or a ghastly row. The waitress arrived with a bowl of fresh anchovy salad, some warm bread and two large steins. He began to apologise, thinking they had ordered coffee but Helga quietly thanked her, shaking her head.

"You must eat my king. You are so thin, I can blow you over!" She picked up a chunk of bread and tucked lustily into the anchovies with her fork. Sunlight spilt over the table in dazzling pools as the trees swayed gently above them in the warm breeze. Around them, students were chatting and laughing, and somewhere someone was strumming the inevitable guitar and smoking a joint. Three floors up on the far side of the courtyard a stocky woman in a starched white smock leaned out the window to turn a duvet.

He decided to skip the row and smiled gratefully at her. "Thank you for this, Helga. You are very perceptive, I do get grumpy when I'm hungry, I keep forgetting." For some reason he thought of Christine at that moment and wondered if she was happy. Now he was alone again, he missed her badly, though they would often go weeks without seeing each other.

Helga gazed steadily at him, mildly encouraged. She found his tall wiry frame rather ungainly. Though he seemed well-coordinated enough, he was completely unaware of his awkward posture and strange loping gait. At the same time, he had a handsome roguish face, with strong inquisitive jaws and high prominent cheek bones protecting deep-set startled blue eyes. His unruly mop of blond hair was unfashionably long for a student she felt, quite down to his neck. It seemed to hang around him in long lazy coils, never quite managing to lay flat, the whole effect bouncing along slightly as he walked.

His whole manner was strangely tense and inarticulate in a way she found curiously seductive, though in truth its origin was more mundane. From birth, David suffered from a mild short-sightedness in one eye, which from an early age he had learned to accommodate through an unconsciously close and leisurely study of his surroundings – including faces – often with startling effect on the opposite sex.

* * *

Helga chatted continuously it seemed. She moved about a great deal too he noticed, tossing her hair back excitedly, causing her breasts to dance languidly beneath her top. The salad too, was delightful, and the beer perfectly continental. From nowhere at all, a perfect day had materialised. He listened to her happy inane chatter and smiled contentedly, chipping in with a few meaningless comments. Before he realized, they had finished the meal. She stood up, seemingly bored now and in a hurry to leave. The waitress arrived and glanced at David. He stood up too quickly, steadying himself on the table as he rummaged in his jacket pocket. Helga smiled at the waitress and paid the bill, carefully including the expected tip.

"Come my brave knight. It is time to find your professor." She led him away still fumbling with his wallet. Delicious smells wafted through shop doorways and the strong sunlight dazzled his vision, jumbling his thoughts and emotions. Trams plied effortlessly up and down the tree-decked avenues, stopping now and then to disgorge unruly packs of small children strapped into huge satchels.

They turned into a quiet leafy road lined by tall apartment buildings and stopped in front of a large deeply-carved oak door. An angry buzzer sounded when she pressed the button and pushing open the door with her foot, she gently guided him through. The building was cool and silent inside, with high walls lined in dark wood panelling. The air smelt deliciously foreign, a heady cocktail of cigar smoke and herbs, tinged with a whiff of drains. They quietly made their way up three flights of stairs and stopped outside a small door.

"Ernst Flaubert lives here?" he whispered in surprise. She opened the door with a key and threw her jacket over a peg. Turning, she smiled, and reaching up, gently pulled his head down to kiss him generously on the lips.

"No David, I live here! We have an important assignment. Then I take you to meet your professor."

"What are you talking about? I've come to ask for a job, not hand in some bloody homework." He stood rooted in the doorway, staring into her small chaotic bedsit.

She shook her head slowly and gazed into his eyes. "Crazy bloody Engländer!" she exclaimed softly, as she crossed her arms and pulled her sweater over her head. She stood quite still, naked to her jeans, thumbs curled provocatively into her waistband. A broad smile played over her soft lips, as her pendulous breasts bobbed gently outwards beneath his startled gaze. It was a while before he remembered to breathe again.

* * *

Many people believe your whole life flashes before your eyes the instant you die. Ernst held little truck with the notion, being too unscientific for his taste. Unfalsifiable, as Karl Popper would say. An idea which cannot be tested and offer at least some opportunity of being proved false, has no place in science, wherever else it might appeal: religion, politics, love or philosophy perhaps, but not science. But what clinched it for Ernst was that it seemed so contrived, so naively human and parochial. He didn't doubt there was something to it, but not a video rerun of one's life.

A deep wave dread and anger swelled inside him as he tipped slowly backwards over the ledge. A tremendous pain beat at the entrance to his brain, clamouring to be admitted like a mob at the castle gate. As the sky rolled over him, he heard his mother warning him not to look directly at the sun. Of all the ridiculous things to tell an inquisitive child. He remembered too, the smell of snowy pine forests thawing in the first hot rays of spring, the gushing streams of cascading melt water beating its tortuous way down the mountainside to swell the charging river below.

As the panorama rotated, he saw beneath him the blinding ice sheet that would shortly be his grave. He recalled with intense sadness the day he buried his father and wished now he had spent more time telling him what a wonderful father he was. Now as he plunged to his own death, he wondered if had done enough to please him.

The rational side of him calmly noted, not without a little malice, that his mind was reliving the past. But this was no replay, he argued, more a random string of images flashing through a highly charged mind. His natural defences were in overdrive, pumping adrenalin and other fight and flight hormones through his bloodstream, in an instinctive effort to keep him alive.

His body would fight for him all the way down but his mind had accepted the last rites with a calmness. It would use its final moments doing what it did best – observe, associate and analyse.

He wondered how it had all come to this. True, he had decided to end his life, but changed his mind a week ago. It was still his mind to change, after all. Surely that was allowed, he had no pact with the devil. How clear it all seemed to him now, his hand hovering over the little brown bottle, every day for a week. And how every day for a week, his mood had lifted, little by little, until finally, with the fresh spring oxygen and the scent of pine resin coursing through his lungs, he had burned through the fog of depression that had crept up so insidiously the last few months. Some unknown side effect of the pills perhaps, stoking a deep-seated anxiety. He was glad he discovered it before …

For some reason the girl's face returned to mock him. That she had murdered him he had no doubt, though her innocent looks and steady gaze sickened him. She said she was a student but he did not recall her, and in his heightened state, he nailed her lie. What, then? Had her father abused her or her mother abandoned her? Was she bleeding internally, a slow painful death? How had she come to this, so young and indifferent? As he gazed into her eyes he saw terrible things and shuddered. He had seen her before, but she was no student.

It was two months ago, in his laboratory. She was with Slimeball. Even now he marvelled at the fabulous recall his new awareness afforded him. He had returned unexpectedly for his laboratory notebook, anxious lately for its safety. Slimeball was showing her around his laboratory, strutting about, examining the apparatus. One experiment in particular it seemed, involving a heavily-shielded radioactive source and murmuring quietly as to its likely purpose. At the time he assumed Slimeball was showboating with the pretty young thing, showering her with his shameless patter. But now he wasn't so sure.

An industrial spy then perhaps, recruited by one of the multinationals with whom Slimeball cultivated such lucrative contracts. He was glad he had surprised them, though at the time he was far too angry to see the implications. He wished now he had retrieved the entire set of notebooks recording his experiments over the last sixteen years, but it was not to be.

Anyway, the last journal was the key, and now they would never find it. For the first and last time in his life as an observational scientist he had left no record of his last experiment, its expected conclusions, or any of the questions leading up to it. Did they know anything of his final experiment? Were they watching a week ago when he left home with the quartz detectors?

It hardly mattered. The experiment was complete, though he would have preferred to examine the crystals and record his results. He calmly reminded himself there was precious little time to examine anything now. In the end he concluded, it was always a case of knowing when something was simple, when you were gazing at the simple naked truth. Such moments had been few in his life. Feynman and other great scientists had spoken of them with a quiet pride.

There was an instant when I glimpsed the simple truth and for some brief moment, knew only I had seen it.

He remembered only one such moment in his life and it was only a small truth, but he had always treasured it and it brought him great comfort on sad days.

But now he knew for certain he had glimpsed another truth, a far deeper truth, and though he had so little time to covet it, he felt content. The science was simple though scarcely credible, exactly what one would expect from that strange child of modern physics, the Quantum Theory. The repercussions for mankind and its role in the universe were profound. Would historians use it to check their elaborate tapestries of fact and fantasy? He scarcely cared one way or another. What fired him was the thought that science would use his discovery to explore the history of this beautiful planet, its creatures and their place in the universe. His love for his work, the world, its peoples and all its lifeforms, filled him with a contentment that had eluded him all his life.

And now with great sadness, he realised in René a different kind of truth, a truth which to his immense regret, he had found neither time nor courage to pursue. He hoped she would find a fulfilling and rewarding life for herself. She certainly deserved it, though he knew that counted for little in the great scheme of things. He felt the cold shudder of a man grown old with no one to hold his hand. He hoped she would understand his failings, perhaps one day forgive him and not make the same mistakes herself. He said a small prayer for her and kissed her goodbye.

* * *

Depending on its exact orientation on impact, it takes about one thousandth of a second for a human being travelling at two hundred kilometres per hour to come to a complete halt. The average deceleration suffered is therefore about 700g. Destruction is caused not so much from the deceleration itself, but from the fact that different parts of the human body decelerate at different rates, the softer parts detaching themselves after the more rigid parts have come to rest. Fighter pilots are trained to cope with momentary blackouts of 8g but anything above 15g causes permanent damage, death mercifully intervening at about 50g. Death is not however, instantaneous. It never is in nature. But as blood vessels rupture and nerve endings sheer in tiny fractions of a second, Ernst's death was quick and relatively painless. Professor Ernst Flaubert was smiling as the pink ice exploded around him. He had remembered a good joke to tell the Ferryman.

Chapter 4

Helga was a mistake, he knew that now. It was perhaps the only thing he knew about her. She had tricked him back to her flat and quickly seduced him, and like the fool he was he didn't think much about it until she kicked him out, two days later. Not that she threw him out of course – just picked a silly quarrel and let him to walk away, dazed and confused.

She was a kind and generous girl, but in the end she grew bored with all his science and not being first in his thoughts. It didn't take much; a few brooding silences, as he lounged comfortably on the floor against her legs, reading and scribbling his equations. Some deep sighs, which he took to be her need to talk and his to listen, though when he did he heard nothing she hadn't said before and he could think of nothing useful to add. And while he sensed she was looking for more, he had no idea what, and she could not – or would not – explain.

The end came suddenly enough while he was poring over Flaubert's last paper, trying to visualise in his own mind what the equations were saying. She was chattering contentedly enough in the background, when he looked up suddenly, alerted by an unfamiliar tone and abrupt pause. And while his face still registered a dreamy lost smile, it was a smile too closely recalling their tender moments together. She recognised it and grew angry. A dull uncomprehending panic swelled within him, dissolving his thoughts in a pool of confused silence.

"Of course you can stay," she said, "until you find somewhere …" If her words were empty and ambiguous, her tone was definite enough. By the time he deciphered her meaning, the matter was apparently settled and his smile had disappeared. So too had Helga, to make some farewell coffee. He was a heartless brute to walk out now, but she would be loving and generous to the end.

Waiting for the bus he was drenched in a sudden downpour and growing irrationally angry with himself, resolved perversely to trudge on by foot in an effort to stoke his black mood and cauterise the pain. Besides, he could hardly get much wetter.

Eventually, cold and tired, he found a cheap room and stripping out of his sodden clothes, stood for a long time under the hot shower. Then he drank an expensive bottle of cheap wine from the mini bar and climbed into bed, obsessing over a sour quote he'd read somewhere and never really understood. *Even if man could understand woman, he still wouldn't believe it.* As he lay waiting for the wine to numb his thoughts, he scribbled a mental footnote. *Even if he believed it, he still wouldn't remember.*

* * *

He slept late, and lay listlessly mulling over the wasted weekend and another inexplicable rejection. It was mid afternoon before he summoned the courage to face the world again and make his way back to the *Poly*.

This time he studied the name board carefully. The solidstate laboratory was on the second floor, Lab 2J. Ignoring the lift, he bounded up the stairs, grateful for a chance to calm his nerves. The building was quiet and he felt strangely conspicuous. Don't be daft, he scoffed quietly to himself. Students come and go, nobody knows or cares, everyone too busy with their own work. Besides, foreign visitors were always dropping in.

He checked off the doors as he walked along the quiet corridor. Should he knock? He decided to walk straight in. Keep moving, that was the thing apparently. The lab was lined with dark wooden workbenches along every wall. Two large peninsular tables occupied most of the central floor space. Every available inch was taken up with carefully constructed equipment and instrumentation. At the far end of the aisle stood a cleaner with her back towards him, rummaging clumsily through a large wooden crate. In the distant corner he saw a partially glazed door and strode over purposefully towards it.

The office was empty, empty of human life that is, though there were papers and files strewn everywhere. This was not the Professor Flaubert he remembered. Picking up a neatly written journal from the floor he began to leaf through for dates. The sudden noise of tinkling glass distracted him, and laying the journal open on the desk, he returned to the lab. The woman had evidently broken something and was now hurriedly clearing away the mess.

"I don't think you should be doing that," he said awkwardly, standing behind her. She hesitated fractionally, then continued, pointedly ignoring him. "Do you hear me? I do not think you should be handling the equipment." The woman turned slowly towards him. She was younger than he imagined, and quietly athletic, with shoulder length auburn hair drawn fiercely back into a small provocative pony tail. Her face was freckled slightly with a light natural tan and a darker colouring now suffused her finely sculpted cheek bones. She stood motionlessly gazing at him, a quiet intensity smouldering behind her liquid brown eyes.

"Have you seen Professor Flaubert?" he asked in careful English. She continued to stare at him. "Is he here today? Perhaps you can tell me where he is? It is very important I find him."

"He is not here," she said finally in perfect English and returned to her work. She appeared to be dismembering a large piece of equipment.

"Here, shouldn't you be tidying up? I very much doubt Professor Flaubert will be too pleased to find you dismantling his experiment. What on earth is going on in here?"

"He is not here today," she repeated, her back towards him. "Perhaps you may call again tomorrow?"

"Now look, I don't wish to intrude, but really, don't you think …" She spun round violently at the touch of his hand and he sheepishly withdrew.

"I'm sorry. I didn't mean to startle you." He paused awkwardly again, wondering how to proceed. "My name is David King. I collaborated with Ernst, sometime ago. I am visiting Zürich for a few days. I thought I'd drop in and say hello."

The collaboration he alluded to was three years earlier at a New York conference, and amounted to little more than listening to the professor deliver some startling results in a little known backwater of solidstate physics. David felt her eyes silently assess him and the hair tingle down the back of his neck.

"I am René Schante," she said simply.

"Well, look here René, I'm sorry to ..." He stopped abruptly.

"Schante? You are R. M. Schante? Co-author of Spontaneous Large-scale Quantum Anomalies in Quartz Crystals?"

"But, you are a ..."

"A woman?" she offered carelessly, completing his sentence.

"Well obviously, what I meant, I thought you were ..." He floundered again and this time she did not help him.

"Yes David, I am a woman. A woman and a mathematician. I performed the mathematical analysis and all the calculations. I developed the algorithm. I wrote the computer program. It was my work. It was supposed to be my presentation but he wouldn't have it, said it was too incomplete, too controversial for my first presentation. They would tear me to pieces, me being ... just a woman."

"He's dead," she added coldly, turning away, "a climbing accident. They found his body. That is why no one is here this afternoon. Nobody speaks to him, but now he is dead, they go to mass and say goodbye. Typical Swiss hypocrites! I come here to find something, while it is quiet, to rob his grave. I say my goodbyes another day."

She was leaning over the bench, her back tense and rigid as she worked ineffectively against a large metal flange. He laid his hands gingerly on her shoulders, bracing himself for her reaction. Instead, she stopped fumbling with the wrench, turned and sobbed quietly against him, months of stress, turmoil and final rejection spilling into grief.

"It is no use," she said after a long silence. "We should leave." Just then a man's voice rattled angrily down the corridor. She gasped quietly, stiffening in his arms. "Professor Rheinhalter, Head of Department. He comes to ..."

"It's alright René, calm down. It's his department, he's supposed to be here. I imagine he's locking up or something. Perhaps I should introduce myself. Maybe we can help you find what you are looking for."

A look of abject terror overcame her as she backed away from him. "No, you do not understand," she whispered. "He is an evil man. He always hated Ernst, tried to get him fired. He is the cause of all this ... misery."

"Look René, you're understandably upset. It's hard to see things clearly when ..."

"Get yourself in here and find the fucking things. Search all night if necessary."

They heard his footsteps resume towards them. David quickly backed her around the bench into the small adjoining office and quietly closed the door, flicking off the lights as they crouched behind a row of filing cabinets.

The professor stopped abruptly outside the laboratory and looked in through the open doorway. The lights were on and the scene appeared much the same as the previous evening when he had searched fruitlessly for Flaubert's detectors and notebook. Still he hesitated, sensing something amiss. He walked around the room to Flaubert's office and gazed at the mess. Not that it mattered, he would have the office cleared out and tidied by morning.

Switching off the light, he locked the door and paced thoughtfully around, pausing to examine the wrench and abandoned equipment. His gaze fell questioningly on the partially glazed door. The small tidy office was unlit and belonged to Flaubert's attractive young assistant. Perhaps with her interfering boss now out of the way, the delightful Fraulein Schante would come to her senses and accept his generous offer to help. He smiled knowingly and reached for the door handle.

His mobile rang again. "Ja sicher. Ich kommt direkt." He rang off abruptly and left, turning out the lights and locking the door behind him. They listened in relief as his footsteps faded away.

"Come on René, let's get out of here. Do you have a key?"

"Yes, but we might meet him on the stairs."

"So? You work here, and I'm just an old friend visiting. What could he possibly do?"

"You do not understand. Things are very tense at the moment. David, please! You hear how angry he is."

She led him out, relocking the laboratory door with thoughtful deliberation, and marching him quietly to the far end of the corridor, almost running down a small flight of steps and bursting through the swing doors that by day formed a jostling short cut for students from the faculty of Astronomical Sciences.

They sped down another flight of steps and into a dimly lit lobby where a small group of students stood around a snack machine, sipping hot chocolate and taking a noisy break from their early evening practicals. René linked her arm through David's for effect as they walked past, grateful for the reassurance. She was shaking gently as they bounded down the steps and out onto the street.

The cool evening air, the bustling crowd and chaotic rush hour traffic all helped to dispel their fears, and drew them irresistibly to a lively bierstube already packed with noisy students. After the tense atmosphere of the lab, the smoke filled beery air soon had them grinning like teenagers again, and with a few delicious beers they fell to chatting and laughing about their little adventure.

* * *

"So where did you get to with the quantum anomaly?" David asked finally, unable to maintain the small talk.

"Ernst was convinced the blister formation was the result of two distinct processes. The first process remained unobservable and mysteriously random, but was somehow necessary to trigger the second process, which we thought we did understand. We also discovered quite by accident that if you zapped the blister with a laser in just the right way, it popped! Disappeared completely, as if it had never been there."

"And there was something else," she added quietly, looking away and recalling with deep sadness the last days alone with Ernst, when time stood still and they felt they were making history. David looked up, puzzled by her abrupt silence.

"What?" he asked. "What something else?"

"There was an emission. Shortly after the blister popped, something came out. A light pulse."

"Impossible," he said, shortly.

"Yes," she said. "Impossible. So we repeated everything, again and again, more carefully and with better equipment. It was true. A brief pulse of light was emitted a few nanoseconds after laser stimulation."

"A defect of the laser probably."

"No, nothing to do with the laser. It was different for each blister, that much we could tell, though at the time we had no idea how to analyse the pulse."

"Well then, perhaps the laser was picking up a local impurity in the crystal and doing something with the light."

"No David, not an impurity of the crystal. But you are right in a sense. The laser was interacting with the local electronic field of the blister, causing it to collapse and release a bubble of electromagnetic radiation."

"No René, you can't use the word release. Release implies the light was locked up inside the blister before it popped. That's impossible, it violates the Uncertainty Principle. You can't lock up light in a tiny cell and throw away the key, not unless ... oh my god!"

"You see it too! You see it" Her eyes sparkled as she saw the idea slowly form in David's mind, just as it had with her and Ernst.

"Let's go through this again René, slowly, right from the beginning. Something – no idea what – but something very local and energetic, sensitises a tiny part of the crystal surface. While it's sensitized, light falling on that spot can be imprisoned. No, not imprisoned, that can't happen. But the incident light modifies somehow the local electron field in the disturbed region. Then the sensitivity switches off again, very rapidly, leaving the local structure of the crystal permanently altered in a way that echoes the incident light. It's like, it's like a ..." he groped around for an analogy.

"Christ almighty!" he exclaimed loudly, causing a few students to glance at him. "It's like a bloody camera, recording the incident light at the instant of excitation. Good God, René. Nature's camera!"

"But without the lens, David."

"Oh yes, that's right, no lens. Phew! Got carried away there for a moment. Still, a very useful effect. You could use it for all sorts of things, a historical record of light intensity, for example. That would be useful somewhere, I imagine."

"David, listen to me. You don't need a lens," she confided in a whisper.

"What? Of course you do – I mean, either a lens or a pinhole. Every camera has one. Every eye in nature has one or the other. If you haven't got a lens – like plants – you can only detect the presence or absence of light. No René, you have to have a lens."

"David, look over there," she said suddenly, nodding across the crowded room.

"Who is it?"

"No, not who is it, David. What is it? What do you see? Tell me David"

"Nobody, nothing, just a wall."

"No David! You can do better than that."

"It's just a white wall. Have you gone nuts?"

"Come on David, be *precise*. Tell me what are your eyes are detecting."

"Oh I see ... *precise*," he mimicked, gazing at her with a gentle mocking smile. "Well, let me think. My eyes are detecting incoming photons, previously scattered from a partially reflective surface – the white wall. Photons which, given their uneven intensity, I infer were emitted originally from two distinct sources of light. Namely, the two electric light bulbs on opposite sides of the ceiling."

"Yes, very good," she said. "You're getting there – slowly. Your brain has worked out, through historical association over many such experiences, that this particular wall is illuminated by two separate light sources. You don't have to see the two sources directly. Just the two pools of light on each side of the wall are enough to intuit their presence. If there was a third light source and you studied the wall carefully enough, you could probably figure out its presence and approximate position too. And if there were other illuminated objects in the room, not just lights but say people, which of course there are, and if your eyes were sufficiently sensitive and discriminating, you might be able to intuit their presence too. Don't you see? Purely from the light striking the wall you could reconstruct the entire scene facing the wall. It is the proverbial fly in the wall."

"Fly *on* the wall," he corrected her.

"And you don't need the whole wall either," she said, ignoring his pedantic interruption. "The light falling on each tiny bit of wall contains enough information to reconstruct the entire image, as seen from that spot. It's just a case of figuring it out."

"Well alright, miss smartypants. I stand corrected, in the detail. But that's essentially what I meant. It's true, all the information is there, just hopelessly tangled up and impossible to untangle. That's why you need a lens René, to stop it getting tangled up in the first place."

"No David, that's why you need a mathematician. That's why you need me," she said, her eyes wet with excitement.

"How do you mean?" he asked warily.

"Mathematics can untangle it. It's difficult and so far the results are very crude, and it's unbelievably expensive in computer time – not exactly unique selling points for a new kind of camera. But in theory it can be done, if it's worthwhile enough." She paused expectantly, gazing into his eyes. A slow thoughtful smile formed on her lips while he sat immobilised in thought.

"Speaking of expense David, would you pay for the drinks and buy me a nice bottle of red wine? I have to give a long lecture tonight on Matrix Theory."

"A lecture, at this time of night!" he asked incredulously, "who on earth to?"

"To you, David. Come on," she said, gathering her things.

Chapter 5

"Simon? Get yourself in here, at the double. And bring your passport."

"Yes sir." Simon lay motionless in his bed rewinding the previous thirty seconds of his life. It is 03:51 and the phone has just rung. I answered, and now I am going to work – with passport. He checked his phone. The last call was 03:49 and lasted nine seconds. No dream then.

He called a cab and was showered and dressed in time to hear it pull up outside. He made it to the office in twenty-three minutes, shaving on the way.

The home secretary was still in evening dress. An untidy trail of the morning's first editions lay scattered across the floor.

"You're off to cloud cuckoo land Simon," he said brightly. "There's been a death. A Professor Ernst Flaubert, Swiss national. Suicide, they are saying. Life too rich for the poor old sod. Slipped off the edge, quite literally, according to the Swiss. But we know better, don't we Simon?"

"We do?"

"Yes Simon, we do. Because against all sound advice, the good professor has been very stubborn lately. Poking around where he shouldn't be – and I don't just mean his damned mistress. These confounded blisters! Worked quietly for years, getting absolutely nowhere. Now, all of a sudden, he's onto something. So what does he do Simon, step off a cliff? I don't think so."

"It turns out Simon, you're due for a spot of leave, a mountain break. Hopefully, nothing as permanent. Talk to Flaubert's colleagues and students – discreetly. Find out what they know or suspect. Everything we know is in this file – read it and leave it.

Don't use your phone except to order pizza. First flight to Zürich and full report on my desk by Friday morning."

* * *

After just a few minutes in the front passenger seat of her tiny car, David became acutely aware of somehow missing a step in the decision making process. Either she had decided for him or simply assumed he had no real objection to driving home with her.

When he finally realised, he became uncomfortable and fidgety, insisting instead she drive him back to his hotel. By the time they found it he had calmed down again, explaining clumsily he just needed to collect a few things.

He entered alone, loitering uncertainly in the small foyer for his key, wondering whether he should summon someone or simply reach over behind the desk. He was startled out of indecision by the desk clerk materialising silently beside him, anxious to be of assistance. Unable to think of anything better, he asked for his bill and wandered off thoughtfully to collect his things. He paid the bill without comment on the way out, retrieving his passport.

He fully expected her to have driven off in a huff, noting irritably the complete absence of her car outside the hotel. He swore loudly into the cold night, just as a pair of headlights flashed at him, and to his embarrassment and childish delight, he saw her little yellow CV lurch out from a prudent parking bay. That's Switzerland for you, he thought, prudent and legal.

As he climbed awkwardly into her car he sensed a gentle understanding pass between them and his early anxieties melt away. Her easy acquiescence to his abrupt and irrational request seemed to calm him. Inside, he felt the first stirring of something warm and momentous.

* * *

He had been playing with the hem of her red and white checked tablecloth, absorbed with brushing his finger along its surprisingly rough edge, while she systematically explained the mathematical mysteries of Matrix Algebra and Fast Fourier Transforms. She gazed at his distracted fiddling and after a hesitant pause, continued in fairly flat tones that she looked pretty good naked, only to be rewarded by his total lack of response.

"David! You haven't listened to a word I've said. I have just explained how it is possible to regenerate the captured image using matrix ..."

"No, no ... I believe you!"

"But you don't understand."

"Well ... no, I don't understand the maths. But it's not just that René, I can't visualise the problem in the same way," he said, immediately regretting it. "No, that's not what I meant," he added quickly, feeling a rising tide of fatigue entangling his thoughts.

"Then what *exactly* did you mean?" she snapped. To her evident annoyance, he began to tell her.

"Well no, I can't honestly say I understand it, not properly," he started out appeasingly. "I suppose I begin with the simplest imaginable scene and ask what kind of diffraction pattern that would create in the crystal field. Then make the scene slightly more complicated, and see how that changes the pattern. Carry on like that, bit by bit, until I've built up the complete picture. Only it's not a calculation, it's more a ... visualisation." He trailed off lamely, wishing he hadn't tried to explain, it all sounding so feeble now in plain words.

For her part, René wished she hadn't asked. She was very proud of her analysis and not at all receptive to somebody telling her it could all be done with simple visualisation or some such Zen nonsense. All the same, another part of her became intrigued with the mathematical possibilities of his perspective and she made a mental note to consider it again in the morning.

Not for the first time that evening she marvelled excitedly how different they were in outlook, at the same time feeling a inner sense of warm contentment with him. Well, they say opposites attract. It had certainly been some time since she felt so relaxed with anyone, apart from ... She looked up suddenly. He was talking again.

" ... thinking again about the first event, what could possibly trigger the photon capture. I can't help thinking it's key to understanding the whole business. Didn't Ernst ever discuss it?"

She started visibly that they should both be thinking of Ernst at the same moment and wondered if he had read her thoughts somehow. Yes, undoubtedly, Ernst had talked about it, Ernst was always talking about it. That was how Ernst did science, though she rarely listened. At first, she felt she didn't understand because she didn't know enough of the physics. But in the brief time she had known David he had taught her something quite profound. It wasn't that she didn't know enough – she just didn't look at it the same way. It wasn't good and it wasn't bad, it was just different. She sensed suddenly how useful it could be sometimes, to view a complex idea from more than one perspective.

"Here," she said, dumping some bedding in his lap. "We both need some sleep. You here, on the couch," she emphasised, in case her rash boast had lodged somewhere in his subconscious. "You need all your energy tomorrow," she added, eying his tall wiry frame with a smile. "In the morning we climb a mountain – I show you where I go to think."

* * *

She was up bright and early the next morning, clattering happily about in her tiny kitchen, intent on warming some par-baked rolls and making fresh coffee. When he finally emerged from the tangle on her sofa, she was startled at how incoherent and dazed he looked. It even crossed her mind whether he had helped himself to her Eierlikőr during the night, sneaking quietly off to check, and returning with a sheepish grin, though he appeared not to notice. As she worked, she found herself looking forward to the day with quiet excitement, showing him the prettiest views, pointing out the hardy but delicate-looking wild flowers nestling among the crags, and the impressive glacier of course. Maybe though, she wouldn't show him the ledge.

After coffee he appeared to perk up a little, muttering a faint good morning and fiddling absently with one of her ornaments. She marvelled at the way his fingers led an independent life of their own, undertaking delicate investigations without apparent supervision from their owner. Last night while she chatted about her childhood, he had absently fixed her radio, which for months had developed an ugly rasping edge, simply by reseating the aerial connection. The drawer which ran jerkily and jammed occasionally was now smooth and obedient. And all the while, his mind seemed elsewhere, or perhaps entirely blank, she wondered. She flinched visibly when he started up suddenly, almost as intensely as the night before.

"It needs to be discrete. It needs to be random and spontaneous. And it needs to be highly energetic," he added. For one dizzying moment she wondered if he was talking about sex.

"That's all we know about the trigger mechanism. Something happens that for a very brief interval causes a tiny part of the crystal to become electrically distorted and sensitive to incident light. Then it snaps shut again, locking up a signature of the light inside the crystal lattice."

She gazed at him as his he toyed with the wooden coffee grinder her mother had thrown out one Christmas, delicately tensing the knob that controlled the grinding action. She wondered if his mind also worked that way, whether it had to feel its way around an idea before making sense of it. It took a little while for her to realise his fingers had ceased their urgent enquiries – jammed worryingly mid-task on something. She looked up and was surprised to find all his attention now directed on her. Well, not on *her* exactly, more on the wall behind, and wondered if he had spotted an indiscreet photo.

"What is it?" she asked, turning about to find nothing more incriminating than a smoke detector, and wondering if now of all times, he had decided to check its alarm function. She sincerely hoped not, she detested its piercing shriek which startled her so badly whenever she made a slice of toast or fried an egg.

"What?" she repeated, when he still didn't stir. "The smoke alarm? I hate it, but the landlord insists. It is part of the insurance. They check, frequently. What is the matter? David, for God's sake say something!"

She poured him another coffee and waited anxiously for the next caffeine rush. At last his lips began to labour their way around a reluctant sound.

"Americium 241," he managed finally.

"What! What about it?"

"It's a man-made element. Radioactive. Often used in smoke detectors. Radiation, René! The trigger!"

"What are you saying?"

"Radiation – a highly energetic particle striking the crystal surface! Small, energetic, discrete and very local. And very random too," he added, excitedly ticking the boxes. "That would explain why your detectors deteriorated so rapidly in the CERN environment. What did Ernst do with the detectors, René? What kind of equipment was he using to examine them? And where are his notebooks?" He couldn't stop talking now, and it was her turn to be struck dumb.

After a while he seemed to lose interest again, content now to fiddle aimlessly with one of her CD's, gently running his finger around its sharp edge, assessing its tiny imperfections.

"Come on," she said. "We can talk about it while we walk. The sun's getting up and we need to be on the higher slopes before noon." She quickly packed a few provisions and gave him a man's jacket to wear. "It can get cold up there," she added quickly, "even on a day like this."

There was no need for careful explanations. He was busy flexing the disk in a shaft of brilliant sunlight, absorbed with the flash of spectral colour as it danced across the ceiling.

Chapter 6

When they eventually set off, he was stunned by the beauty of her small garden and the surrounding hillside. Now with the sun shining across the valley, the warm rising air brought the scent of hay drying in the meticulously tended meadows below. Thoughts and conversation melted away as they adapted to the rhythm of walking together.

They strolled along the edge of a meadow, happy with each other's company and comfortable in the silence. An old man scythed methodically, gently rocking his way uphill through the still damp grass and David found himself wondering about the mechanics of the scything action. Small delicate white flowers grew around the foot of each fencepost where the blade avoided, giving the effect of neat and purposeful planting. He stopped to gaze as a large brown bird took sudden flight across the meadow, lazily beating its great wings. It seemed hardly possible such a slow effort could keep the huge creature aloft but somehow it managed to gain height. Gradually its wings beat less as it circled in the warm rising air with elegant grace.

She was chatting happily about village life, how things were changing even here, miles from the *Poly* and occasionally cut off briefly from the outside world by snow blizzards sweeping down from the mountains. He recalled the pictures on the walls of her cottage; simple mountain scenes, wild flowers, mountain panoramas and a small group of huts perched high in the hills; a small faded print of a smiling young man in uniform, standing behind a mountain rescue sledge.

He asked her about her childhood and what first drew her to mathematics and recalled to her his only previous visit to Switzerland, a school trip to some ski resort with an unpronounceable name. He had hated it. Tall and not particularly athletic, he spent a miserable week on the slopes. They had travelled by coach and the journey seemed endless. On the way he tried to make friends with a pretty girl and failed miserably.

The trees opened out now onto a large expanse of steep meadow. A small vigorous stream rushed down its edge, its sparkling waters bouncing off large boulders and arcing gracefully through the thin air as the ground gave way unexpectedly beneath. She sat down on a smooth rock and waved to him.

"Come and sit down – we should eat something." He rarely ate in the morning, and dairy foods first thing set him coughing for hours, but to his surprise he found himself enjoying the rich bread roll.

She handed him a small flask. "Real coffee, just for the tourists – locals drink from the stream," she joked lightly with him, smiling steadily into his friendly blue eyes. The coffee smelt luxurious in the keen mountain air, and he carefully poured a small portion into the delicate white china cup she had packed for him.

"This is so nice," he told her. "There's plenty left, would you like some?" But she shook her head, smiling slowly as she repacked the flask. He gently brushed a small insect from the back of her neck, running his fingertip enquiringly down the line of fine hairs. Ridiculously, he started shyly when she turned towards him. She stroked the back of his hand as they gazed quietly into each other's eyes. A flock of chuffs took off from a nearby outcrop of rock, scoffing at their coyness.

* * *

"What did Ernst do with the detectors," he asked again eventually, when they set off.

"I don't know," she sighed, shaking her head. "I keep reliving the last few weeks, trying to recall something. Despite everything falling in around him, his only interest was the quantum blisters. Perhaps he took the detectors home with him. He spent most of his time there towards the end, just coming in for lectures. I began to worry about him. He was avoiding all his friends and the few colleagues who were still on speaking terms."

"I pleaded with him, reminding him I only had a few months of contract left and that there was little sign of the faculty offering me anything else. He just shrugged it off, saying it would be fine, he would sort it all out. He had always been so particular with the admin, but now it just accumulated in an untidy heap on his desk. Slimeball dropped in most days on some pretext, probably just to gloat. Once, when Ernst was in Genève, he suggested he could help me in some way."

"Then I heard from a friend there had been a terrible row with Slimeball and the Dean. I was away, at my parents. My father had fallen and hurt himself. They said Ernst had lost his temper and thrown coffee over the board of faculty. I just couldn't believe it. He was always such a calm, softly-spoken man. I suppose I never realised how tense and angry he was inside."

"He wrote to me, care of my parents, though I hadn't told him where I was going. His letter didn't make much sense, he sounded a completely different person. He said he understood, and that I was doing the right thing. At first I thought he was trying to say goodbye, but couldn't summon up the courage. That was the last I heard from him, apart from the mobile. The next thing I knew he was dead ..." she sobbed gently against his shoulder as a silent wall of guilt rose between them.

"The afternoon you came to the lab I was looking for the detectors. I wanted to save something of our time together, a memory. I didn't know what else to do really, I was always much more on the theoretical side."

She sighed deeply. "I never managed to make the computer program work efficiently enough, but he was always kind and encouraging. He said he had complete faith in me, said he knew I would solve it one day and not to worry about the departmental politics and the stupid deadlines. I suppose I knew he was being unrealistic. Well, he was of course, I realise that now. Perhaps if I had worked harder he might still be alive."

He gazed at her, unable to find the words to comfort her, unable either to admit his own guilt and hating himself for it.

"Either he destroyed the detectors or Slimeball found them, though why he should want them I cannot imagine. A cruel memento of his final victory perhaps. He was searching for them that evening, I'm sure of it. Perhaps they found them after we left?"

* * *

The gradient was steeper now and they were scrambling hands and knees over gnarled rocks and stunted trees. But with the hard climbing she seemed to recover, as if a weight had lifted from her shoulders.

"What did Ernst say on his mobile?"

"When?"

"I thought you said he rang from his mobile."

"Ernst? No, I don't think so – he hated them. He rang me on my mobile, but I was too angry to answer. I was feeling sorry for myself I suppose, worried about the future. He left a strange message, saying how he understood everything. He sounded ... well, a bit incoherent, but also strangely excited. He said it all made perfect sense. One more definitive experiment and not to believe anything I heard at the *Poly*, it would all work out. Then he rang again, almost immediately, and very emotional. I wanted to talk to him, but I just couldn't find the courage. He said he was going to do something, something he should have done a long time ago. I think he was very upset at the end."

"Did he mention the experiment before?"

"What experiment?"

"One more definitive experiment, you said."

"I don't think so, no. Well, maybe. He was always doing one more experiment, always checking the same thing a different way."

She was distant again, anguishing over her private thoughts. "René!" he repeated gently, when she gave no sign of hearing him. "Were you, you and Ernst I mean, were you ... lovers?"

She didn't answer and continued climbing, gazing into the distance. It was an intrusive question he realised, and a fairly pointless one at that. They continued climbing in gloomy silence.

"Four years ago," she answered softly, as if the intervening silence was a gentle sigh. "He was just beginning to make significant breakthroughs, attracting international attention and leading a respected research group. I was a raw postgraduate, recruited to help with the mathematics. I was overawed, I suppose. I fell in love with him. Everything was so new and exciting. So hopeful."

"They were beautiful days. We went for walks, it was the only way. We photographed wild flowers and made love in these beautiful hills, and once up there on the ledge, like crazy teenagers." She nodded ahead, and it was clear where her thoughts had been all along. "I can't remember if it was his idea or mine. His, I suppose."

He felt out of his depth with her sudden intimacy, drowning in her pool of emotion. Maybe she sensed his discomfort somehow, for she stopped suddenly, put her arms around his neck and kissed him slowly on the lips.

"You are a beautiful man David," she said. "But right now you have to be very brave and help me." At that moment he would have done anything for her.

* * *

Ten minutes later he was not so sure. She brought him out through a tangle of stunted trees to a large outcrop of rock. As they moved around it, the path narrowed and then fell sharply away on one side as it led out onto the ledge. Earlier, from below, it had seemed picturesque and remote, but now as it dawned on him she was about to venture out along it, a primitive fear seized him, pinning him to the rock face, his legs refusing all further commands.

"René, don't go out there, please. René I can't do it!" She didn't reply and he could no longer see her, only the smooth curve of rock around which she had disappeared. He felt a cold fear in the pit of his stomach and his palms sweating against the cool rock. He looked down stupidly at his feet. The ledge was not that narrow he conceded, perhaps as wide as her pretty garden path down in the safety of the valley below. The rational side of him recalled he had few problems negotiating it this morning, or last night for that matter in the pitch blackness, tripping hesitantly along behind her. It was simply the fact that one side fell away for hundreds of metres, that was all.

That was all? It was enough! And anyway, why take the risk? What was the point? The point he realised quite suddenly, was ahead and calling for him. If she thought it worthwhile risking her life, then maybe it was worthwhile for him too. He quickly silenced the part of him that questioned the circularity of this logic. This was no time for logic.

He was sweating profusely and stiff with fear by the time he edged slowly round to her. She was sat, back to the wall, her legs dangling lazily over the edge, gazing thoughtfully across the valley towards the distant wall of smooth rock.

"For chrissakes René," he hissed. "What is this all about?"

"I don't know David," she answered him flatly. "Maybe it's about me, Ernst and me. Maybe it's about finally saying goodbye."

He turned his head slowly towards her, carefully maintaining his balance, his face strained in nervous anguish.

"Oh David!" she laughed. "Your face!"

He gazed silently at her, wondering if she was actually quite crazy or whether it was perfectly normal for every woman to suffer moments of sheer insanity. The little experience he had inclined him to generalisations. Certainly she had her moments, witness poor Ernst. Somehow he rather doubted it had been Ernst's idea. He sincerely hoped she never tested his affections so recklessly.

* * *

He had been gazing inanely at her for some time before it registered, a tiny glint of light high in the rock face above her head. At first he guessed it must be sunlight reflecting on a small pocket of water, but then realised with a start it was above his eye level. Whatever it was, it wasn't water. But then, so what? Now was hardly the time to go clambering around on a whim risking his life – or hers. He gazed at it intently. The reflection was remarkably steady. He moved his head slightly to one side. A colourful flash winked in and out like a ...

Like a what? He tried to think clearly as he stood rigid, hands clinging to the rock face as if by suction. A mirror perhaps, he wondered, slowly moving his head from side to side. Another dazzling spectral flash burst through his vision. No, not a mirror. More like a diamond, or a prism. Or possibly ... a crystal! He tried to focus through the after-glare but gave up, waiting impatiently for it to clear.

Slowly, he edged his head around, careful not to stare directly into the beam. He could just make out some surrounding detail now, a black metallic edge encasing a small rectangle, fabulously smooth and flat like a mirror. A small ribbon of multi-coloured wires ran off for a few centimetres to a miniature connection block.

"Oh my God, René ... the detectors! That would be it, of course. Cosmic rays, Pic du Midi, the first experiment of high-energy physics! Immensely energetic particles from outer space, origin unknown, possibly flying across space since the beginning of time. Then crashing down through the air, most of them annihilated high in the atmosphere, but some reaching ground level. Lots more reaching mountain tops. Hence the Pic Du Midi experiment. Hence Ernst's last definitive experiment."

"No expensive equipment, no fiddly experiment. Immensely powerful and random cosmic rays – free of charge, courtesy of Mother Nature, just one pleasant day's stroll away. One pleasant stroll, followed by one seriously unpleasant clamber along a dangerous ledge, he thought more soberly.

"René, how many detectors?"

"What?" She was elsewhere, quite unprepared for the sudden interrogation.

"How many detectors? Come on! You were searching for them that afternoon. You must know. How many? What do they look like?"

"Two I think, maybe three. Small and grey, rectangular with a flat slice of bevelled quartz. There's a group photo at home, from a science fair in Genève. I'll find it when we get back ..."

"Stand still!" he screeched, as she stood up and moved towards him. He was reaching high above her with his left hand, back to the wall, searching blindly along a narrow shelf. His fingers inched methodically along, almost jumping with fear at the first touch of something smooth and angular. Gently they continued their sightless reconnaissance, probing its weight and shape, sensing its centre of gravity and surrounding obstructions, then finally closing around the object and carefully lifting it down.

She gave an audible gasp of surprise.

"Here, take this. For chrissakes don't drop it, put it somewhere safe." She flashed a strangled look at him but he was already reaching high above, pressing tightly up against her. It was all very unnerving; one moment he seemed paralyzed with fear, the next he was prancing about like a mountain goat.

"David, please …"

He ignored her. "Stand still René … think of England," he added on some daft impulse, wondering about the phrase and what she might make of it. His fingertips reached a second object. Cold, metallic and smooth, but not angular – heavier and more rounded.

"What the hell …" he started, as he rocked the object gently, trying to lift it with outstretched fingers. "Move along a bit, René!"

But she had reached her limit and refused to budge any further. It was maddening. He backed off and she began to follow. "No, no. Stay there!" he hissed, slowly twisting his shoulders around until he had to change his footing. For an instant he felt the ghostly tug of gravity as part of his body moved briefly over the edge, but in a cold sweat he twisted himself around until his hands and face lay hard and motionless against the cold rock face.

Now he was crabbing back towards her again, stretching his right leg around her and pinning her hard against the wall. Their gaze met, his with fear and exertion, hers with wide-eyed astonishment. He stretched up again and felt along the shelf. As his fingers closed around the object he became aware of a peculiar sensation in his groin. Stifling a cry, he started to shake inwardly.

"For God's sake René, where did you put it?"

"Don't ask," she breathed, summoning her last grip on reality. "Hurry up, David."

His hand clasped around the heavy object and gingerly lifted it down. "Fuck this," he said with a finality. "Two will have to do." He carefully slipped the heavy lead parcel into his jacket pocket and edged back along the wall. "Come on," he said, "I've lost the urge." She was well past humour herself now, and followed him lamely back to safety.

* * *

"Of all the stupid things to do," he told her, when they were lying safely on their backs, basking in the warm sunshine and laughing nervously at the clouds passing above.
"What else was I supposed to do?"
"I have no idea. I hope you haven't ruined the experiment."
The tension broke suddenly and they began laughing nervously in each other's faces, rolling over, kissing and trembling uncontrollably as the adrenalin started to drain from their bodies. Relaxing eventually, they lay quietly, gazing at each other. A mischievous twinkle appeared in her eyes.
"It's no good David, I am so sorry, it will never work." He was quiet for a while then sat up awkwardly, gazing nervously into her eyes. "Sex, it can never be the same for me again," she explained seriously, then spluttered suddenly, her body shaking uncontrollably as she clasped herself tightly between the legs. Her composure was helped by David, fisting her playfully in relief and gently fondling her breasts.
It was late by the time they made their way down the hillside in the gathering gloom. They felt strangely subdued and thoughtful, trudging arm in arm along the steep lane to her cottage. But they had found the detectors, something Ernst held so important he had risked his life. Gave his life for, perhaps.

Chapter 7

"Ladies and gentlemen, much has transpired since our last discussion, so I will try to summarise developments. Both the Americans and Chinese have launched dedicated space probes to rendezvous and observe L4 from close range. We believe the Chinese are still intent on annihilation, but so far they seem happy to watch the show. The Americans have promised a complete data share, but we know what that means in practice. In contrast, the European Space Agency has been slow to respond, fossilised over costs, but is finally beginning to act and hopes to have a satellite ready for launch in two weeks. It may well be too late."

"All attempts to establish communication with L4 using visual, radio and radar signals have so far failed to elicit any kind of intelligent response. The Americans have confirmed and refined many of their earlier findings. The mass of L4 exceeds twelve thousand tons despite being only ten metres across at its widest point. The surface material is rich in iridium, a element rare on earth but a common constituent of asteroids apparently."

"Recently, the Americans obtained further startling results. Ten days ago a faint halo was detected surrounding L4 which appeared to reflect sunlight in a peculiar way. Speculation that it was simply fallout from the copper slug impact, has been discounted. Further studies suggest the material to be surprisingly discrete in nature. Calculations based on its transmission spectrum, imply a cloud of some 10,000 optically translucent lumps of material. The Americans are adamant the cloud is a very recent phenomenon and definitely not present when their probe arrived."

"Two samples were acquired and successfully returned to earth via a small courier pod. They are now the subject of intense examination. It's not known if the Chinese secured a sample, though it seems likely. The only other point is that the American satellite now seems to be drifting away from the object. Whether this is intentional or not we have no idea."

"Suggestions put forward by our scientists as to the nature and purpose of L4, roughly in order of plausibility, are as follows."

A natural object for which our observations are misleading
A natural phenomena, never observed before
The work of another nation to spy / distract / intimidate
An alien spy device now obsolete, malfunctioning or dormant
An alien conditioning device, prior to contact with humans
A warning beacon, either for us, or indeed, another species
A beacon warning that humans are now space cognisant
A device to lure us into a cosmic trap
An alien homing device for invasion or extermination
A planetary bomb which is now armed – and counting down

"Clearly, it is absolutely vital that none of this finds its way into the public domain. Obviously for something as unprecedented as this, speculation would be rife as to its purpose. This is what I wish to discuss today, together with our response. Perhaps we could begin with your thoughts on the subject, home secretary?"

* * *

As the weeks passed, René and David worked feverishly to extract the images imprisoned within the electronic blisters. Their natural friendship deepened until they virtually excluded the outside world, finding time only for each other and their work. David set about building a device that could systematically scan the crystal surface for the tiny blisters, prick the electronic skin and capture their precious contents. It was exactly the kind of challenge he craved, as he began salvaging laser drives and control motors from second hand computers and ordering specialised equipment online. He set about redesigning the control circuitry, and with René's help, wrote and tested new programs for controlling their stepping motors. When he was satisfied, he burned the control programs into EPROM chips for permanent and rapid scanning action.

Modifying the circuitry, trying and failing and succeeding, fooling around with René and cooking her meals, David couldn't remember or imagine a better time. It became his routine to start early and work through until noon, often dozing lightly on the couch after lunch, only to find René asleep in his lap when he woke. Then they'd work through until evening, when he cooked dinner, before collapsing into bed, while René worked on intently through the night. Each day he learned something more beautiful about her and each day she found something intriguing about him.

The blissful existence recalled within him something of the way his grandfather's face would light up when he reminisced on his carefree days as a young man, returning home to London's East End after five gruelling years as prisoner of war, safe now, but ill, jobless and forgotten. He recalled with fondness his stories of scavenging a broken-down old van from a distant relation, stripping it down, and lovingly restoring it. They were one of the first families on the street to own a car. Delivery van actually, but it was just as good, for he had installed extra seats and windows and forgotten to tell the tax man. He took his young family for outings to the seaside; Brighton, Margate or Clacton, and on one memorable occasion, a fourteen hour trek to Devon for a week's camping. *Best days of your life son!*

At the time, David didn't understand the phrase, nor did he think to ask. But years later, watching a movie, he recognised it with sudden poignancy as an old army expression, barked out by screaming sergeant majors to calm their nervous charges.

Meanwhile René continued to refine her calculations and algorithms for untangling the captured images. She smouldered with a suppressed rage and determination she herself had difficulty explaining. Her own blossoming confidence and single-minded sense of purpose to vindicate Ernst surprised her. She was aware too of blurring the emotional boundaries, but felt Ernst would understand, and perhaps even approve.

After five weeks of intense activity they were ready to reconstruct the first image. One morning David came into her study to find her reading a book.

"Seeking romance, sweet pea?"

"I wish, David! I'm searching for a more efficient algorithm to invert anti-symmetric matrices."

"You mean they're all out there, ready to use – off the peg answers? I wish my job was so easy. Here I am, burning bloody holes in my fingers, soldering all your equipment and what are you doing? Feet up, getting it all out of a book!"

"Why re-invent the wheel? If someone has gone to a lot of trouble perfecting something, why not use it? There's no copyright in mathematics."

"What on earth is that," he asked suddenly, distracted by a colourful flickering on her computer display.

"It's a screensaver, my background program searching for extraterrestrial intelligence."

"Good grief woman! We've no time to go looking for aliens."

"Don't be silly David, it's a screensaver. It runs automatically in the background, whenever my computer has finished its work and has nothing better to do. It helps the international SETI project, analysing radio signals from outer space, searching for anything remotely interesting or intelligent – obviously nothing for you to fear!"

"Ouch! Where did it come from?"

"It's called distributed parallel processing, you can download them for free. There are hundreds out there – for all sorts of things. Some people say the military use them to steal processing time. I have this one installed to make sure my computer doesn't do anything I don't want it to do. Besides, I like to think I'm helping with something big."

"Finding aliens? Bloody hell! Does it work?"

"Who knows – it seems to have dragged you in here. What exactly do you want David, or are you just lusting after my body again?"

"I have the first batch of blister files ready," he said, handing her a memory stick. "Pop it in girl, let's sit back and enjoy the show. How long does it take?"

"It's not so straightforward, David. The calculations are still very demanding. I have to run a low resolution program first, to rough out each image, like a thumbnail sketch. Then we can run the high-resolution program on the more promising images."

"Sounds very sensible. So how long is that?"

"Twenty minutes or twenty-four hours, depending on which you use."

"What! That's no good," he gasped, towering over her and rubbing her shoulders. "There're thousands of images to untangle on this one crystal alone. There must be another way," he said, tentatively slipping his hand down her blouse.

"Well if you're so clever, perhaps you should try some of the programming yourself. You seem to have plenty of time on your hands at the moment."

"I might just do that smartypants. Listen darling, what do you say we set the low-res program running on this first batch and then go for a good long walk. It's been ages since we had some fresh air together and I reckon we're due for a break. When we return we can select the most promising image and feed it to the high-res monster. Then perhaps open a bottle of wine. Who knows, I might even get some sex at last."

"That's fine by me big boy. But you might like to treat me to a nice meal first, I'm getting fed up with your lentil stews every day."

Their banter had grown in confidence over the weeks, though lately it had become tinged with something of an edge, perhaps in growing anxiety of a deeper intimacy. Privately, each suffered a guilt that was difficult to admit, even to themselves. As one felt released the other became blocked, in what was fast becoming a frustrating cycle of behaviour. Each longed for the other to break the deadlock and sweep aside their anxieties.

René loaded the data and set the program running, happy with the decision to get out at last. They had been cooped up far too long with each other. She phoned *Die Post*, her favourite restaurant over the ridge and down into the next village. And it was about time he showed a little more physical interest in her, she thought bluntly. Ever since his stunt on the ledge, she had been looking forward to having him securely between her legs. He'd better be worth it, too. All this science was making her fidgety.

* * *

After packing a light lunch and donning her walking gear, she returned to check the program. The first image was just coming through, a disappointing grey swirl for the most part. She knew most of the images would be uninteresting of course, but she badly wanted their first picture to show something encouraging. She rotated it about the screen trying to pick out the vertical.

To reduce processing time, the images were generated in sixty-four shades of grey. To reconstruct the colour balance she needed to identify three objects whose colour she could guess. Rather arbitrarily, she allocated light blue for a large featureless area she took to be the sky and grey-brown for a flat area she guessed was the ground. The whole picture now took on a drab brown shade, rather like the old negatives her mother kept of her childhood. She searched around for something to fix the third colour component.

There seemed little else of interest, just two hazy patches on opposite sides of the image. The one at the top right seemed a foreground object and slightly more discernible. The one near the bottom was unclear, though it too seemed part of the foreground, obscuring at one point a strong uniform band running down the centre. She heard David yelling and called out to him.

"Damn, I knew it! Can't leave your baby alone for five minutes. Come on, René, put it to bed and let's get going."

"*Our* baby," she said wistfully, staring at the display. "What do you make of this?"

"Why is it round?"

"Why is what round?"

"Why is the image round?"

"It just is David, you don't get nice sharp rectangles in nature. Straight lines are a human artefact. Anyway, what does it matter, I'm trying to figure out the scene."

"But it's not even circular. More like oval."

"For Heaven's sake, David! Maybe the screen aspect ratio is off, I don't know. Forget the shape. What is this?" she said to distract him, pointing to a fuzzy patch near the bottom.

"It's a person obviously. Young, female, attractive. Good body."

"What! It can't be. How can you tell?" she asked, peering intently at the image.

"I haven't the faintest idea, René. I was just kidding. Now, can we get going? I really don't fancy being out all night in the hills with crazy-girl again," remembering the last time and rather deciding it was exactly what he fancied.

"No, you said it spontaneously, without thinking. You must have sensed something. What did you see David?" They both stared at the image.

"It was nothing, darling, honest. It's a male thing, we're wired that way."

"Well if it is, that would be her face I suppose," she said, pointing to a vaguely oval patch. "I'll set it light pink."

"That's a bit presumptuous, isn't it?"

She looked at him warningly as she rapidly typed a few commands. The whole scene took on a slightly more discernable appearance.

"So why is she lying down? Oh God no, David – don't tell me. Do you know what, you remind me sometimes of those Lissajous cards psychiatrists use to get people talking about their sex lives."

"You mean *Rorschach Inkblots*. And no, I'm not like that René, you know I'm not. Anyway, you brought it up, perhaps you're the one with the problem."

They lapsed into a thoughtful silence after that.

"Hey, René. That reminds me of a joke. There's this lady psychiatrist see, and a bloke stretched out on her couch ..."

"David – shut up! I want to sort this out. Go take a long cold shower." He ignored her and continued to stare at the image. "So what's the red patch over her right shoulder?" she asked finally.

"You mean her left shoulder. You've just painted on her face, remember. Besides, if it is a woman, she's not laying down, women don't look like that laying down. How do you know which way is up, anyway?" he asked, twisting his head round alarmingly.

"That's not the ground, René!" he exclaimed suddenly. "Or if it is, it's not the horizontal ground. Can't you see – it's a vertical wall of some sort and she's standing in front, not laying on it. Turn your head this way and look. That's the sky alright, but the bit we see is the top left of the picture."

René tapped a string of keys and the picture rotated itself with the brown wash cancelled.

"How on earth did you do that?" he asked in astonishment.

"You need to know matrix theory to understand that," she replied icily.

"Why would I ..."

They both gasped simultaneously, as the picture deciphered itself in their minds.

"It's the ledge, she whispered. The white band must be the glacier below and the dark strip the valley wall opposite."

"I wouldn't know," he replied cuttingly. "I didn't have much of a view myself."

"There was nothing wrong with your view buster," she said, fisting him playfully in the ribs and realising with a start she was beginning to talk like him, even adopting some of his mannerisms. Perhaps frighteningly, she was even beginning to think like him.

"So who is this?" she asked quickly, shivering nervously at the thought.

"God knows. Some tourist I should think."

"A pretty brave tourist to be out on the ledge by herself."

"She's definitely pretty, that's for sure. I might order a few enlargements for my collection." René shook her head, muttering a German obscenity. "Come on René, give it up. Feed it to the high-res monster and we'll take a good look later. I've got to get out of here."

"OK, I'll just tidy up a bit."

"Oh God no, René. Don't start the washing up!"

She tidied her work away and carried the coffee mugs back to the kitchen.

"Right, that's it!" he yelled, hearing the clatter of crockery in the sink. "I'm off!"

"I'm coming," she yelled out excitedly, smiling slowly at the thought.

* * *

They quit the cottage and headed off carelessly down the lane. Two pairs of expressionless eyes watched them from within a nondescript utilities van.

"Well, that has just about buggered it," the man said, flicking some switches to standby. "We better inform Control and squeal this off to her straight right away. She was in the foul mood this morning at briefing, it will be meltdown when she gets this lot. Follow them and see where they go. Did you check their walking mikes?"

His companion nodded fractionally. "Good. Well, stay out of sight and keep me informed. And lose that bloody jacket."

She slipped out the van, eyeing him coldly. "Listen Mischka, don't go soft on me. I don't like soft partners. Neither does control. You might like to think about that while I'm gone. And just remember, if you hadn't botched up on the old man's pills, we wouldn't be out here now, chasing around after these two."

Chapter 8

"What the fuck were you thinking," yelled the prime minister in a rare display of unguarded emotion. His words were addressed to the only other occupant of the small soundproofed room, somewhat to the rear of 10 Downing Street. The haughty figure of the home secretary, parade ground erect and a full head higher, was at that moment favouring the prime minister with a well-practised sneer of contempt.

"The Swiss professor knows ... knew ... nothing. The girl has nothing to do with us, hired by a privately owned weapons contractor. She overreacted. It's completely unattributable. The Swiss have it all tidied away with their usual efficiency."

"Of course it is not unattributable, you damned fool! You sent the gay buffoon over there, stomping about like some Etonian Miss Marple, asking damned silly questions about the professor and his sexual proclivities. Do you take them for complete bloody fools? This isn't some CCF training romp over the South Downs! I want your resignation on my desk, first thing in the morning," he added more evenly.

"I think you will find, prime minister, that you do not, not if you sit down and think about it. Too much collateral damage, as our American cousins would say. I bid you good day, prime minister." The home secretary paused dramatically for a few seconds after seeing himself out, awarding himself a brief congratulatory smile.

* * *

The meeting had been long and inconclusive, chiefly because there was little to conclude. But since when, mused the prime minister dryly, was nothing to say ever a hindrance to a gifted politician? Meetings were the bread and butter of politics, never to be ceded lightly. Scale back on meetings and there's no telling where it might end. After a brief coffee in the lobby and a few carefully chosen words to some of his junior ministers, he bade them goodbye. Tompkins sidled up to him.

"Prime minister, there is something else you should know. I didn't want to mention it earlier, because it didn't seem relevant. They're known to science as large-scale quantum anomalies – naturally occurring bubbles of light, captured on the surface of crystals in the form of minute quantum blisters. They've been known for years actually, although their true significance was not really appreciated."

"Blisters again! So that's what they are. No more science Tompkins, please! Whatever happened to the good old days, when politicians were left to get on with things they understood."

"Inventing new taxes and starting old wars, prime minister?"

"I was thinking more of statesmanship and entertaining foreign dignitaries, though it probably amounts to much the same."

"Yes sir. Anyway, if the technology to read these blisters develops much further, the implications could be immense. Besides the obvious security issues, we might face a deluge of revelations on royal indiscretions, religious inconsistencies, political intrigue, judicial interference, military cover-ups and industrial espionage. Even our own national heritage and royal accession might find itself answerable to independent arbitration."

"Good heavens, Tompkins! It sounds worse than Armageddon. At least there we all get to die in positions of power."

"Yes sir."

"So how is the technology developing?"

Tompkins proceeded to give the prime minister a brief summary of recent developments, deftly avoiding the innate ability of some of his departments to foul things up on a regular basis. As always, the prime minister went straight to the point.

"Let me see if I have this straight, Tompkins. Two jobless misfits, without funding, facilities or resources, apart from some plasticine and a piece of string, have apparently succeeded in the space of three months, where a multi-million pound program has failed to make discernable progress in fifteen years?"

"Plasticine, prime minister?" queried Tompkins, deciding the moment ripe for diversion.

"Before your time. Where are our lovebirds now?"

"The last we heard they were ensconced in the picturesque little village of Dieterfeld in Switzerland, perfecting their technique as it were. David King is a British citizen, jobless and fairly guileless, René Schante, a Swiss born doctorate of mathematics who seems genuinely fond of him. I'm sure we can haul them in if we have to."

"I'm damned sure you can't, Tompkins. Not if Swiss Security gets wind of it. You'd have trouble smuggling out a Toblerone without their nod. No, they may be multi-lingual but there's only one language they really understand – money, and lots of it. We'll just have to pay for the privilege I suppose."

"Prime minister?"

"Never mind, Tompkins. As it happens this is the best news I've had all week. I would like you – with the full Swiss blessing – to quietly coax our lovebirds out of Switzerland as soon as possible. I want them tucked up safely on this side of the Channel. Spend some money on them, flatter them – praise, sympathy, the works. Use that GCSE in people skills I saw on your CV. Promise them whatever they want, within reason. I want everything they know about blisters – facts, figures, technology, intuitions, dreams, fantasies, nightmares the lot. If they're harmless, we'll drop them back in their fairytale existence with our blessing. If not … well, we'll think of something. We don't have a thousand years of unwritten constitution on computer file for nothing. Do you know, Tompkins, I'm beginning to feel very much better about this whole damned business. Good work my boy."

* * *

Before she could think of something more romantic he was talking science again.

"I just can't see why Ernst got so excited about the detector experiment."

"Maybe he thought it would vindicate all his work, silence his critics. After months of frustration and disappointment, he felt he had discovered something really important. Perhaps he thought he'd get his old job back, and the CERN contract. Even ..." she trailed off.

"No, he must have known he'd burnt his bridges at the *Poly*. And his detectors were still no good for CERN. They want a device that detects high-energy particles, not one damaged by them. He must have seen something else. We're missing something."

They sat down to catch their breath. "What possible interest could anyone outside science have in nature's box brownies? It's just so difficult to generate a decent image, and the results don't even begin to compare with a cheap camera."

"Don't get me wrong René," he added hastily when she glared at him, "I'll follow this wherever it goes. I just can't see Ernst getting so excited about it."

"You didn't know Ernst," she breathed with a sigh. "He was obsessive when it came to science." Not as bad as you, though, she thought in quiet frustration. They sat gazing distractedly across the valley, René lounging comfortably between his legs, leaning into his chest as she watched a large black shadow sweep majestically up a distant hillside and disappear rapidly over the top. The warm breeze blew her hair into his face. He leant down and kissed her ear, brushing his lips softly down the side of her neck and tasting her delicate natural scent. For a long moment they were still, savouring each other's sexuality, her deep sighs gently lifting and swelling her breasts.

"David," she murmured eventually, finally seizing the moment. "I saw a book on your desk this morning."

"Well I can read – on a good day, like."

"No, I didn't mean it like that. I meant fiction – romance."

"Oh *that*," he sighed heavily. "It's not mine, René. It belonged to a friend who ... who said I should read it."

"I was wondering, David. You know, we always seem so busy these days. Maybe we should talk more about ... our feelings."

"I don't understand it René – I was hoping you did."

"What are you talking about!"

"Well you're a woman, for heaven's sake! You're supposed to understand these things. I barely managed the first chapter. The main character seems to be a comatosed cat – and a pink pashmina. I never really got into it."

"David, will you forget about the stupid book! I want to talk about *us*. We don't seem to be progressing, emotionally."

He grew uncomfortable at her sudden intimacy, surprised at the direction and intensity of her thoughts. A vague dread stirred ominously inside his chest as he groped blindly about for something to say.

"These are beautiful," he said quickly, delicately lifting the top of her blouse with his fingertips. Her eyes narrowed quizzically in quiet acknowledgement as she let her head fall gently onto his shoulder, feeling the warm sunlight caress her throat.

"Beautiful and delicately shaped," he continued oddly, closely examining one of the stones in her necklace.

"For God's sake David," she hissed, sighing so deeply it hurt, and gazing forlornly into the deep blue sky. One of the stones glinted brightly as she shifted irritably in his arms.

"What are they?" he asked, obliviously.

"Amethyst. Beautiful, though not especially valuable." Rather like me apparently, she thought sourly. "Found all over the world David, the product of millions of years of heat and pressure." She mused sadly whether her analogy still held good.

"David, can we stop all this thinking for a moment, and start making love. Raw physical love, without all the clever words and deep thoughts? Perhaps if we just let …"

"Christ, René – that was it!" he exclaimed, sitting up excitedly and jolting her neck. "That's it, don't you see?" She pulled angrily away from him and jumped up unsteadily, searching his face in her confusion.

"No!" she cried, now shocked into temper. "No David, I don't see it – I don't see it at all. You don't love me enough, is that it, is that what you're saying? You don't trust me to be kind and gentle and loving with you? No David, I don't see, please explain these things to me, you cold-blooded Englishman! Explain them to me right now David, before I die inside."

* * *

They walked for miles in the suffocating silence, he in a bewildered numbness at her outburst, she angry at his ineptness and moody withdrawal. It was better than just sitting there, she conceded, though not very much. As they trudged on, dark thoughts stalked their minds, both hating the silence but unable to break its paralysing spell.

"It's found all around here," she offered finally. "Amethyst, I mean. But most of it comes from the Jura Mountains. I have a large cluster of amethyst crystals at home. You like to play with them sometimes, when you talk to me." She smiled faintly at him, encouraged to see a glimmer of humanity return to his fixed and wounded expression.

He recalled the delicate cluster of lilac crystals she stacked her letters and bills behind. "You don't believe he jumped, do you René?"

She shook her head slightly.

"Neither do I," he said. "Not anymore."

"The inquest found no evidence of suicide and returned a verdict of accidental death arising from a climbing accident. A tragic lapse in concentration, brought on perhaps by stress, illness and overwork. No suspicious circumstances to delay the funeral. But ... I don't believe he fell either," she added, breathing deeply.

"So now we have a third possibility. Maybe he was pushed." She looked at him strangely. The day was turning out a far cry from their early optimism. As if to seal the gloom, the sun winked out behind an angry black cloud.

Chapter 9

The restaurant was reassuringly full and lively after their long walk back, with couples and young families talking excitedly over their evening meal and young children playing contentedly between the tables. The waiter led them to a table near the *kachelofen*, a large ornate wood burning stove. René took him eagerly through the menu, though he had quietly decided already on schnitzel and chips. As he played absently with the pepper grinder, listening to her thoughts, his gaze fell on a young couple seated in the far corner, seemingly absorbed with avoiding each other's gaze.

The waiter arrived to take their order and by the time René had finally chosen her dish, and duly chastised him for his, he was at a loss to recall what is was exactly about the couple that had attracted his attention. After a few moments thought he gave up, putting it down to the drama of the day's events, and shuddering inwardly over the painful misunderstanding with René.

He leaned over the table and gently squeezed her hands, so abruptly that she stopped talking and gazed at him anxiously, wondering if something had upset him again, but he smiled longingly at her and gently stroked her fingers. They were still making love when the wine arrived. David poured two generous glasses and smiled happily, marvelling at her innate ability to calm his spirit and soften his thoughts.

"David, what happened this afternoon? Why did you get so upset?"

His soft thoughts evaporated abruptly as he bristled under her accusation. "Why did *I* get so upset?"

"Yes, why were you so angry with me? What were you thinking."

"René, I have no idea how I upset you. Tell me."

"You were thoughtless and uncaring. You hurt me, jolting up so suddenly. I felt I didn't understand you anymore."

"René, I would never hurt you, never."

"But why were you so mean to me?"

He sighed deeply as his mind misted over with the debris of crashing thoughts. A cold dull ache seeped into his chest as his gaze drifted across the room like a boat slipping its moorings, scanning the horizon of human imponderables for signs of the approaching storm. Long forgotten anxieties materialised with a hard-edged reality as he became suddenly world-weary of human distress.

He had learned to dread such moments in his life, and his chronic inability to avoid them. Should he try something touching and sensitive, steer the conversation back to calmer waters? Perhaps touch lightly on male inadequacy, a self-mocking joke perhaps? Or would a diversionary display of gushing emotion be more effective? In the end, he could find nothing adequate to say before the familiar blind panic consumed him, suffocating all thoughts. It will be here David King, he said to himself miserably, right here and right now, that you will lose her. Your whole world will unravel once more.

His tired gaze fell once more on the young couple as he suddenly recalled a movie he had watched with Christine. After, they had argued about it, though now he could recall nothing of the plot, just a jarring sense of too many extras overacting in the background. Somehow their phoney mannerisms, strident walks and over energetic miming annoyed his sense of reality, distracting him from the story. Perhaps it's very difficult to appear natural when you have so little to do, he thought charitably. Somebody ought to study the problem and write a handbook.

The only thing that struck him as genuine was the girl's chestnut hair and the intermittent glare she offered her disinterested companion. For his part, the young man appeared to have problems of his own, touching his ear tenderly from time to time and looking down into his drink. And not once did either of them show the slightest interest in their lively surroundings, much less in René or David, now teetering on the verge of a hurtful row.

"David, please don't look away from me when I talk to you. Tell me why you were so upset. I want to help."

"I wasn't upset, René. And I wasn't mean to you. How was I mean, tell me that? I can't ever remember being mean to you. I was trying to think, trying to remember something. Sometimes when I get a really good idea, my mind gets overexcited and confused, and promptly forgets what it's thinking about. It is incredibly frustrating. I have to stand motionless, deaf to the world, trying hard not look at anything and grope backwards through my thoughts. But if I try too hard, I frighten it off for good. It's just something I'm not very good at René. I can't seem to think straight from start to finish like normal people. It all gets tangled up and lost."

"But why be so horrible about my necklace!"

"For chrissakes René!" he said, raising his voice and immediately regretting it. "I was not horrible about your necklace. It was nothing to do with your necklace. I love that necklace, I love the stones, their weight and glassy translucence. I love the story your mother …"

"Hell's bugger, René – that was it! That's what started it all, your necklace, and the fact that the stones are really made from quartz. That's what I was thinking about!"

"My mother told me they were amethyst."

"Yes, they were, they are, she's right. But amethyst is a common form of quartz, there are many different … but I think amethyst is one of the most beautiful forms," he added hastily, acutely aware how rapidly their earlier conversation had dissolved into a strange maelstrom of emotion and anger. He hurried on.

"Anyway, pure quartz itself is colourless and visually uninteresting, as a gem that is. It's the tiny impurities that give amethyst its delicate rose colour. Iron, I think. Or is it aluminium, I'm not sure."

"Anyway, quartz is just silicon dioxide." He stopped abruptly. "Now where did that come from? I've been trying all day to remember that. One atom of silicon attached to two atoms of oxygen. What's more, silicon and oxygen are two of the most abundant elements on Earth, so quartz is literally the stuff of the Earth – well the Earth's crust anyway. Sand is more or less pure quartz, you're walking over miles of the stuff when you stroll along the beach. Ocean beds are covered with it. Granite rock contains large numbers of tiny quartz crystals, you can see them glinting sometimes in the sun."

"So are you saying there's a chance of finding blister images in rocks, virtually anywhere on the Earth?"

"Yes, because quantum blisters are very, very tiny – only a few hundred atoms across – so even very small crystals could accommodate many hundreds of blisters. You don't need large crystals like your detectors. And the trigger mechanism, cosmic rays, are also everywhere, even at sea level. Imagine it René, a vast picture gallery of the world's natural history locked up in billions of tiny quartz crystals, all laying around waiting to be picked up, just like those diamonds on a beach somewhere in Africa. Thousands, millions, perhaps billions of years later. Crikey."

"Of course, it's not *that* easy," he added after some reflection. "You need some serious equipment, and a substantial effort to collect and decode the images. And there would still be the difficulty of dating the images I imagine. Still, immense value to science."

* * *

Their meal arrived and they fell to a hungry silence, devouring their food with a sudden and overwhelming appetite. As their hunger eased they began chatting once more.

"David, is there one moment in history you would liked to have witnessed, if you could?"

"I've always wanted to know what really happened to Neanderthal man. How did they get on with Homo sapiens? Imagine having two distinct species of human beings around at the same time. Did we drive them to extinction? Did we all really originate somewhere in Africa, then walk out to the far flung corners of the Earth? What did we look like? Did we live in small families or large groups? Maybe we'll find a complete time-line of images going back all the way – and for all the other species too, a definitive record of life on earth. What's your favourite moment in history, René?"

"I'd love to see some real dinosaurs. How they lived and why they died out so suddenly after ruling the planet for hundreds of millions of years. Did we really evolve from the small furry rodents that survived that era? It hard to believe without photos. And mammoths too, roaming freely, right up to a few thousand years ago. And cavemen and women, painting beautiful murals on the walls of their homes."

"Or the Scottish mountains when they were young and majestic," he added excitedly. Some people say they were higher than the Himalayas and nearer the South Pole than the North. And where did all the water come from? That's a crucial question."

"Wasn't it always here?" she looked up in shock.

"No, the inner planets were too hot when they first condensed; any water would have boiled off into space long before the surface cooled enough for liquid oceans to form. Some people believe it all came later, after collisions with millions of comets. Who would have guessed it René, comets, the water carriers of life? That's what I'd like on my wall, the print of a comet crashing to earth and forming a lake. I'm Aquarian by the way," he added with a laugh.

"And was God a space man, *Chariots of the Gods*, and all that. Was life seeded by beings from another world? Were we ever visited by curious space travellers? Perhaps we'll find images of space ships landing on Earth!"

"Eat your heart out, Von Däniken!" he laughed easily. "And it's not just here, on this planet, René. Silicon and oxygen are two of the most abundant elements in the universe. So if it happens here, it happens everywhere else too, on all the other planets. Did life ever get going on Mars and Venus and then die out? One day we'll know for sure. Hell, they've even found meteorites here on earth that were blasted off the Martian surface. Perhaps they contain blister images of little green men!"

"Some things we'll never know, I suppose. Like how things were before the rocks solidified. How the sun and planets formed, the evolution of stars and galaxies. *The First Three Minutes*, now there's a film I'd like to see! No distracting extras there, everyone a star!" he exclaimed loudly, laughing helplessly at his own jokes and glancing again at the young couple.

"And that's another thing. What with the surface of the Moon being so old and unchanging, its rocks might hold a complete historical record of the changing face of our planet. Pictures of Earth as seen from space going back millions, perhaps billions of years. Some of the moon rocks are over four billion years old."

"They would surely record the Earth's continental drift, perhaps even the changing face of our planet as the plants evolved and poisoned the atmosphere with free oxygen – the first great environmental catastrophe. Then there's that first great continent, Pan Pan … whatever it's called, and the gradual rise and fall of great mountain ranges, the flooding of vast ocean basins, global warming and global freezing down through the geological ages. Phew René! Do you think we'll get the Nobel Prize for all this?"

Chapter 10

It was at once a statement and a goal. From his elected perspective Silicon Valley started at the smooth rolled edge of his empty walnut desk and continued uninterrupted to the foothills of the Black Mountain. Landscaped fingers of sparkling blue water, refreshed daily by the Pacific Ocean, lapped the shoreline of San Francisco Bay.

His office was both expansive and minimal. A huge plasma screen filled the left-hand wall, his portal to the universe. At the touch of a pad or a tone of his voice, any one of eight trillion web pages collating and analysing every human activity in the outside world, would summon to view. The lower nearby corner carried a discreet inset revealing the first three significant digits of his personal fortune. Today it hovered at just under $68 billion, greater than any national defence budget outside the United States.

His calm reverie was interrupted by the dulcet tones of his PA.

"L4 meeting in ten minutes, Ben."

"Thanks. Any news from the Swiss camp?"

"Status is unchanged. SAP squads remain on standby two miles offsite."

"Thank you, Frances. Keep me posted."

He stood up and strolled to the en suite bathroom. The cabinet mirror returned a lean, handsome face, a youthful looking forty he preferred to believe, with short cropped hair masking the first grey flecks around the temples. Clear blue eyes bore out challengingly onto an uncluttered world. A clever agile face, lined with intensity, worked well with his easy lopsided smile.

In dress he preferred comfortable looking clothes, invariably soft-tailored jeans with a white open necked shirt, a small inverted triangle of black cotton registered his only protest to the white vest code of Middle America. In shoes he preferred crocodile loafers, the older the better.

* * *

As a nerdy teenager in the fledgling computer industry he had tasted early success and failure and emerged distracted by neither. He was remarkably untroubled by common reality. All his visions were realistic, *de facto*, all criticism irrelevant. In his dealings with friends, partners and employees, his mind remained uncluttered. There was but one topic of conversation: his latest vision. No small talk, no empathy, no sharing of mutual experience. He lurched from one startled victim to another, searching intolerantly for the next piece in his one-dimensional jigsaw. If by good fortune you happened to furnish it, that was great. You were great. The world and Benjamin Khoeller were great. For all of ten seconds. If you sought so much as gentle clarification, you were shit and the world was shit. End of conversation.

In the commercial world he wove for himself, his binary-man strategy worked phenomenally well. He had the charisma and wealth to attract highly talented, dedicated staff and he maintained the tunnel vision to focus their skills into furthering his vision, step by remorseless step. He could be unbelievably generous or ruthlessly mean and heartless. If you stood up to him and argued with his naive pretentions you risked equal chance of being fired or promoted, with little inkling of either. He possessed inner goals beyond human imagination. Today he aspires to a world superpower enshrined in a single corporate ethos.

Ben Khoeller had fulfilled his ambition to create and dominate the global information industry. He distrusted to a fault conventional hierarchy and wisdom. If information equated to intelligence, Ben ran the biggest intelligence service in the world, more or less openly, at least as open as any privately owned organisation can be, and certainly a lot more openly than many public organisations. What's more, he did so in his own flamboyant style, as original as it was envied. Style, it had to be said, was very important to Ben Khoeller.

Having realised his ambitions ahead of schedule he suddenly ran out of ideas. He could sit on his hands, allow his empire to evolve the established norm. That had its attractions. Find a soul mate perhaps, start a family. Or he could sell out, start another impossible dream and spend the next fifteen years route-marching it to reality. Just as he feared he might flounder between the two, it happened.

Later, he would recall the exact moment. A stray report on the discovery of a new moon flashed across his screen as his thumb brushed the mouse pad; one of a billion mundane items by every two-bit Jack with an axe to grind. The web service requested authenticity and reader verification. There was neither. But there was an authentic quality to the report. It seemed authoritative. It had style and a lingering integrity. He tried to trace its author and failed. He tried to locate the web service but was frustrated there too.

That surprised him. He was unaccustomed to people and organisations avoiding his attentions and greatly irritated by the slightest reluctance to furnish any of his requests. His current managerial mantra was *three clicks or less*. He ordered his best technicians to track the source and analyse its technique, for as an experienced hacker he sensed instinctively that here was something more valuable than the news it carried. In truth, he was furious with the notion that someone was hiding out there, playing games with him.

After a half-serious attempt to finger one of his business associates, his technicians reported back in trepidation they were now unable to locate the original webpage, much less its author. He told them he was staring at it this very instant, and to either locate its source or another job before they went home. Life for Ben Khoeller was simple and uncluttered.

* * *

He reread the report and followed an inconspicuous link. Another report on the new moon, same content virtually, but different style, and mentioning off-hand a name, L4. Hardly a name, but he chased it down nonetheless. Fourteen million results in 0.3 seconds, the first helpfully listing the contact details of over two hundred local businesses with matching zip codes. The second was a devoted doctor's reply to a patient suffering in the L4 and L5 region of her lower spine. The thirty-second reference mentioned a science fiction genre, whose space colonies were sited at L4. L for Lagrange, an 18th century French mathematician.

He was beginning to tire of the adventure, having forgotten or exhausted his initial curiosity. Suddenly before him was another report, equally informative, equally uncorroborated, citing international connivance at withholding details of L4. Top heavy with technical jargon and reeking of conspiracy theory, the report gushingly featured a photograph stolen from the Hubble telescope. In a Boston art gallery it might boast a title, *Grey Smudge on Black Canvas*. Or it might be a child's first attempt to photograph a potato at night.

Another link led him to an internal NASA memo, listing details of American and Chinese space missions which, in a palpable gesture to cementing a new spirit of international cooperation, had been hastily rescheduled to observe and study L4. The science seemed less consequential than the politics. He checked official sources wherever he could, but preferred the stray technical reports which flew around the web, their authors trading a lifetime's professional reputation for a few moments of global recognition.

Despite drawing a complete blank, he began to feel an odd sense of presence. A sense that he need only formulate in his mind a question, for the answer to emerge at the next link. Precise answers to still half-formed questions. He wasn't at all surprised by this mental prescience. He quite accepted his own mind as insightful and profound. Here now, was a second. But when it struck him how rare this experience was in practice, he became thoughtful.

Gradually his obsession for the identity of the source blurred with a thirst for its knowledge: another report confirming earlier measurements of size, mass and spin. The scientific units were not immediately helpful and when he tried to make sense of them he grew irritated with his own arithmetic for yielding absurd values. He calmly reminded himself he was no mathematician and besides, there were other ways. Suddenly from nowhere – he was quite certain this time he had touched no links or even hovered above one – a one page synopsis of the L4 phenomena flashed across his screen, confirming all previous observations, his own arithmetic, and drawing particular attention – in terms even a politician could not fail to register – to the staggering incompatibility of the size, mass and spin values.

The report was written with an easy technical competence but the author went out of his way to convince the reader of the profound social implications of the data. And it did seem to be *the* reader – singular. More a private memo than a report. An urgent and confidential memo from a trusted technical advisor to an important decision maker. It concluded the matter would be quickly settled once the samples were analysed, but stressed urgent consideration be given immediately to the likely affects of the news becoming public.

For eight hours he researched and redirected his quest, ordering in pizza and cola, and delegating all incoming business. Then suddenly he had it. Not suddenly, he realised. He had already sensed something for a while without understanding. He didn't understand it now, he just knew. By the time he stepped out into the balmy spring evening of his rooftop garden he knew his goal. He felt in awe of himself and clarity of vision.

Fate, destiny or providence. He cared nothing for these labels, lame excuses to justify unfounded intuition. Benjamin Khoeller needed no justification. Self and style were his axioms. A new life stretched before him, perhaps a new Benjamin Khoeller too. But a new life already battle-hardened in finance and corporate warfare. As he stood alone in the leafy luxuriance of his rooftop garden overlooking the bustle of downtown San Jose, his gaze lifted to the Black Mountain and beyond, into the black uncharted depths of space itself.

* * *

David was thoughtful again, brooding over the day's events and fiddling with his napkin. René gazed at him anxiously.

"David, when you think about it, rock has been used as a building material down through the ages, I mean the temples,

Stonehenge and the Pyramids. Perhaps we'll get to see how they were built."

"I guess so René," he conceded weakly, laboriously trying to untangle his emotions. "Large amounts of quartz are also found in clay, another ancient building material. And bricks of course. And sand! Vast quantities of the stuff are used in the manufacture of concrete and plaster. There must be photographic records of every civilisation that ever walked the Earth – what they looked like, how they lived and how they died out. Imagine, the very walls and ceilings of our homes and offices, factories and cathedrals, court rooms and parliament, the very streets of our cities, all recording history down through the ages! What was that famous old wartime poster? Walls have ears? They got that wrong – walls have eyes! You were right all along René!"

"What?" she asked vaguely, unsettled with the thought everything she had ever done in the privacy of her home might be on record somewhere.

"Our first evening together René, in the bierstube. The proverbial fly in the wall, you said. You were absolutely right. And paint! They mix powdered quartz in paint to make the colours more vibrant. Imagine Michelangelo painting the Sistine chapel with millions of tiny cameras! Maybe some of them actually recording him, labouring beneath his masterpiece. Perhaps every painting contains a secret record of its creator at work. I can see that causing a few red faces at Sotheby's! And who was the Mona Lisa? Perhaps one day we'll know. My God, it's endless."

"And all that tedious history René! Was there really a wooden horse at Troy? Was Helen of Troy as beautiful as they say? Did the Red Sea part? Who killed the twins in the tower? Who was Jack the Ripper? Who shot JFK? And the whole dreary Shakespeare-Bacon saga!" he shuddered, recalling the endless mind-numbing literature lessons at school.

"Oh, David! Don't be so shallow, of course it is interesting. It's your cultural heritage, waiting to be retold. Accurately this time."

"Hmm ... maybe. Actually, I can't see the historians being too pleased about it, too many brittle reputations at stake. But I'd quite like a print of Leonardo De Vinci testing his helicopter, or Galileo telling the inquisition where to get off!"

"What about the religions, David, have you thought of that? The star of Bethlehem? Did Jesus really live, the crucifixion and all the miracles? Who rolled back the stone?"

"Debunking the Turin Shroud's got nothing on this lot, René. I can't see the Pope being best pleased!"

"Are you sure it's all a good thing, David? Perhaps our ability to interrogate the past will turn out to have a sinister side, more like opening Pandora's box than peering through nature's Box Brownie."

"I can't see that, René. I mean, why go to all that trouble to confirm something every sensible person has already guessed? It might make people a bit more honest, I suppose, knowing it's all on record somewhere. I doubt it will make much difference to politicians of course. A bit more devious perhaps."

"Or a bit more ruthless ..." but he had already moved on.

"God, no wonder Ernst was excited. Do you think we'll get the Nobel Prize for this? I wonder why he didn't publish it straight away? Tell the whole world. Post it on the internet before someone else discovered it?"

"He was a very cautious man. He'd want to check it all thoroughly first, he never did anything on impulse," she said.

"Well he did once, I seem to remember."

"Scientifically I meant," she added, blushing quickly and looking away. Her gaze fell on a quiet young couple seated in the corner. The young woman was staring at her, a slow lingering smile spreading across her moist lips. René smiled back instinctively, trying to place her face and where they might have met. Her companion was staring fixedly down at the tablecloth, speaking quietly and pressing his ear. The girl seemed to be listening to him but at the same time smiling overtly at her.

"What did you have to eat?" he repeated eventually, apprehensive now at her distant gaze and the thought he had upset her again.

"Sauerbraten, it's my favourite," she said, coming back to him. "I won't tell you how it's made, not on a full stomach. Would you like a dessert, *Schatz*? They do a gorgeous stem ginger ice cream – homemade," she added quickly, embarrassed she had slipped into the intimate form of address.

"It sounds gorgeous René, but let's go straight home. Maybe get a nice log fire going and open a nice bottle of wine? This is turning into the best day of my life!"

"*Our* lives, Schatz," she said slowly, in her best come to bed eyes. David smiled, on the edge of tears, wondering how anything could ever be better.

* * *

From the top of the col the view was breathtaking. Not so much the flickering lights of the villages below, but the sky arching over them like a black fathomless cauldron, far darker than anything he had experienced in England. As he gazed into its black depths he recalled with intensity the moment he grasped his first great mystery, perhaps the greatest of all mysteries, one that even a child of five could appreciate. *Does it all go on forever, or does it all just stop somewhere?* He spoke of it in hushed tones to René and of cosmology's modern day answer.

A gibbous moon was just rising to the south-east, lingering over the distant peaks with a cold, pale green light. Mars hung like an angry red beacon high in the southern sky and the Milky Way sprawled over the entire sky, a tiara of scintillating stars.

They had heard it for some time, its deep rhythmic drubbing of the air, churning their insides uncomfortably as it drew relentlessly closer. For a while it seemed to pass along the valley wall below, but now it returned with a brutal urgency, hugging the terrain until finally bursting out over the ridge, its intense searchlights blazing down on them, immobilising their thoughts. As it swooped down towards them a blinding explosion threw them to the ground, stunned and disoriented. Two figures in grey jumpsuits, abseiled smoothly down and cantered effortlessly across.

They stood a little distance away now, alert and purposeful, knees slightly bent, silhouetted in the brilliant blue searchlight. Addressing René in German, the shorter man explained that with the deteriorating weather conditions they were being advised to leave the mountain at once. Where were they heading? René replied weakly in polite German.

"That will not be possible," he replied. "We must ask you to come with us."

"Bad weather?" David asked, trying to make out the stars through the glare.

"Weather conditions can change rapidly in mountain regions," explained the man in perfect English. "It is our job to ensure your safety. Your insurance is invalid if you do not leave the slopes when requested."

"But we are just walking to the next village, twenty minutes away. Did you think we were mountain climbing this time of night? Anyway, what insurance? I'm not even insured," David laughed.

"In that case, I must insist you come with us. I am sorry, nobody is allowed up here without the requisite insurance. It is contrary to Swiss law. This is not the European Community you understand."

"This is such nonsense," David snapped, backing off and feeling a sudden painful stab in his thigh. He turned, astonished to see the taller man pointing a gun at him.

"Mountain safety is our first concern. There is no time for discussion."

As he sank to the ground, suddenly nauseous and groggy, a last foggy awareness of the tall quiet man turning slowly away and shooting René.

With their clothing loosened, they were bundled unceremoniously into the helicopter and strapped tightly into their seats, one of the men returning to check over the ground. The helicopter took off slowly, but instead of heading down into the valley, it dipped its nose determinedly and began pounding its way up the hillside.

The pain started immediately, quickly followed by a buffeted falling sensation. David's eyes were dry and burning as he watched the moon fall out of the sky. A deep beating wail filled his head and for a long time he seemed to hang upside down, unable to breathe and convinced he was dying.

Chapter 11

"You will have read Tompkins' report, ably summarising the position to date," the prime minister announced, looking his home secretary in the eye. "I think it worthwhile reviewing the L4 phenomena since events are so unprecedented even our best interpretations can quickly turn out to be misguided. This, I am sure you realise, is why for now all knowledge surrounding the discovery of L4 must remain an absolute secret.

"Unfortunately, with our eastern friends so heavily involved, this situation cannot last for long. Already critical information is appearing in the public domain. A number of anonymous reports have appeared on the internet, ranging from international exploration on the far side of the moon, to the discovery of nearby asteroids rich in diamonds and plutonium. All attempts to identify the source of these reports have so far proved unsuccessful, but it is merely a question of time: perhaps our inscrutable friends operating beneath the friendly guise of some East European intermediary."

"Prime minister, I was led to believe that every internet transaction is logged on an audit trail, with each user and service provider indentified by a unique address. How is it possible Her Majesty's government is unable to trace these hackers and bring them to justice?"

"Let me assure the home secretary that all the relevant branches of our security forces are working around the clock on this breach. And while I suspect the home secretary already knows the answer to his question, let me remind him – and everyone else here – since it will avoid unnecessary misunderstandings at the next reshuffle."

"The fundamental problem is not one of examining the audit trail and verifying bone fide URL's as they are known, but in verifying the *individual* using that URL. Ultimately, a computer responds only to voltage at its electrical inputs, not from whence that voltage derives. The same pattern of voltage elicits the same computer response. If the identification codes are bona fide, the user supplying them is accepted at face value."

"All the groups investigated to date as originators or intermediaries of the rogue reports have turned out to be bona fide users and well respected groups. Good heavens man, even NASA and the Pentagon have been penetrated and hijacked into authenticating and disseminating reports. The world has moved on a little from your halcyon days and *The Right Stuff*. But be under no illusion, the culprits will be apprehended and dealt with severely. Someone will be crucified." The prime minister's gaze rested fractionally too long on the home secretary as the two men glared at each other with poorly veiled contempt. "Does that answer your question, Hugh?"

Pre-empting further inclination on the part of the home secretary to muddy the waters, the prime minister proceeded lead with his trump card.

"However, we digress. Our main purpose today is to introduce Professor Angor, who has very kindly taken time out from his important researches at GCHQ to brief us on some remarkable developments."

* * *

The professor started straight in, unaccustomed to the world of politics and having waited in the ornate drawing room long enough to conclude a child of five might have read and digested his report by now.

"Since the American flyby, L4 has been the subject of intense examination. One month ago NASA launched a dedicated probe to study the object from close range, as did the Chinese. ESA is about to launch a satellite in the next twenty-four hours."

"After six days of continuous observation, NASA observed a faint halo surrounding the object and manoeuvred its probe closer to investigate. It acquired two samples of the cloud which have been returned to earth via a small courier pod. They have been safely recovered and are currently the subject of exhaustive investigations. The best available information is that the Chinese also returned a sample."

"Initially, the intention was to investigate both samples at undisclosed locations on American soil, but under intense lobbying from the prime minister, together with technical support from myself and other experts in the UK, it was agreed that a British led group of experts at GCHQ, liaising continuously with the US group, should investigate the second sample. I shall only discuss progress of the GCHQ group today."

"The samples turn out to be translucent spheres roughly the size of a large grapefruit. They appear to be made of a clear colourless material not dissimilar to quartz, though slightly denser. They have an indeterminate bluish haze, due to the surface not being perfectly smooth at atomic dimensions. Electron microscopy reveals in fact the surface to be covered with a gigantic number of tiny bubbles or pits, like a modern compact disk but of far higher density, something like 10^{19} in total – that's a one followed by nineteen zeroes. As far as we can tell, all the bubbles are identical and therefore almost certainly not of natural origin."

"The spacing between the bubbles is not uniform, but neither is it random. The most obvious conclusion is that the pattern of bubbles and gaps forms a coded message – rather like Braille or Morse code. If that is the case, it is an incredibly long message – equivalent to some 10 billion distinct volumes of the *Encyclopaedia Britannica*. That's roughly one volume per every human being alive on the planet."

"Professor Angor, could all of this be some elaborate Chinese scam to economically sidetrack the west?"

"Unlikely, but we can't rule it out at this stage."

"But if this were an attempt by an intelligent species to communicate with Earth, surely Morse code is rather primitive?"

"The binary nature of the code is indeed primitive, but at the same time, very fundamental. All modern digital communication is based on something similar. The primitive aspect of this code is more likely to reflect limitations of the reader rather than the author. Someone has gone to a lot of trouble to make this message understandable."

"Intense efforts are underway to transcribe and decode this message and I will report our progress shortly. At this stage we have no idea how the message proceeds beyond the first few million bubbles. After an easy introduction, the language may well become much more sophisticated very quickly."

By now most of the ministers were waking up to the fact that this was almost certainly the first physical evidence of extra-terrestrial intelligence. There was a hushed pause around the table as the implications of this momentous discovery began to sink in.

"Prime minister, can the globes be considered in any sense alive? Should we not be taking all sorts of precautions and quarantine measures? Even if they are not alive, is it wise to place these objects at centres of national security?"

"Obviously, extremely stringent precautions and decontamination procedures have been taken to ensure the globes are nothing more than what they appear to be – a durable solid matrix for carrying a physically imprinted message. Professor, please continue."

"However, we get ahead of ourselves here. Decoding the message is not the most pressing problem. A more immediate difficulty is that current technology is unable to read this quantity of information at anything like the speed necessary to make significant progress. First estimates suggest that at current rates it might take something like ten thousand years just to sequence the message, that is, read and transcribe the sequence of bubbles and spaces. Once sequenced, the message still has to be decoded. Obviously, we can't expect it to be written in the Queen's English."

* * *

If it was intended as a joke the professor had badly miscalculated. Instead, there was a mounting concern as the political dream of appearing on *Newsnight* clutching a globe and promising a new prosperity for all, faded rapidly from the expectant faces around the table.

"Prime minister, we fully appreciate the pace of technological progress over recent years, but ten thousand years! That is quite intolerable. What are our scientists proposing to do about this?

Even a hundred fold improvement in speed would still mean ..." but here the minister for sport and leisure stumbled visibly with the arithmetic, " ... quite a few generations of delay. Suppose the message is out of date by then? If it's a warning, we will miss it." There was a quiet fury around the table now, directed mainly at Professor Angor. The prime minister cleared his throat.

"Professor Angor is merely quoting these figures to give us non-specialists some idea of the technological leap required to make significant progress. Obviously, considerable efforts are under way to improve the reading process and I am pleased to say this nation has taken a leading role."

"Quite so," continued the disgruntled professor. "Ultimately, we aim to have the reading and translating steps automated and running in parallel, once we have the final codebook. That is not possible at the moment, as the first section of the message contains detailed instructions critical to decoding subsequent sections. The one abiding principle we have assumed from the outset is the author's wish for the message to be understood, and as a consequence, provide the reader with every possible assistance along the way – quite unlike our own intelligence services of course."

Good for you, thought the prime minister, warming to the professor's performance. Nevertheless, he sensed the meeting was becoming restless with the professor's excessive caution and decided the firm hand of authority might prove timely here.

"It may be useful to recall, for the benefit of our younger colleagues here," the prime minister intoned, glancing casually at the minister for sport and leisure, "of a less than glorious moment in our island's history when this nation stood alone, once more, on the brink of crisis. Several years before the outbreak of World War Two, the British Secret Service was offered stolen intelligence of the German enciphering machine, Enigma. From the French, I seem to recall, though we mustn't blame them for all our troubles. Secrets, ladies and gentlemen, which I am sorry to say we politely declined, on the basis of some home-spun defeatism that it would still take thousands of years to decipher just one Enigma message. History fails to record exactly who offered this advice and what became of him. Given the politics of the day, I imagine he was knighted."

"History does record, however, that just one month before the outbreak of war, this nation went cap in hand to a trio of Polish mathematics students who, with no training and scant resources, had been breaking the enigma traffic on a daily basis, right up to the moment their country was overrun. Remarkably, all three students evaded capture and two of them made it safely to this country, hauling their homemade equipment and expertise with them. Expecting little more than a modicum of gratitude and the opportunity to continue their cryptographic attack on the common enemy, we promptly interned them for the duration. Presumably they lacked the rolling Oxbridge tones, so enamoured of our security services."

"Not one of our better decisions, ladies and gentlemen. So, no more defeatist grumbling! Let us take heart and have confidence in our home grown geniuses. Let us offer them every assistance and encouragement for the challenge ahead and try to conduct ourselves with a little of the selfsame conviction and belief. Let us stand firm in the face of adversity, our backs to the wall, noses to the grindstone. Be bold, ladies and gentlemen, history will judge us."

The prime minister seemed quite carried away with the moment, but at this point a rather pale Tompkins entered the room, handing the prime minister a folded note. The prime minister read it twice and glanced up.

"Ladies and gentlemen, we are receiving reports of a thermonuclear explosion in the vicinity of L4. The Americans are pointing the finger at the Chinese, while the Chinese, remarkably, appear to be blaming both the Americans and L4 itself. Privately, the Americans are admitting the Chinese were successful in securing a sample, so detonating an explosion now would conveniently stem all further supply. As yet, no public announcement of the explosion or its cause has been made by either side."

"This is a grave development, ladies and gentlemen, with potentially catastrophic and escalating repercussions. I suggest we return to our departments and quietly review contingencies agreed in the event of widespread nuclear hostilities. We may call it a surprise rehearsal, which is exactly what it is. Lack of notice we will attribute to the need for realism. In addition, each of you will gather your best intelligence on events leading up to this disaster. We reconvene here at 14:00 hours to review the situation and decide immediate policy. Good day ladies and gentlemen, and godspeed."

By the time he stood up, the prime minister's agile mind was already grappling with his next engagement, a roast beef and yorkshire pudding lunch with lashings of his favourite horse radish sauce.

* * *

The sickening motion had stopped. He lay bathed in a pool of sweat, clinging to a delirious all devouring sleep. He was at school again, playing football in the quad with René. Suddenly he grew tired and lay down, only mildly surprised to find the asphalt as soft as his bed. It's only a dream, his mother was saying, stroking his forehead. Of course it was. He knew it was all a dream.

Strange voices floated above him. Why am I dreaming, mother? He felt her hand stroke his head. Sweet dreams, darling. But a dark foreboding welled up inside him, hammering in his ears; a whirring, beating, screaming pain with tilting horizons and plunging moons. He felt her soothing caress consoling him again, telling him he was safe. Think of something nice, David. Think of René. Are you happy, David? Do you love her? Does she enjoy all that science? What are you doing there, you two, all day long? Tell mummy, darling. But when he tried the words came out tangled and confused and his limbs screamed with a searing pain.

He scarcely felt the second stab. Go to sleep, darling. You've hardly slept at all. You were dreaming of René and her crystals. Such a clever girl, finding all those pictures. Where is her professor friend? What are you looking for?

He dreamt of René and her necklace. He had known crises before, when the world fell in on him and dark shapes stalked the shadows. He had learnt a way to survive, to focus on the small details. His face itched ferociously but when he tried to scratch it, his hands screamed with pain. That was a small thing, but still he did not understand.

His mother had gone now and René was with him, soothing his burning face and gently massaging his penis. You had a bad dream David, but I am here now. I love you David, you know I would never hurt you. Do you remember this morning darling, in the grass?

He tried to sit up and felt her naked breasts brush his face. She whispered wet thoughts in his ear, feeding his erection. Good boy. Do you love me? Tell me David, I love to hear your voice. Tell me about the picture, David. The girl on the ledge! So clever. How many pictures David? What can you see? Where is Professor Flaubert? Have you seen his friend, Professor Rheinhalter? Did you kill Professor Flaubert, David? Why are you so interested in the quartz crystals?

He tried to tell her, really he did. He pleaded with her. So many questions but he could not find the words. He understood that now. That was a big thing. He strained violently as she worked him to a climax, arching his back, the cable ties biting viciously through his wrists, while his mouth worked silently, foaming with effort.

* * *

Now all was quiet again and René had gone. He was waking up, his eyes conjuring terrifying shapes in the darkness. He lay still, listening for familiar sounds but could hear nothing beyond his own breathing. Why am I listening? He couldn't remember. Find a sound, something small, something to fix on. Listen for the hum of electric mains, pipes creeping with the heat, or floorboards creaking as they dried. Hear the clunk of metal on metal, the wind and the rain. Birds.

But he could hear none of these things. Maybe I am dead, he wondered. But then he did sense something, something about the air. Not actually a taste, or a smell. Not a dampness either, but a certain dryness perhaps. A lightness, a lighter sensation at the back of his throat as he breathed. The air was lighter and thinner. Was he flying? He suddenly recalled the helicopter and a sickening panic seized him.

He should find a window but had forgotten how to move. To his surprise his fingers moved a little, then stopped hastily as the hot blood shot pangs of glass needles up his arms. Slowly his feeling returned and the tingling died away. He stiffened suddenly at the sound of an anguished moan beside him.

"René, is that you?"

He was alive. René was alive. His fingertips gently stroked the raw groove around his wrists, as his mind and body slowly began to function.

Chapter 12

The lights dim, a screen glows. Words fade in, accompanied by soft momentous music.

A New Age Dawns

Hushed disciples file into his darkened suite in silent anticipation. This is Ben Khoeller's way, his magic. Even diehards succumb. It was after all, why they were here. Serious eyes scan the room. The email cited a life-changing experience. They always did, and they always were. Life-threatening too, if you got in his way. The strange thing was, by the end, everyone was sold on his vision and fired to make it happen.

An irregular lump of rock floating in space, fades slowly into view, gradually depixelating on ever finer scales. A general outline at first, then one large indent. For a while nothing more seems to happen, then a few smaller craters appear, then a rush of new detail. Suddenly the whole object snaps into stereoscopic clarity with mesmerising detail. As their eyes grow accustomed to the startling image, they see it is moving, drifting slowly across the blackness of a space studded with faint stars. No one had ever seen anything like it before.

This Is Our New Moon

He says the word 'our' as if he had just bought it, which he may well have.

"I say new, actually it's as old as the Earth. Newly discovered, forty-three weeks ago. It has circled the Earth for four billion years in the same orbit as our Moon, but always 60° ahead. In astronomy, its orbit is known as L4. There is a second orbit L5, its mirror image, 60° behind. Together, they comprise the only two stable solutions of the famous three-body problem of astronomy."

"Three things are known about L4, as the object itself has become known. It's size, mass and spin. It is the size of a bus, the mass of a destroyer and it has zero spin – a truly impossible combination of statistics. These three numbers alone scream out …"

Extraterrestrial Intelligence

He had reached the incredulity stage in his presentation mantra, the point at which each participant privately accepts that Ben Khoeller has slipped off the edge of reality.

He pauses dramatically, gazing at his followers. "But there is more," he adds quietly. "Seventeen weeks ago, in a last minute detour to its planned Mars mission, NASA fired a high velocity copper slug at L4 in an attempt to learn more about the object. The results were not startling – typical asteroid composition. But since then, L4 has displayed certain signs of consciousness. One week after the impact, the object underwent a remarkable change in its electromagnetic character. Pulsed variations in both its emission and absorption spectra were observed at red, green and microwave frequencies."

"Then, five weeks ago, in great secrecy, the United States and China launched dedicated probes to rendezvous with L4 and examine it at close range. Since then the US, UK, China and Russia have gone to enormous lengths to restrict and monopolise knowledge of L4 and obscure their interest in the object. Today we become the fifth superpower with an interest. Tomorrow, effectively, we will be the first."

"Last week L4 showed further signs of awakening, spawning 10,000 globes like this one. A globe materialises on the screen, iridescent in a shimmering blue lustre. The American satellite acquired two globes and shipped them safely back to earth. They are the subject of intense study, one by the NSA at Langley, the other by GCHQ at Cheltenham, England. The Chinese acquired a third globe, of which nothing further is known. Then yesterday, L4 detonated a nuclear warhead onboard the Chinese probe. Yes, you heard me correctly. The Chinese probe was carrying a nuclear weapon and L4 detonated the device."

"At first it was thought only the three globes survived the explosion. It is now evident that L4 also survived intact. In addition, several additional globes have appeared randomly scattered across the surface of the Earth. How many, where, when, how ...why ... nobody knows."

"With the supply and demand of globes completely unfathomable, they command an extremely volatile price on the black market, with reports of globes selling for millions of dollars."

From nowhere it seems, a globe appears in the palm of his hand. He lets them stare at it, then places it carefully on the desk in front of his nearest disciple. Nobody stirs as it begins to move, rolling towards the edge of the table. In sudden panic, the unwilling participant catches the globe just as it rolls off the edge.

"Don't worry, they appear indestructible. So simple, so perfect, so stunningly beautiful. Hold it, examine it, stroke it. Take your time, pass it around the room. There is no rush. To date I have acquired four others like it – at considerable expense."

"But the cost, boys and girls, is insignificant when I tell you each globe carries a stupendous amount of information in the form of nanoscopic bubbles just below the surface. A binary message of phenomenal length, far exceeding the sum total of human knowledge. There is no question this message is written by an alien intelligence far more advanced than our own. So where are they? What are they saying? And what do they want?"

He waited. Nobody stirred. Neither questions nor answers were taken when Ben Khoeller was speaking and to touch his white board was to court excommunication. Our mission is simple, he informed them flatly.

Let's Find Out

The words fade in, centred on a pristine white screen. On cue his audience erupts with spontaneous applause and relief. They had reached the 'band of pirates' phase, ready to follow their inspired leader anywhere around the world in search of bounty.

"Each globe carries 10^{19} data bits together with 10^{15} high quality images encoded in the form of quantum blisters, also variously known as large-scale quantum anomalies or quantum electromagnetic bubbles (QEBs). When decoded, each blister produces a one gigabyte image, over a thousand times the resolution of the human eye. If all 10^{15} images were viewed as a slideshow, it would take 30 million years to watch."

> *Touch me Frances. Stroke me. I am soft.*
> *I am smooth. Hold me in your hands.*

"Quantum blisters have been the subject of classified research for some time, but only recently has their true significance become clear. Lately, this information has begun to appear in the public domain, whether by accident or design no one is certain. It is clear these captured bubbles of light will play a fundamental role in the information industry of the future."

"That the globes employ this technology is of huge significance in itself. But for us their key role will be in decoding the message. The message is our holy grail. Our mission is simple."

Decode The Message In Twelve Months

"By anyone's estimation, the information content of each globe greatly exceeds the storage capacity of the human brain. There are more facts here that the human brain has molecular pathways to store. Not to be too Freudian about it, the globe that Frances is so lovingly caressing, is effectively an alien brain ... Frances? FRANCES!"

At the far end of the table a distracted young woman with large moist eyes and hot red cheeks, starts violently from a daydream, the globe still rocking gently in her cupped obliging hands. A moment of sheer panic flits across her features, as she stops to examine her hands, and with deliberate effort, pass the globe to her neighbour. With a defiant shrug she returns to stare down at her notes, slowly guiding an imaginary strand of ash blonde hair behind her ear.

"But as you all know, I dislike the term alien, loaded as it is with historical associations of fear and belligerence. So that's another thing. We will need to build a new vocabulary in the months to come."

The meeting now reached the third stage, 'man the ropes'. "Your goal is to decode the holy grail in twelve months. Just twelve months boys and girls, for something that takes 30 million years to watch as a movie. How is that remotely possible?"

"Simple. We engage free of charge the entire human race in the gainful employment of decoding the message: compiling, cross-referencing, comprehending and commenting. No one person will ever know or understand the entire message, but everyone will know and understand parts of it. We coordinate the work using the powerful new search engine this project will develop and continuously upgrade. The age of the polymath is over. The age of island nations is over. We all need each other now."

"To coordinate and empower this effort, the world requires a new kind of superpower, one that transcends political boundaries. Traditional superpowers are congenitally incapable of cooperating on a task like this. National jealousies and suspicions, historical grievances, racial distrust and hatred, economic enslavement, all these things mean that if traditional governments ever attempt such a task they will fail disastrously, precipitating perhaps something far worse. Already a huge covert operation is underway by the big four in the name of international security to impound all free globes."

"Boys and girls, this is our moment, this is our destiny. The whole world will decode the message. That is their right, that is their destiny. We will coordinate all their efforts. We will provide the storage, the software, the upgrades and the guidance as and when needed – uncensored, immediate and completely free of charge. We already have our motto, *do no evil*. Now we strive further and higher."

Do But Good

"For this venture we need foresight of historic proportions, an international powerbase and an invulnerable search engine. The first two we have enjoyed for many years, courtesy of my great enterprise. Today I reveal the third. Boys and girls I give you the most powerful search and collate engine on the internet ..."

Googal L4

"There is more, much much more, but we must depart. My luxury Googal jet awaits at FSO to fly us to Genève. From there we transfer by helicopter to the five star Hotel Grindelmark for a brief rest and inception, before starting work, daybreak Thursday at the Flaubert institute, my brand new Googal infoplex high in the Swiss Alps."

"On board Googal-jet, a program of technical seminars and strategy meetings will bring everyone up to speed, together with some luxurious entertainment and relaxation. Make full use of it boys and girls, it may be your last for the next twelve months."

"The moment we arrive in Swiss airspace, Googal L4 goes live. I conservatively predict 10 million hits the first day, rising to one billion daily by the end of the month. We will be in the news. We will *be* the news, permanently. Leave your mobile phones and all electronic equipment on the desk in front of you, they will await you when you arrive, together with any belongings you request. Arrangements will be made for your immediate families to live onsite or visit on a regular basis. Come friends, let us depart."

Chapter 13

"What do you think?" asked the older man.

"The girl is the real brains, gave us all the technical details. She developed the mathematics and all computer programs. Impressive woman."

"Impressive looks, too."

"Yes sir. At least, Doctor Curtis thinks so, seemed to spend an awful long time questioning her. As for Mr King, it seems he's better with his hands."

"I bet he is, the bugger."

"Not like that sir, although the girl is besotted with him, fairly explicit at times. But there's no real physical side to the relationship. He designs and builds the equipment, makes it all work. She's unclear how he does it."

"Anything else?"

"Not really. He's not very logical, has problems thinking in straight lines, he can hardly talk straight, most of the time. Doctor Curtis is still working on him."

"Dismantling the poor sod, more like. Scary woman, our doctor. Still, might save us a job."

"Yes sir."

"Do we have a forwarding address?"

"There's a sealed tunnel leading under the glacier. It's used by students twice a year to collect ice samples and measure the glacier's speed. With a jet of hot water it is possible to melt a small hole in the base of the glacier. After a few days the hole fills up and the glacier moves on. No trace, not for a thousand years anyway."

"How long?"

"Twelve hours."

"Too slow, we must be out by midnight. Rig a boost pump and a hot water supply – use more hoses."

"Yes sir."

"In the meantime, have them flushed out and sobered up. Lock them in the service apartment, warm and comfortable. Let's see what they have to say. And keep the sadistic bitch-doctor off their backs. In fact, slip her some of her own dream juice, we'll put all three under ice when we go. The woman's become a damn liability. I'll talk to Rheinhalter."

* * *

"What are they going to do with us?"

"I don't know René. What did they say to you?"

"I can't remember anything, just sleeping forever – and dreaming."

"Dreaming! Dreaming about what?"

She blushed violently. "Oh, about our work, mainly. It all seemed so clear, like writing a report. Strange really, I always dread writing up."

"Yes, I had a vivid dream about … about you!" He seemed startled at the memory, then turned away and began rooting slowly through the cupboards. "Do you suppose there's anything to eat here?" She didn't respond, overcome by her thoughts and a strange tenderness.

"Hey René, there's a kitchen through here. Cooker, sink, everything. Even wine in the fridge. And a bathroom! Probably some sort of holiday chalet. What about fixing something to eat René? I could do with a shower."

She set about organising a simple meal, clattering unsteadily with the saucepans and pasta while he ran the shower hot.

"Did you see any canned tomatoes?" she called out, searching through the cupboards and almost toppling over him, as he crouched down on the floor in his underpants to examine the door hinge. He threw her a conspiratorial glance and smiled boyishly, motioning her to continue with her preparations. With a skewer and a few carefully timed taps, he began to loosen each hinge pin. He returned to steal a quick kiss from her astonished lips, and relieve her of a bottle of olive oil she was holding. She watched as he carefully directed a thin stream of oil down each hinge pin, vigorously shaking its head, until it rotated smoothly between his fingers.

Very pleased with himself and smiling broadly, he returned the bottle to her still outstretched hand, kissed her again and disappeared into the bathroom singing quite horribly out of tune. She returned thoughtfully to the boiling pasta. Quite her little hero, she thought dreamily, with a yearning smile.

"The shower was truly wonderful, René. Go and enjoy yourself, I'll keep an eye on your feast. Then we need a serious chat, I've just had an idea." He searched the kitchen while she showered, finding a candle and even some music, together with a few more useful items which he carefully tied in a tea towel and stowed by the door.

"Wow! You should wash more often," he effused, as she emerged pink and radiant, her luxurious dark hair slicked provocatively back.

She fisted him meaningfully. "And so should you!"

* * *

They ate well, though neither of them could face the wine. After their meal David became suddenly quite amorous, even trying some of the sensitivity in Christine's book, but with disappointing results. In the end he turned the music up and dragged her squealing towards the bed. She seemed quite startled by his urgency, though her resistance proved strangely ineffective. He dowsed the lights and pulled her under the covers, kissing her hungrily and groping beneath her shirt.

"Not now," he whispered incongruously in her ear, as her hand slipped eagerly down to his zip.

"Not just yet, René, we're moving out," he breathed softly, his body still writhing hungrily over hers. "Come on René, make it sound realistic."

"Oh great," she sighed, ruffling his hair. "Our first time, and we're both faking it."

* * *

"Ladies and gentlemen. The L4 conflict remains critical but stable. It has been agreed that none of the big four will make any statement concerning the explosion and will deny all knowledge of the event if necessary. Privately, the Chinese and Americans are accusing each other, without citing any credible motive. Probably, the whole affair is of great convenience to them both. Although the nuclear flash would have been visible from earth, reaching the brightness of full moon for a second or so, by good fortune it occurred at a time when L4 was close to the sun in the sky and largely unobservable."

"More problematic is the continuing media and internet speculation. There have been several unattributed reports of an explosion in space, in addition to a large number of hoax photographs. One spectacular image even carries authentic-looking Hubble sequence codes. NASA is denying all knowledge of an explosion, maintaining the Hubble telescope was undergoing a software upgrade at the time.

Unfortunately, NASA's recent admission to publishing Hubble mosaics – two or more separate images superimposed to appear as one – has not helped. For its part NASA maintains the practice is purely aesthetic, necessary to maintain public interest at times of uncertain funding. All the same, it is now distinctly awkward to accuse others of the same deception, especially when it's done so spectacularly."

"Lack of credible information from the big four is only fuelling public frustration. Now Googal has entered the fray by launching a massive new search engine, Googal L4 if you please, ostensibly to coordinate and authenticate news and public opinion worldwide. They have published a remarkably accurate history of the L4 phenomenon and are alleging L4 remains intact. In a clever bit of PR they claimed over ten million hits yesterday, with the Googal Sky satellite apparently streaming live and detailed images of L4. The elevation of L4 to global status could prove disastrous if it continues."

"Prime minister, why don't the Americans simply close the service down?"

"Technically, it appears that's not such an easy thing to do. The relevant computer equipment is not sited in any one location, and much of it is not even on US soil. Moreover, as quickly as one site shuts down, another can start up, almost instantaneously in fact. In addition, Googal appears to have brokered a data sharing deal with the Swiss, in return for a secure neutral site. The White House privately admits that to close Googal down at this stage might precipitate a global panic. However, my American counterpart believes the new web service will prove a short-lived affair, and Googal will soon be retiring from its latest space venture with severely burnt fingers." The prime minister permitted himself a faint knowing smile.

Chapter 14

"So, what now Mr Bond?"

"I haven't a clue René. I thought we were in a ski chalet, with a handy chair lift down to civilisation. We seem to be stranded on top of some bloody great mountain, miles above the tree line. That dome looks like some sort of observatory. Where do you suppose we are?"

"It must be the Blofeld laboratory, 007."

"Stop arsing about René, this is serious. There's bound to be a phone somewhere. Perhaps we can call someone."

"Who do you suggest, mountain rescue?"

"It's getting dark and I'm already frozen. Let's get out of the wind and try to think of something."

"David, can you fly?"

"Can I what?"

"Over there. Can you fly?" she repeated, nodding towards the helicopter.

"Are you completely off your head? Driving your car around these hills makes me queasy. Let's look for somewhere to hide up René, then sneak down at dawn."

"Didn't you learn anything useful in the Boy Scouts?"

"Camp fires and animal tracking – I got a badge once for map reading."

"Wonderful, David. You can be navigator. Come on, I'll show you what we learned in the Girl Scouts."

"Girl *Guides*, René. Are you seriously suggesting you can fly a helicopter?"

"Of course, every Swiss Girl Guide can. It's now or never David," she said, scanning the horizon. "Thirty minutes flying time at most. Hurry up."

They skirted around a storage depot and climbed the steps behind the helipad. "Oops, someone's going to be in serious trouble."

"Helicopters have ignition keys? It never occurred to me."

"Some do, David. Right, you go around releasing the safety strops. Make sure you don't miss any. I'll do the flight checks and warm things up a bit."

"That's right bossy pants, hog all the cosy jobs. René, are you sure about this? Why don't we just start walking?" he asked, crouching down in the snow to release the first shackle.

"We'll just take a short ride, a quick hop over the ridge and down into the first valley. Then we'll dump it somewhere and disappear on foot. You don't really want to leave it behind for them again, do you? And seriously David, if you start any of your 'just a woman' nonsense, I'll tip you out at two thousand feet."

"Roger, Kapitän! I'm all yours. Just don't ask for help. My eyes will be glued tightly shut all the way," he said, leaning over and fingering the intricate grey helmets strapped above the seat.

"Well don't close them just yet, Schatz. I can't find the fuel boost."

"Could this be it?" he asked, pointing to a small button labelled *Fuel Boost*. "René darling, are you sure you've flown this type of helicopter before?"

"Many times David, I'm just trying to keep your mind off things."

"Well you're succeeding brilliantly darling, it's gone completely blank," he said, fiddling absently with the intricate helmet attachments while she systematically stepped through her checklist.

"Engine heat, fuel heat, cockpit, harness ..."

"Where's the wheel?"

"What?"

"Where's the steering wheel?"

"Helicopters don't have steering wheels David! They're just like small planes really, apart from an extra column to control rate of climb. OK darling, now strap yourself in securely," she cautioned, muttering something under her breath.

"Doors, controls, fuel, environment ... Oops, forgot the clutch," she added with mischief.

"René, this just isn't funny. We need to be getting out of here."

"David, be quiet. This is important. Make yourself useful. Get the GPS working."

He leaned forward to configure the GPS and noticed two small cylinders clamped beneath the flight panel, with an empty bracket for a third. Carefully releasing one, he studied the bright yellow lever and its retaining clip.

She pressed the red start button until the engine caught, throttling it up for several seconds before easing back and engaging the clutch. With the rotors engaged, she increased the RPMs until the craft shook with startling power and noise.

"Christ, that's bloody loud," he shouted, peering anxiously over his shoulder. She was easing the collective back, intent on the ground ahead, her hands working simultaneously at the separate control columns. At last he felt the helicopter juddering on its skis.

"David! Are you sure you released all the straps? What's the torque?"

"Yes, absolutely. Hurry up! Here they come!"

He caught a rapid movement in his peripheral vision and turned to see two jump-suited figures take up firing positions behind a low wall. They'll have to report back for instructions he thought, as the machine lurched again and tipped forward alarmingly on its ski tips. "Eighty-five per cent torque," he shouted shrilly.

They lifted a few inches and hopped forwards, David uttering an involuntary croak as the craft landed heavily on one ski, bounced a little to one side, then steadied and lifted clear of the ground. They were moving slowly forwards, the rotor wash sending a tremendous swirl of snow and ice into the faces of the two figures sheltering behind the wall.

"Keep going René ... as fast as you like," he added, struggling to maintain an even tone. The machine was gaining height steadily and was now clear of the landing pad. They're waiting for us to clear the buildings he realised suddenly, loosening his harness and opening the door.

"David what are you doing!" she shouted, staring intently in front of her as she struggled desperately to keep the machine on an even keel.

"Brace yourself René, keep looking straight ahead. Squint your eyes shut and fix them on the skyline."

"Fly with my eyes shut?" she shouted back, incredulous.

He edged open the door, pulled the retaining clip and tossed out the stun grenade, aiming at the last moment for the bright flash of gunfire. As he struggled to close the door a vivid blue flash erupted beneath them and a tremendous percussion wave blasted his eardrums. Dazed and disorientated, he felt the straps cutting viciously into his shoulders as the craft plunged earthwards leaving his stomach far behind. "Bastards," he yelled weakly.

Instinctively, he moved to brace himself as a white wall of ice raced up towards them and then slipped silently beneath. Glancing over, he saw René stiff with fear and concentration, straining intently ahead, her mouth moving rapidly as they descended the hillside into the gloom. He could hear a faint screaming sound and realised she was shouting.

"David! Are you alright?"

"Yes – I love you," he shouted back, unhelpfully.

"David, the GPS. I need a bearing. And shut the door!"

He pulled the door shut and began fumbling frantically with the helmet.

"David, we are not going to crash! The GPS is right in front of you," but her frantic appeals seemed to have little effect on him.

"Here, try this" he shouted, easing the helmet over her head and slipping the night sights gingerly down over her eyes. She uttered a small gasp and sighed deeply, relaxing her white knuckled grip fractionally on the controls.

"We're not far from Interlaken," he said suddenly, working the GPS. "Why don't we land there, preferably in the middle of a great big field."

"Interlaken? Interlaken! Oh David, of course we are! That's the Sphinx observatory, in the Jungfrau mountains. That's why there was no cable car. It's mountain railway all the way, a tunnel constructed entirely through the rock. No we can't go to Interlaken, they'll be waiting for us."

"Who will?"

"Not Mountain Rescue, that's for sure. But Schatz, it's fine. I know this area. Give me a bearing for Kristalberg – Kristalberg with a K."

"I have it!" he announced abruptly. "It's already on the display, one three zero degrees, seventeen kilometres. Christ René, I can hardly see a thing. Are you sure you can do this?"

"OK here we go," she said ignoring him. She banked the craft steeply, her eyes darting continuously between the skyline, compass and artificial horizon, then levelling out smoothly as she came round on one three zero degrees.

"Are you sure about the bearing, David? We seem to be heading for a very large hill."

"Yes, one three zero check ... Christ!" he shouted, as the nose eased up and an enormous mountain reared up right in front of them, the last rays of sun picking out the skyline high above them.

"Fucking hell, what was that?" he screamed, as the craft lurched violently.

"It's OK, David. It's OK. We were just a bit ... low."

"You mean we hit something? A crash!"

"No, of course not! I had to pull up sharply, that's all. Let me concentrate!"

"Oh God, I'm feeling sick."

"Later darling. We'll be fine, I promise."

She throttled to maximum and eased the collective back, engaging the rotors ferociously with the night air. They began to rapidly ascend. Even so, the summit loomed over them with oppressive menace.

"David, what's the torque?" she demanded a little quickly.

"One hundred and twenty percent. Well into the red."

"OK. We're going around" she snapped, banking the craft steeply and side-slipping ferociously across the steep hillside, causing his stomach to lurch sickeningly to one side. "Sorry darling, that was a bit fierce, the controls are more responsive than ... than I'm used to."

She levelled the craft out shakily and he could see they were following a slowly ascending contour of the hill, heading steadily for a high mountain pass between the peaks. He let out a long heavy sigh, relaxing limply into his seat, then jumped violently as the radio blasted his right eardrum.

Chapter 15

Advanced computer equipment crowded the benches. High above, a large plasma display flickered with status reports. Text and high definition images scrolled rapidly through a lattice of window displays.

Across the laboratory hung an imposingly framed mission statement, strategically sited above the refrigerated water dispenser. A penetrating high-pitched whine seeped from a large enclosure festooned with high visibility warning symbols. Two young researchers sat perched on stools, huddled over a large computer display, their pristine white vests reflecting brightly in the screen.

"We'll have to report this, Joe."

"Sure thing, along with the remaining extracts."

"No, now I mean, Joe. Regulations."

"There's nothing definite yet."

"That's not really our decision, is it? Our job is to check the message as it's translated and report back. Inform, not assess. Remember?"

"Ease up buddy. We'll talk to Ralph when we're through."

"Sure," said a voice behind, causing them to jump.

"Ralph! We were just about to call you."

"What's the problem, Johnson?"

"We're strategic ranging sir, as directed in the last mission briefing. It's this section of the message, third level segment J5 – lots of good data, much of it standard and decipherable, but also quite a few gaps. It looks like an important document of some kind. It's all logged and appended sir, as procedure. There are images too. They're still low grade, as of this moment. We're still waiting for the high-res frames from the SuperCray."

"What do the images show, Johnson?"

"The planets, sir – our planets. Earth and Moon in the correct proportions. Jupiter and Saturn with the familiar banding and ring systems. Mars and its polar ice caps. Also well-known local nebulas and distinctive star clusters. It's like an atlas of local landmarks, a tourist guide I guess, except ... Well sir, identity is not the problem."

"Then what is the problem, Johnson?"

"This last bit of text sir. It's different from the usual stuff. Kinda stiff and formal, like a legal document. We're a long way ahead sir, so it's only a partial decode. We can't expect one hundred percent accuracy, there's gonna be errors. But it seems important enough to ... well sir, we thought you ought to ..."

Ralph indicated to the young researcher to be silent while he read the message for himself.

****** reviewed all data **** *** *************, the supreme ******* ********* a 95% attenuation of principal lifeforms to ************** planet, third distant **** stellar centre. In ****** this decision the supreme ******* postpones total sterilisation for ten megaperions in the event of ******** lifeforms arising. The supreme ******* ****** charges *********** hercules cluster with *********** the above decision, which is final and of immediate *****.

Decrypt sourcefile US1/3J5/000139
Codebook VS #001B5F

"How does megaperion translate?"

"We don't know at this stage, we think it's some unit of time, but we have no scale factor at present."

Ralph examined the text again carefully, slowly marshalling his thoughts. "You were right to call me, but you should have reported this immediately. I'll file for an immediate assessment and notify the director. In the meantime, keep your mouths shut and look darn hard for corroborative data. Report only to me. Is that clear?"

* * *

Ralph duly reported to his director, who no doubt duly reported to his. By late afternoon, a substantial military presence had quietly installed itself throughout the facility and all leave was cancelled. Research civilians were reminded of the terms under which they operated and Ralph was reminded of the terms under which he received a sudden and substantial promotion. As dusk fell over the base, two young researchers were quietly led into the back of a military vehicle.

Later still, when a set of high resolution prints were delivered to his office, Ralph saw to it they were inexplicably misfiled, alongside some dubious expense claims he had been examining. It had after all, been a very long day.

* * *

"We're showing up on radar René. Now what?"

"David, give me another landing site, twenty kilometres beyond Kristalberg. Quickly now, darling." Her brisk manner calmed him and the urgency caused him to forget his vaulting insides.

"OK, Feldstadt … twenty-five kilometres further, and more or less on the same heading."

"Charlie X-ray Echo Four Niner, Zürich Control. Repeat your flight plan."

"Zürich Control, Charlie X-ray Echo Four Niner. Medical emergency flight from the Sphinx Observatory, landing out at Feldstadt, estimate twenty minutes. Firearms damage to control surfaces, requesting urgent medical assistance on landing."

"Jesus Christ, René, was that necessary? Now everyone knows where we're going."

"No they don't. And we'll be down at Kristalberg in three minutes." They were skirting the mountainside, hugging the terrain frighteningly close.

"Tell me when we're on a direct bearing for Kristalberg David. Check the fuel and find the landing lights."

"Christ woman, I'm supposed to be the passenger here, remember? OK, fuel is good, more than half. Can't find the landing lights yet."

"We're coming up on the bearing for Kristalberg ... now. René, why Kristalberg?"

"OK straightening out." Suddenly they were plunging over a mountain track as it hair-pinned down into a steeply sided valley. "I can see it, it's beautiful. David, the airspeed – give it to me every five knots."

"Airspeed fifty-five now. Oh my God René. What about cables? Do they show up in your night sights?"

"I can't see any. Have you found the lights?"

"Airspeed forty-five. Got them, just above your right knee I think. Airspeed now forty." She leaned forward gingerly, examining a bank of small switches and flicked on a pair. Two elongated pools of blue-white light materialised on the ground ahead, racing across the slope towards a small collection of huts.

"David, this is where things get ... busy."

"I thought take off was supposed to be the difficult part."

"Thank you, David. I love you too. Look out for obstructions and keep feeding me the airspeed." She eased the collective back again and edged up the nose. There was a nauseous sinking feeling while she struggled to bleed off the speed.

"Airspeed thirty-five. Five hundred metres." She was lining up with the centre of a gently sloping meadow.

"No sign of cables. Here we go," she added, a little needlessly.

Coming in high to avoid obstructions, René eased the collective back and pulled up the nose, until they were barely moving, then let the nose down again slightly, adding a small burst of power to slow their descent. All the same, a heavy landing seemed just seconds away, causing David to stifle a sharp gasp.

She gave another small burst of power, as she was struggled to keep the craft steady, the control column now appearing to jump about in her hand chaotically. She was slightly late with the power, causing a heavy bounce and another sickening tilt forward, but cutting the power and easing the stick back she was rewarded with an almost perfect second landing.

Reluctantly, as if distrusting the controls to behave themselves, she slowly relaxed her grip, then cut the engine and lights and shrank slowly back into her seat to ease her crippling stiffness.

"That was ... unbelievable, René."

"You don't really know the half of it Schatz" she whispered weakly, unbuckling her harness. "Come on darling, I'm exhausted. Let's get out of here. Mind the rotors."

She unbuckled and left, pocketing the key, while David carefully removed the last remaining grenade and set off unsteadily after her in the darkness.

* * *

"Where on earth did you learn to fly like that?" David wheezed, now bent double and fighting for breath as the shock began to express. She stood over him with a bemused expression, gently rubbing his shoulders with both her hands.

"Where on earth did you learn to make love like that Schatz?" she replied reasonably, smiling fondly down at him. She turned her head slowly and peered through the gloom at the distant machine. "But you were right though David, I hadn't flown that type before, but there seemed little point worrying you."

"Well you did brilliantly darling," he said, straightening himself carefully and hugging her appreciatively. "So what types do you fly, normally?" he asked eventually, as they picked their way carefully along the rough stony track.

"I prefer the old biplanes really – gliders too sometimes, if I need to relax. But I have played with most types on MX Flight Simulator. I did try the Bell chopper a few times, but I always ... it was awkward to handle. That was my first survivable landing. It's a great feeling David!"

He faltered suddenly as the blood drained from his face. "David, don't look at me like that. You said the situation was desperate."

"Not that desperate, René."

"We all got down in one piece, didn't we?"

"Three separate pieces, thankfully."

"Well, serves you right. Maybe now you won't be so mean about my keyboard skills."

"René Marlene Schante. You are single-handedly responsible for four of the most terrifying moments of my life. Why on earth do I love you?" He kissed her tenderly and deeply, with overwhelming affection. Then again more urgently, edging her back against the stone wall. After a long appreciative embrace she pushed him away.

"Come on 007, let's get inside first." He followed her unsteadily along the path which led around the rear of a large shuttered barn and up to a low deep-set doorway. "After you, Mr Bond," she whispered impishly, following him into the dark passageway, and bolting the door behind them.

"René, where are we?" he whispered, nibbling her ear and urgently unbuttoning her jeans. A faint strip of light glowed beneath the door at the far end of the passage but she sighed contentedly, muffling her face in the crook of his neck just as the door suddenly opened.

A large stocky man stood silhouetted in a bright rectangle of light, one hand grasping the doorframe, the other extending stiffly towards them. A thin pencil of light gleamed eerily along the polished black barrel of his Luger.

* * *

Inspector Migrane climbed down from the Swiss Army helicopter and trudged wearily through the snow towards his sergeant.

"They're on their way down now sir, due here at the Eigergletscher station in twelve minutes; a Professor Rheinhalter and Doctor Curtis. Officially, we're responding to a helicopter distress call, as requested. No sign of the helicopter yet, but we found three sets of ski tracks leading down from the top station. We have mountain search squads out looking for them. The observatory is currently being searched. Two automatic rifles hidden in one of the stores, both recently fired. Also a medical kit, complete with used syringes and empty vials."

"Thank you, Jules. Extend our esteemed guests a friendly welcome when they arrive, then escort them to Zürich barracks by army chopper. Arrange for medical examinations and full forensic swabs for drugs and explosives – lots of calming chat and refreshments, routine form-filling etc. No questions until I arrive. It really is astonishing Jules, don't you find, how much time can be spent on paperwork?"

"Yes sir!"

The sergeant's earpiece crackled suddenly through the icy darkness, attracting an immediate and curt retort from its wearer.

"They've located the helicopter sir, down safely at Kristalberg. Sergeant Tuschman has a squad moving into position."

"Good. Tell him to hold back under cover, I'll be there in twenty minutes. Who is the stiff-looking tourist in the overcoat?"

"A Mr Simon Hamilton-Jenkins. Very British sir. And very concerned for the young couple's safety. Nonstop on his mobile since we arrived."

"Alright, I'll have a word with him. Now run over and welcome the professor and his colleague. Take great care, Jules."

A short boxy train appeared from the mouth of the tunnel and eased its way silently towards the low platform.

"Professor Rheinhalter, Doctor Curtis? My name is Sergeant Franz. I am very happy to welcome you down safely after your accident."

The professor looked about in some bewilderment at the bustle of troops, mountain rescue teams and police. "You seem very busy Sergeant. Is there an emergency of some kind?"

"A helicopter has gone down, professor."

"In the mountains? Oh dear, how dreadful. Was anyone hurt?"

"Too early say for definite, professor. No news of any survivors as yet. The accident investigation team is on its way."

"Furchtbar!" breathed the professor.

* * *

The overcoated gentleman finished his phone call and strode confidently towards the inspector.

"Good evening, Inspector Migrane. My name is Simon Hamilton-Jenkins, Personal Assistant to the Right Honourable Hugh Mallison, Home Secretary to Her Majesty's Government. We have reason to believe that professor Rheinhalter may have information critical to the safety and wellbeing of a British citizen, David King and his assistant. We would very much like to ask the professor a few questions."

"I am sorry, that will not be possible at this stage. My earnest regrets Mr Hamilton."

"Inspector Migrane, you do not seem to understand. The couple in question urgently require our medical assistance and protection."

"The couple in question are already receiving urgent medical attention. And protection, sir, is courtesy of our famous Swiss neutrality. You are cordially invited to seek further details through the usual channels. I believe the British embassy in Zürich opens at nine o'clock Monday morning. The last train down leaves in three minutes. Enjoy your stay in Switzerland, Mr Hamilton."

Chapter 16

David eased himself gently forward in his most appeasing manner as the old man squinted alarmingly down the barrel of his pistol, cautiously waiting for his vision to adjust. Worryingly, he seemed neither impressed nor appeased, and David's composure was not helped by René's indignant struggles behind.

"David for heaven's sake," she hissed, finally wriggling past with a sharp distracting prod and rushing the old man in a desperate attempt to overpower him.

"Papa!"

"René! Mein Gott in Himmel, I did not see you. Go say hello to your mother, she is in the kitchen. I deal with this," he indicated, with an angry nod of his pistol.

"Papa, this is David!"

"Herr Schante ... hello. Very nice to meet you."

"So, David. It is you. We expected your safe arrival."

"Did you really? It's more than I did," David admitted, embracing the old man gingerly.

"David," René called out excitedly, "come and meet my mother."

"Mench René, sehr schöne! But so thin! You must feed them, Liebling! So David. You look after our baby, ja!" she commanded, crushing him to her vast bosom.

"Yes well, Frau Schante. I try."

"Come and sit down, sit down. You are exhausted David. Claus, quickly! Some schnapps! And your pistol old man, put it away before it lets off!"

"But you know I always clean it, woman. Gott in Himmel."

"Come, Liebling. We make your handsome man some honest Swiss food, put some meat on his bone. Schöne Raclette! Also a great favourite of Ben! René, where were you, we expected you yesterday!" They left the two men talking and went through to the kitchen.

* * *

"So, David. You fly the helicopters?"

"Me? God no, I mean ... nein, Herr Schante. Not at all. Your daughter ..."

"Ja, ja, I too fly, but long time ago! I remember ..."

David sat down on the small sofa and smiled politely as he sipped the blistering spirit and listened to the old man's stories, grateful finally for the chance to breathe evenly and marshal his thoughts. It would be just a matter of time before they tracked down the helicopter and someone came banging on the door. Now they had involved her parents. It would have been better to hide in the woods or a deserted cellar maybe.

He flinched visibly when he heard Frau Schante's excited banter from the kitchen followed by peels of raucous laughter, but the old man rambled on obliviously. David struggled to blot it all out. Now more than ever, it was important for someone think clearly and carefully.

"René, fetch me a schnapps, and make sure David has something to drink. Don't let papa guzzle it all, you know what he's like!"

René returned to the kitchen with two glasses of schnapps and a thoughtful smile. "It is fine, Mama. Papa is entertaining David with his old flying stories. And David is ... very comfortable. But I don't think he is eating with us."

"Pah! Quatsch, René. Of course he eats with us. He is so thin. Schöne Raclette! And we have guests coming."

"Guests! Mama, what is going on?"

"Guests, I tell you. They telephone, before you arrive. And yesterday, Lieber Gott! All day long! Ben and Inspector Migrane. But you don't listen. You never listen, even as a baby. Always the little madam. You know best!"

"Mama, don't start. Anyway, you don't have a phone. Who are these people? Maybe we should hide in the cellar."

"Ja ja child. Hide in the cellar. But first we eat! So now, here is Ben!" There was a gentle tapping at the kitchen window as a beaming face pressed up against the glass. She heard her mother shouting to her father as she pounded down the passage to welcome her guests.

"Ben Liebling! Come in, just in time. And Inspector Migrane! We are all going to eat. Claus! Claus! Come, inspector. Sit down by the oven and warm up. Claus! Schnapps! Aber schnell, Mann!"

They all trooped into the tiny kitchen and introduced one another. "But you have not yet met David! Where is he, Liebling?" René nodded carefully over the top of her glass to the corner of the sofa where David sat propped, head tipped back, gently snoring.

"Claus! Imbecile! What have you done? Lieber Gott! Aber es macht nicht! He must sleep, inspector. It is hard work looking after our little girl. So we eat, and I save some for David. Come inspector, by the oven."

* * *

They sat down around the small wooden table and started to talk, Frau Schante waddling around her guests, cackling relentlessly at no one in particular, but favouring her husband now and then with her more irreverent comments. Ben and the inspector sat with polite bemused expressions, quietly exchanging the odd subdued comment. Such was her mother's overpowering banter, René was unable to hear any of their exchanges, though occasionally one or other would glance inquisitively in her direction.

She looked up and caught her father's admiring gaze, beaming guilelessly at her with paternal pride. She blew him a kiss, while her mother hovered over them all like a school matron, recharging their plates with steaming potatoes and slices of the molten cheese, before waddling back to the glowing embers to melt another smoky layer of the delicious cheese.

It was only when everyone had eaten their fill of the simple meal, and the inspector, apologising profusely, hurriedly departed for Zürich, that René had the opportunity to approach Ben. During the meal she contented herself with a study of his lean face and easy lopsided smile, inwardly intriguing how a complete stranger – a foreigner at that – could ingratiate himself so completely with her parents.

He was American, she discovered, who spoke fluent German with a slight international accent. Well dressed, though not overtly so. A bit too smooth for her taste, but genuine she felt. She was amazed to discover he had never met her parents until tonight, but had chatted to them extensively by video laptop which had arrived by special courier.

She listened to his easy patter as her parents began tidying up around her, shooing her dismissively back to the sofa when she started to help. "Sit down and talk René. You can work tomorrow," her mother chided her with a meaningful smile at Ben.

* * *

She sat down beside Ben and began telling him about herself, her relationship with David and the harrowing experiences of the last few days. As they chatted, she slowly realised Ben already seemed to know everything about her, and David, and even poor Ernst. With exhaustion seeping through her body and dulling her mind, she had the curious sensation of knowing Ben intimately too, not as a lover or old friend, more as a long lost brother.

Later, she was unable to recall how long they talked or what they said, just a lingering impression of friendship and an overwhelming certainty that he would help and protect them. She kissed him lightly on the cheek and promptly fell asleep, her head nestling against his warm chest.

Ben sat deep in thought as the beautiful girl slept peacefully in his arms, enjoying her closeness and scented warmth. Eventually, after checking his watch, he gently extracted himself, tucking her into the feather duvet Frau Schante had left to warm by the oven. He checked David was still comfortably asleep, then slipped quietly out into the raw night, the valley floor now ablaze with the violet-white glare from batteries of powerful floodlights.

* * *

When Ben returned around 3 am, René and David were awake and chatting over a hot mug of coffee. More precisely, René was awake and chatting and David was sipping a coffee.

"That smells darn good," Ben said, smiling broadly, the cold night air following him in and making them shiver. René poured another steaming mug and handed it to Ben with a warm smile while David looked on questioningly. It was quite clear he hadn't taken in a word of what she'd been saying.

Ben sat down with them at the table and opened his case. "Ever seen one of these before?" he asked, carefully lifting out a round object and resting it on top of the small sugar bowl.

"A crystal ball," murmured David reviving. "How original."

Ben smiled as he rolled the globe towards him.

"Or a souvenir? Something to take the folks back home? Hey!" he said suddenly, shaking it. "What happened to the snow?"

"David, please," said René, cuddling up to him possessively. Ben was unperturbed.

"Take another look, David."

"A badly designed doorstop? The sort of thing an overpaid company executive might buy? Who exactly do you work for Mr. Ben?"

"It's more the sort of thing a billionaire entrepreneur might buy. I paid nearly two million dollars for that one. So far I have acquired another five like it."

David put the globe down carefully. "Is that supposed to impress me?"

"Here David, it's OK. Take a closer look. Did you not notice anything strange about it?"

David picked up the globe, hefted it gently in the palm of his hand and ran his fingertips delicately over the surgically clean finish. He held it up at arm's length and carefully examined the light grazing its surface.

"A little heavier than I'd have expected. I can't see a single blemish, not even a tiny scratch, just a faint blue haze, which is rather interesting. Warm too – no fingerprints," he exclaimed, breathing heavily onto its surface. "That's odd …"

Touch me, David. I am smooth.
I am hard. But also soft.

He suddenly became quiet and thoughtful, turning the globe over inquisitively in his hands, his fingers working delicately at the smooth surface.

"Despite your flippancy, I'm impressed," Ben continued, as René gazed carefully at David's absorbed expression. She thought she understood his fascination for texture, rich information his fingertips could sense and analyse, but here was just a smooth blankness without form or content. She watched as his fingers gradually slowed in their meandering and began to move with greater purpose, as if finding a door, they now sought systematically for the key, while their owner gazed hypnotically into the globe's silent depths.

What do you see, David? Texture? An edge?
And here, a button? Touch the button David.
See, an image? It moves, it evolves.
Follow the image David, and learn.

"David?" she enquired, lightly touching his cheek, alarmed at his complete withdrawal. He nodded fractionally in acknowledgement.

* * *

With David's scorn abated for the moment, Ben proceeded to tell them the story of L4 and subsequent events.

"What's all this got to do with us?" René asked, inwardly irritated by David's complete withdrawal.

"The samples from L4 were covered in quantum blisters."

"I imagine they would be, bathed in cosmic rays for billions of years."

"But they weren't just *samples* René," Ben said, nodding meaningfully towards the globe in David's hands.

"Are you saying that globe is one of the samples?"

"Not one of original three, no. But identical, as far as we can tell."

"So what is it? What does it do?" she asked.

"It doesn't appear to do anything. Everything we know comes from a microscopic examination of its surface. It's covered with minute bubbles, about 10^{19} in total."

"Then they're not bubbles," said David dismissively. The other two looked up in surprise. "Well for heaven's sake," he continued, "you're practically down to atomic dimensions at that level. What are the bubbles going to be made from if they're as small as atoms?"

After his brief and unhelpful return to consciousness, David lapsed back into his dreamy séance once more.

"Nobody knows what they are," said Ben, a little defensively. "The techs called them bubbles because that's what they looked like in the first electron micrographs. The bubbles – or whatever they are – are all identical and laid out neatly along an enormous spiral, which winds its way around the globe a billion times from one pole to the other."

"How are the poles identified?" David asked, gazing into the globe.

"Simply by the ends of the spiral, it would seem," Ben answered, lamely.

"How are the bubbles spaced along the spiral?" asked René.

"Ah," said Ben, grateful at last for a constructive question. "It's as if someone marked out equally spaced ticks along the entire length of the spiral. If a bubble is anywhere, it's on one of the ticks, but there's also plenty of vacant ticks – statistically, about fifty-fifty, in fact. The techs have nicknamed them *dots* and *nots*. If a tick has a bubble sitting on it it's called a dot. If it hasn't it's …"

" … it's called a not," David said in monotone.

"Shut up, David" said René, finally exhausted with his grating attitude toward the ever-tolerant Ben. Privately, Ben too was beginning to wonder about her surly and unappreciative companion.

"It's a message, a binary code!" exclaimed René suddenly.

"Yes! At least to begin with, but we've hardly started René – barely through the first two million ticks."

"So what does it say?" she asked, enthralled.

It starts out counting, just like a child. One bubble then a gap, two bubbles then a gap, three bubbles then a gap, and so on, up to nine bubbles. The gaps are all four ticks long.

"That's incredibly crude," said David. "Even the Romans did better than that, after three."

"Or incredibly careful," said René. "Ignore him Ben. What comes next?"

"The same thing, almost. Sequences of 1 to 9 bubbles again, but this time, each sequence is followed by an eight-bit group of dots and nots. Look, I have a listing on my laptop. The eight-bit groups don't seem to follow a particular pattern, except they're are all distinct.

"It's a little table of eight-bit binary codes, their symbols for the first nine numbers, just like our ASCII code in computing. But why nine, I wonder? Perhaps they have nine fingers on each hand!"

"Perhaps they have three fingers on three hands," murmured David, apparently into the globe.

"What's next, Ben?" she asked.

"A long list of numerical statements, each consisting of five eight-bit groups, so five symbols. The first, third and fifth symbols are just our old friends, the digits 1 to 9, but the second and fourth symbols are new. Look, we've substituted punctuation marks for the unknown symbols."

$$2\,?\,3\,!\,5 \qquad 3\,?\,4\,!\,7 \qquad 4\,?\,5\,!\,9$$

"Well, that's easy!" said René excitedly. "Adding ups! My favourite at Kindergarten. The first unknown is their symbol for *plus* and the second is their symbol for *equals*. This is amazing Ben!" she said, her eyes bright with excitement.

"You can't say that René!" David said, irritably. "It might be a complete fluke, something completely different. Five digit numbers in base 16 or something,"

"So, we try out our guess and check. Any more, Ben?"

"Yes, lots!"

$$4+4=8 \qquad 6+3=9 \qquad 2+6=8 \qquad 5+?=5$$

"Could still be a fluke," David said, less convincingly.

"Hello, what's with the last one?"

"It's their zero! We have their zero! Any more Ben?"

"Yes loads," said Ben helpfully, bringing up another screenfull.

$$4 + 9 = 13 \quad 0 + 8 = 8 \quad 9 + 8 = 17 \quad 7 + 16 = 23$$

"And base ten arithmetic! Oh my god Ben, this is better than sex!" She danced around the two men, overwhelmed with delight. David looked up in surprise, uncomfortable with her declared priorities. Ben was beaming.

"Any more?" she gasped. Ben happily obliged her.

"Hang on a minute," interrupted David. "Why would they use base ten? It's a bit unlikely, biologically I mean. The chances of them having two hands with five digits must be fairly small. Besides, not every human civilisation uses base 10. The Mayans used base 20.

"I didn't know that," said René. "Where did you read that?"

"I can't remember, one of Feynman's books perhaps." But she had already moved on, and was casually draped over Ben's shoulder peering closely at the screen. David stood by disconsolately behind.

"Next we have a list of the first ten thousand numbers, 0 to 10000."

"You mean ten thousand and one numbers," interjected David churlishly.

"Confirming it is base ten arithmetic, I told you David! It's guess and check, just like our secret codes at school!"

"Exactly right," Ben concluded, smiling fondly at her. "Guess the new symbol's meaning from its context, then check it out with the next few examples."

"After addition, we get subtraction," said Ben, bringing up another screenfull. "Much the same thing again – key examples, lists and tables, just like addition, only now introducing …"

" … negative numbers!" interrupted René breathlessly, unconsciously clapping her hands and doing a little skip.

"Yes! How very clever of you," said Ben, gazing steadily into her eyes as if David was invisible.

"Then, we get multiplication and division. Honestly René, it's like being in first grade all over again, only without the dreary teacher. It's incredibly exciting, not knowing what's coming next, and all the while, having to try out things by guesswork, until suddenly, you find something that makes it all fit together. Some nights I go through the first twenty pages all over again, just for fun. It's mind boggling to find something so momentous that starts out from simple counting. The decrypt teams are well beyond that of course."

"Pages?" queried David.

"No, not pages really, that's just a convenience we've introduced. We chop the message into 8 kilobit segments and call them pages, each segment corresponding in information content roughly to one page of an ordinary novel. It's purely for our convenience, so we can build a cross-reference index. So far we can tell, there is no obvious formatting to the message, just one enormously long spiral, like the groove of an old Sinatra record."

"We're compiling a codebook, a kind of dictionary, adding each new 8-bit symbol we come across. At the moment it's in the form of spreadsheet, with one row per new symbol. The first cell of each row lists the new 8-bit pattern, the next our equivalent symbol, then an example of its use, then the addresses of its next ten appearances."

"Every new symbol adds another row, but sometimes we find we also need another column. For example, some symbols come with a visual reference."

"How do you mean," René asked, gazing at his animated face.

"Well take a look at this, something of a breakthrough for us at the time, although it held us up for quite a bit." The display showed a short list of mathematical statements, not especially complicated, but vaguely familiar somehow, like the cryptic clues of a crossword. "If you were an alien intelligence, what sort of object might you be hinting at here?"

"Well that's π to about twenty decimal places," said René, pointing confidently. "The second line is the formula for the area of a circle. The next is Euler's sequence for the quantity $\pi^2/6$, and that is the equation of a circle. It's all about circles – they're giving us their symbol for a circle!" she exclaimed breathlessly. But what's all this stuff?"

"Exactly what it says René, 23 x 23 = 529"

"Yes, well, I see that. But what's it got to do with circles? And what's that great long list of zeros all about?"

"They're not *all* zeros, René, there are a few one's dotted about, here and there. But 23 is a prime number, so there's ..."

" ... only one way to arrange 529 bits of data," interrupted David, "and that's as a 23 by 23 grid. I'm betting there are exactly 529 zeros and ones in that list. It's a bitmap of black and white pixels – a crude picture René, the picture of a circle! Crikey, geometry!"

"Yes," said Ben, pleasantly surprised. "And it's easy to increase the resolution further to generate detailed diagrams and even crude images. So from here on we begin to see diagrams and pictures illustrating the text, which helps enormously interpreting the more complex symbols and words."

"*Words?*" queried David.

"You can't keep allocating new 8-bit symbols indefinitely," Ben replied, "pretty soon you run out, there are only 256 possibilities. But you can start stringing symbols together to form new words. And then string words together to form new sentences. There's virtually no limit to the number of sentences you can make. Just look at Shakespeare!"

"After arithmetic and geometry, the message moves on to algebra, calculus and topology."

"A gigantic encyclopaedia of mathematics," said David. "God is cruel – and boring!"

"Not at all David," said Ben happily. "Recognise this table of numbers?"

"Of course, the periodic table of elements! Atomic numbers, atomic weights, mass defects. I'm guessing that is their symbol for each element – hydrogen, helium, lithium ... Hello, what's this column? Hang on, where's Uranium? Edge over a bit darling, let me see! Atomic number ninety-two, ah ha, here we go, U235 and U238. U238's half-life should is about six times bigger. Crikey! They're bang on! Now this is more like it, Ben!" he said, completely engrossed in the display, while René and Ben exchanged amused glances above his hunched up form.

"Christ!" he exclaimed suddenly, making them jump. "The atomic numbers go beyond 300! But that means ... damn it, where's the half-life figure? Wow! Hang on a minute Ben, I've got to get this down."

"Calm down David – it'll still be there in the morning."

"Yes, I guess so. What comes next Ben?" David asked impatiently, while René slowly shook her head.

"Further on," continued an amused Ben, "we find some famous equations of physics, Dirac's equation for anti-matter and Einstein's Field equations, only with a few additional terms. Then there are formulas and 3D images for all the well-known molecules of biochemistry – amino acids, proteins, fats, carbohydrates, nucleic acids, alcohols, chlorophylls and pages of stuff we don't recognise, much of it involving silicon."

"Where's the table of elementary particles?"

"There isn't one – not yet, anyway. But we've only just started David, barely two hundred pages into the message – the merest drop in the ocean. But we don't think it's an encyclopaedia, it's too incomplete. It seems more like an introduction, a freshman's foundation course."

"I doubt it Ben. It's more likely to be just enough maths and science to establish a starting language, like a child's vocabulary. How many symbols and words in your dictionary so far?" asked René.

"Nearly six hundred, as of yesterday," said Ben impressively.

"Well that's no good! You won't get very far with just six hundred words, will you?" she said. "I mean, the average human being runs to about 7,000 words, and a good dictionary lists over 300,000 entries. Then there are all the different tenses and technical terms. It's unavoidable if you want to talk about life, which I imagine they do, eventually." The two men looked at her a little crestfallen.

"Never mind the meaning of life, René, I was hoping for an early chapter on nuclear fusion," said David disappointedly, "you know, something really impressive and useful!"

"But we've only just started David, who knows what we'll find further on. That's why we have to decode it, and fast. It's an incredibly long message!"

Chapter 17

"We set up a computer program to automatically translate the binary code into plain English, using the codebook as a look-up table. It worked brilliantly for a while, but when it came up against a new word, everything ground to a halt. Then we had to get our pencils out and wait for human inspiration, just like the circle problem earlier on. We could have done with your input a bit sooner, while you were joy-riding around the Swiss mountainside in your new helicopter." David blanched visibly at the recollection, but René was unperturbed.

"I don't see why everything has to come to a standstill Ben, just because your computer runs into an unknown word. Just program it to highlight the new word, like a flag. The flag says, here is a new bit of gobbledegook I don't understand, but I'm going to carry on translating the next bit of the message, flagging up the new word wherever it appears, so that you humans can quickly figure out what it means. I might even offer you one or two suggestions! Anyway, once you know, tell me, then I'll update the translation and the codebook!"

"Nothing has to stop at all. It's simply efficient multitasking, optimal use of man and machine – something women have been doing for centuries!" She was beaming at them now, helplessly pleased with herself, while the two men stood by in a dazed silence. Ben was the first to recover.

"Right then, René. You better get started, first thing after breakfast. I must warn you, it can be incredibly frustrating at times, but at the same time, totally absorbing. I lost two of my best programmers to the NSA before I figured out what was going on."

"Well, that's the other thing of course," said David morosely. "You'll never keep up with the superpowers. They won't let you

– can't afford to, it's all too big. Who knows what there might be further up the message, weather control, nuclear fusion, quantum computers, thought transference, time travel …"

"Institutionalism has its own problems David, take it from me: top-heavy, over-organised, stiflingly regulated, pointlessly compartmentalised and permanently paralysed by the great managerial-science divide. Large organisations are inevitably riddled with personal jealousies, power struggles and chronic inertia. Look at your own sudden loss of funding at London University. Did you really think that was a coincidence? Or Professor Bennet's sudden departure, quietly resurfacing at GCHQ. Or poor old prof …"

But here Ben made a rare blunder. "Well, the point is," he continued awkwardly, "there are some factors you still don't know about. But we *will* keep up David, we're not that far behind. We'll keep up, and we'll do even better. I'm personally worth over \$71 billion. That's more than any national defence budget outside the states. Also, the Swiss are guaranteeing … well, more about that in a moment. But just imagine guys! Einstein's Field equations, and we're only on page two hundred! What on earth is the rest all about?" he said beaming.

"Let's hope to God it's not all Shakespeare!" said David, finally relaxed enough to rib him on his earlier remark. Ben grinned thoughtfully, noting David's first reference to including himself in the adventure. He pressed on with his trump card.

"But there's something else, guys. Something as big as anything I've told you so far – a second spiral."

"What! Where? Why didn't you say? What's it for?" They were both firing questions now at a bemused Ben.

"But I'm telling you now … trying to. It runs from pole to pole, alongside the text spiral. If you think of the text spiral as the sound stream, the second spiral forms …"

" … the video stream!" they chorused together, suddenly aware of another piece of the human jigsaw falling into place.

"Yes," said Ben reverently. "Blisters. Your blisters, guys. Variously known around the world as quantum blisters, QEB's, light-pods or large-scale quantum anomalies, an entire spiral of pictures! A picture's worth a thousand words right! Who said that, Confucius?"

"No, not Confucius," said David flatly. "He much preferred words."

"Well whatever, we've not progressing anything like as well with the image spiral, even with our massive computer resources. Perhaps we need better scanning technology? Or more efficient software?"

"You're down to individual atoms at that level," said David, thoughtfully. "You need the latest nanotechnology, American of course. But you'll never lay your hands on it, not outside the states, at any rate. And inside, you'll be subject to all sorts of government restriction and control – especially now."

"I have some very good connections in the semiconductor industry – big favours to be called in, bigger favours to be granted. For a project like this I can get equipment and personnel tomorrow that would take six months anywhere else, including the states. In addition, the Swiss have some highly respected nanotech companies coming onboard with us. It all makes very good commercial sense for them."

"You seem very sure of yourself with the Swiss, Ben. My only contact with Swiss authorities has been at the sharp end of a gun," said David uncomfortably.

"Yes, they were very embarrassed about that David. We had hoped for a more conventional meeting of minds, but events rather overtook us. Inspector Migrane came out last night to apologise in person, only … well, you had other things on your mind. In the meantime what do you think of this?" he asked, twisting his laptop around to reveal the aerial view of a large new complex.

"The setting looks vaguely familiar. Where is it?"

"It's the Flaubert Institute, right here in Switzerland."

"Can't say I've ever heard of it."

"That's because it doesn't exist – not yet. This is an architect's animation, very realistic too. Here, we can take a virtual stroll. Beautiful rendering of the light, don't you think?"

"Yes, wonderful," said David with keen disinterest. "But where are you going to build it? The Swiss can get very touchy about foreigners bulldozing their mountains away. It will take years just to get planning permission."

"René's parents have already solved that problem, with a little help from the Swiss authorities," Ben replied, strolling over to the window. "I'm afraid we had to move your helicopter, René. You came down a little short of the proposed helipad."

"Don't worry about that Ben," she said happily, handing him the keys, "I don't think we'll be needing it again. Will we, Schatz?" she asked impishly, smiling at David.

"Absolutely not. And while we're handing out presents Ben, you better take this. And for God's sake don't pull the pin out!"

* * *

Outside, the landscape was crawling with mobile cranes, floodlight towers and frantic activity of every description. Squads of military engineers in reflective hard hats swarmed purposefully over the valley installing enormous container units. Ready-made roads were being laid and bulldozers worked feverishly, excavating huge cut-outs from the side of the hill to accommodate power installations, water utilities and storage depots. Cables, satellite dishes and infrastructure seemed to be going up right across the valley. Further down, a huge army helicopter was ferrying in four container loads of pine trees.

"State of the art, Swiss made field laboratories, previously available only to the military. Battlefield laboratories, manufactured for front line use in the rapid deployment of hi-tech warfare. Delivered and installed in hours, anywhere in the world. Three fully operational labs, up and running tomorrow morning – this morning, in fact. Another seven, in the next twenty-four hours. In a few hours time, the rest of the team arrives. We start with breakfast and a chance to meet everyone. Then a progress meeting to bring everyone up to speed."

"Twenty dedicated and talented young people like yourselves. People who share a passion for their work and a willingness to explain it to me, now and then, in terms my grandmother could understand. Young minds to inspire and be inspired. I don't want people who clam up whenever I ask a dumb question. And I don't want bull-shitters spouting techno babble neither they nor anyone else understands. I want people who can admit to not knowing something when they don't – and then make it their damned business to find out. A modern day Lagrange, in fact. There's not that many of you guys out there!"

"But why here in Switzerland Ben? I'm running out of lives for one thing – I used up most of them yesterday, just getting here!" He was gazing at René, a big sheepish grin on his face.

"We have massive funding and investment, not just from the Swiss, but many smaller nations too, all uneasy at the way the superpowers are monopolising the message and carving up its knowledge for themselves. In addition, the Swiss are providing massive technical and manpower resources, together with guaranteed security and the famous Swiss neutrality."

"Why? What do they get out of it?"

"They're not stupid, David. Switzerland is a small country with very limited natural resources. Information is the new industry and this is the greatest investment in information ever. Information is knowledge, and knowledge is power. Shakespeare, right?"

"Bacon I think," said David, morosely.

"Well, anyway. The point is, this isn't a cosy little research project anymore. People are being killed for their knowledge. Governments will topple and civilisation runs the risk of imploding. We owe it to the free world. Centuries of national inbreeding and military crusading across a world of finite and dwindling resources, means that individual nations are genetically incapable of working together on something this important."

"Already, draconian steps are underway to seize all free globes under spurious pretexts of alien invasion, radiation hazards, biochemical contamination, economic destabilisation, terrorist threat, international intrigue – the list is endless. I run the world's biggest information industry. Our web service has been inundated with millions of reports from all over the world in just the last twenty-four hours. It's getting pretty grim out there."

"Your web service?" queried René.

Ben strolled back to the table. "I give you Googal L4, boys and girls. Its mission: to decode the message in the next twelve months. Here take a look while I make some more coffee. We went live yesterday," he said, staring hard at his watch. "Eleven million hits in twenty-four hours. Quite a debut."

"You'll never do it in just twelve months," said David, "the sheer quantity of information will swamp you. 10^{19} data bits! Have you any idea how much data that is, or how long it takes just to scan that quantity of data? Thousands of years, and that's assuming the latest technology!"

"Slightly more than ten thousand years, with present technology," said Ben, unperturbed. "But we won't be using present technology, will we David?" He was looking thoughtfully into David's slowly comprehending eyes. "And we will have help. Staggeringly large amounts of help," he added, strolling to the window and gazing out.

"They're out there now, waking up, having breakfast, going to work, coming home and having dinner. They're sitting with their families, watching TV, reading bedtime stories and going to bed." Venus hung suspended in the early dawn sky, a sparkling diamond, high above the jagged black silhouette of distant peaks. His own star the Googal Sky satellite was up there, streaming data and live images around the world. A world of seven billion people, thirsting for information and knowledge, impatient with political leaders and their stone age mentality. "We will recruit them all," he promised quietly.

Chapter 18

"Professor Angor, please brief us on your current progress."

"Thank you prime minister. The Cheltenham group continues to make decisive progress decoding the message, recently passing the ten millionth data bit. In addition, thanks largely to the prime minister's efforts, we now have far superior scanning facilities, enabling even more rapid decoding."

"What is your revised deadline for decoding the message?" asked the chancellor, desperate for a booming technology sector to resuscitate the chronically failing economy.

"It's early days yet, chancellor. We are making tremendous improvements all the time. Current estimates are bound to be grossly pessimistic."

"Yes professor, we all understand that. But with the improved scanning, what are we looking at now – five to ten years?"

"It's a pointless calculation chancellor, but something like 2000 years at current rates."

"2000 years! You told us the scan rate was vastly improved."

"The scan rate is much improved, yes. But decoding is becoming more difficult – as anticipated. Much of the decoding is being automated, but some tasks are still heavily dependent on human inspiration."

"Then get more humans! Heavens man, your budget is large enough, we're bleeding dry every scientific facility in the country. There must be battalions of eggheads out there, desperate for work. Rationalise your workforce, restructure, introduce new incentives, ambitious new targets and cut-throat competition. Slash salaries, pensions and benefits for underperformers, cut out the dead wood. Be ruthless man! That's how we get results in the financial sector."

"Yes chancellor, disastrous results, if I may say. Results that the rest of us will be refinancing for generations to come. What century do you people actually live in? We're not talking Global Economic Theory here – you can't just make it all up as you go along. Our only hope as a nation is to invest our few remaining assets into decoding the message, before every tin pot banana republic learns how to generate free electricity from sea water, or make massless plastics stronger than steel, or build the first quantum computer."

The prime minister was thoroughly enjoying the professor's performance but knew he would have to intervene, if only to avoid bloodshed on his Persian carpet.

"Please sit down, chancellor! Ladies and gentleman, can we keep to the brief? What have you found, professor?"

"Well, prime minister, the first part of the message is clearly a concise introduction to mathematics and science. A freshman's course, if you will, all fairly standard stuff. We believe its primary function is to establish a common vocabulary – a general purpose language to enable more sophisticated topics to be tackled."

"And what might we expect to find then, professor?"

"It is difficult to speculate at this stage. Obviously, there is no precedent for prediction. But we are all hoping surely, for some new science and technology to bail us out ..."

"Yes, yes," interrupted the chancellor again. "Kindly confine your comments to the message, Professor Angor, and leave Global Economic Theory to the ..."

"The experts?" interjected the prime minister facetiously. The chancellor subsided in a smouldering rage and the professor continued.

"It is pure speculation what comes next," said the professor.

"Why is it? The Americans are confidently predicting new technology within months – thirty million data bits in the first week alone!"

"That figure is quite misleading, home secretary. We suspect they have decoded only a fraction of that. And while we share all our results, our American partners are not quite so forthcoming. In addition, they appear to be cherry picking, jumping ahead, decoding snippets here and there in the hope of discovering something of great value and importance. It is a high risk strategy. Some of their techniques are fairly dubious, cryptographically. We believe at this stage a cautious systematic approach will prove crucial in the long run. Of course, they do have a far greater budget and access to some twenty globes now, so they can afford to experiment."

"Nevertheless professor, they did recently discover, did they not, an extremely disturbing section of the message, an extract warning all mankind of imminent extinction." The home secretary seemed rather pleased with the consternation this startling revelation caused around the table. The professor glanced at the prime minister who was now fuming at his home secretary.

"And did they not discover this using their superior decoding strategy?"

"It would appear so, home secretary, though at this stage it is quite impossible to be confident of its exact interpretation, the decoding is only partial and there are too many gaps to be certain."

"Have you checked the relevant section of your globes?"

"Yes, and we broadly confirm their translation, which incidentally, spectacularly confirms their dictionary is little more advanced than our own. But as I said, the interpretation is, at this stage, very speculative. May I repeat, the authors of this message have gone to enormous lengths to present the information in the order they do. There could well be grave risks associated with jumping ahead."

"What sort of risks, professor? Do you imagine the globes will all withdraw in a huff and self-destruct?"

"No, of course not! But we cannot speculate here. After all, we are dealing with a far greater intelligence. It is important we proceed cautiously."

"Yes professor, we are well aware of your passion for caution," the home secretary noted dryly.

"Professor Angor, do *you* believe the extract is a genuine warning of mass extinctions here on Earth?" asked the prime minister.

"No, prime minister. The associated quantum blister images show the Earth's continents and oceans, not as they are now, but as they were millions years ago. One image even shows the Indian subcontinent as a large island two thousand miles off the Asian coast. We think this section of the message is nothing more than a scientific account of the Chicxulub impact, 65 million years ago, when a large asteroid collided with the Earth in the Bay of Mexico, wiping out 95% of the planet's lifeforms, including the dinosaurs. A key event in our planet's history and one likely to be of interest to any intelligent inhabitant of the planet."

"So why would the US suddenly propose setting up an international taskforce to safeguard our planet from rogue asteroids?"

"I have no idea, home secretary."

"And why might they be proposing to build a large nuclear facility for the construction of a new type of superbomb? Is it possible they have found something else in the message, something we know nothing about?"

"I don't think so. I'm more inclined to believe their proposals are ... politically motivated. More your line of business, home secretary."

"And if we declined to join the superbomb initiative, and if as a result, the Americans felt unable to support us quite so generously at Cheltenham, could your group continue alone?"

"Yes, I believe we could, thanks largely to the prime minister's efforts in securing another seven globes and the latest scanners."

"Scanners which, I believe, only the Americans are in a position to supply."

"Er, yes. That would appear so, home secretary."

"Thank you professor," said the prime minister abruptly. "You have been very frank and helpful. Let us not detain you any longer from your vital work. Please pass on our sincere thanks and encouragement to all your colleagues at GCHQ."

"Thank you prime minister, I will do so. Good day, ladies and gentlemen."

Chapter 19

After the professor left, the real politics began. The prime minister immediately assured his cabinet that Her Majesty's government would be fully supportive of the US initiative for a new global defence strategy.

"While the slightest doubt remains over the ultimate purpose of L4 and the globes, we must clearly prepare for the worst. I see this as an evolving process. A global threat demands a global response." The prime minister smiled thoughtfully at his unintentional ambiguity.

"We come to the second item on the agenda. Security breaches continue to escalate, with the unauthorised publication of classified documents across a whole swathe of departments: technological advances in blister technologies, satellite reconnaissance, and numerous aspects of L4 and the message."

"Even more damaging is the political fallout on the nation's morale. While the general public may dislike government secrecy, they dislike still more seeing their nation's secrets plastered all over the internet and foreign news channels. From there, it's but a small step to a complete loss of confidence in democratic rule generally."

"Since its inception, the internet has always proved a security nightmare, but one which successive governments have sought to deny rather than tackle. Today, we face mounting evidence that well organised elements of our society are using their technical expertise and international powerbase to undermine democratic rule in the free world. Top of the list is Googal but there are a number of smaller groups and many lone individuals, either acting independently or with common unspoken purpose. A virtual conspiracy, one might say, in modern parlance."

"By its nature, this form of technological attack is difficult to pin down and largely invisible. But make no mistake, this threat is as potent as any the free world has faced in the last hundred years. Because of the speed with which such attacks can be mounted, we cannot afford to delay our response any longer. The governments of the United States and the United Kingdom, together with the full support of the People's Republic of China and the Russian Federation, have therefore agreed to a Global Defence Strategy, a taskforce whose primary role is to identify and neutralise any such global threat. Threats of a physical nature, naturally. But also, more subversively, those of an alien intelligence, supported either wittingly or unwittingly by elements within our own society."

"GL4, as it has already become popularly known, continues to grow in popularity, yesterday claiming 50 million hits daily and predicting one billion by the end of the month. In case it escapes you, that represents 30% of the world's adult population. It is also reporting the existence of hundreds of other globes scattered across the world and is recommending independent verification and documentation of the message."

"Alarmingly, the website publishes entire segments of the message as they are decoded, inviting 'trusted' users to verify accuracy and authenticate content. Once authenticated, the translated segments are instantly uploaded for all and sundry to read, thereby supporting their claim for free and immediate democracy. Every internet user is at liberty to read the message and post criticism, comment and review. Apart from anything else, the practice raises serious patent and copyright issues for the protection of any future technologies we may wish to acquire from the message."

"GL4 is inviting every man, woman and child on the planet to register, whereupon they are supplied free of charge with an entire suite of decoding programs, tutorials and extracts of the message, together with as much web space as necessary to publish their findings. Such programs are designed to run in the computer's background, making the whole endeavour aesthetically pleasing and ecologically satisfying. They even offer to supply state of the art scanning equipment to established groups with a proven track record."

"GL4 is rapidly becoming a popular teenage fad, even hosting an *Alan Turing* competition. My own daughter informs me her mathematics teacher runs a dedicated GL4 group every lunchtime, which yesterday was posted 43rd in the Global Hall of Fame – she has a certificate on her bedroom door to prove it! Obviously, a large degree of this we can discount as pure hype, but if GL4's user base continues to grow, they may well come to challenge and exceed our own efforts. In short, ladies and gentlemen, Googal is making us look like bloody amateurs."

* * *

"So, we come to our response. The NSA has arranged for a number of undercover groups to register and establish a proven track record with the GL4 website. One such trusted group will upload a lightly edited version of the extinction extract, edited in such a manner as to incite public fear and panic once disseminated at large. Shortly afterwards, support groups will bombard GL4 with uncorroborated reports of rioting, looting and troop mobilisations around the world. First reports will be fabricated but credible. There'll be little opportunity for journalistic authenticity, and pretty soon there will be plenty of genuine chaos and rioting."

"Fearing imminent alien invasion and public unrest, some nations may feel obliged to mobilise their troops as a precautionary measure. This may well cause neighbouring countries who suspect their motives to retaliate. Tensions will run high and accidents, no doubt, will happen. Or be arranged. The whole thing may well escalate into a minor international war."

"Other factions of society will be only to ready to believe life on earth is threatened. We can rely on our religious leaders to comment effusively on the subject, offering prayers in our moment of need for the wise and careful counsel of their leaders. For some societies no doubt, the Gods will be angry. Sacrifices will be demanded, punishments exacted and old scores settled. And of course, old prophecies will be revived: judgement day, Armageddon, Nostradamus, Mathias. No, ladies and gentlemen, there will be no shortage of doom and gloom."

"Public opinion will harden once they see food riots in the streets and the breakdown of law and order. Panic buying will become endemic and prices will rocket. Rationing will need to be imposed. If necessary, we will engineer a collapse on the global money markets, inadvertently taking a huge profit from futures and options. The windfall will help finance the GDS initiative and kick-start a rapid economic revival once we reassert control, but more importantly, enforce the political will to ensure this sort of thing never happens again."

"By the time Googal discovers it is all a dreadful mistake, it will be too late. Governments will move in, quietly close it down and replace it seamlessly with a more responsible service. The ringleaders will be arrested on charges of global treason and passing information with the intent to help an enemy or enemies unknown. The internet will be brought to heel. Our trusted judiciary will ensure the legal process remains bogged down for years, possibly generations, thereby solving itself. Major world governments will pass emergency legislation dealing with the threat to global security, as they perceive it. Smaller factions will fall in line once they see what is happening to the big boys, or we'll pick them off one by one."

"Prime minister, this will obviously take months of detailed preparation and planning. Do we have an approximate schedule in mind, at this stage?"

The prime minister looked carefully at his watch. "6pm this evening," he announced quietly, carefully adjusting his new tie. "Just in time for the early evening news."

Chapter 20

"Good afternoon, boys and girls. What a week! It's hard to believe it's just seven days since we first set foot here in Switzerland. I hope you have settled in comfortably and have had the chance to meet everyone. Empathy is the keyword which empowers our venture and I hope you agree with me we have a most talented and gifted group of young people here. I am happy to announce we now have thirty-eight fulltime staff onsite plus a further twelve support staff caring for our every need and comfort, in addition to a considerable number of Swiss security personnel safeguarding our mission. And beyond them of course, our main work force, seven billion of them, all striving towards our common goal. So please raise your glasses to ... decoding the message!"

"None of this would be possible without the world's most powerful search engine GL4, currently streaming sixty terabytes of data, news, analysis and comment on the message around the planet. We now have twelve fully equipped laboratories up and running, together with substantial workshop facilities and a well appointed gym. A further sixteen accommodation units will be in place by Sunday, bringing the total to twenty-eight, although I'm reliably informed Jennifer and Sarah no longer require separate quarters. Boys and girls ... Jennifer and Sarah!"

When the whistling died down he continued. "A machine shop and ultra-clean room comes online tomorrow as we gear up to supply research groups around the world with state of the art scanners and customised computer equipment. I have negotiated a ninety-nine year lease on the adjoining 240 hectares of land for future expansion, accommodation and amenities. We are building for the future, boys and girls, in every sense."

"GL4 is one week old midnight tonight and is due to welcome its one billionth contributor. And perhaps I shouldn't say this, but a significantly large number of hits seem to originate in the Langley and Cheltenham districts. Excellent! We are proud to be of service to everyone!"

"Before I ask section leaders to bring us up to speed, I wish to share with you one brief highlight of my week – a defining moment for me. You are of course familiar with this stunning image of the Hour Glass nebula, posted by René's group earlier this week. The resolution is startling, far greater than anything we've ever seen before, a beautiful cloud of incandescent gas and dust in the back yard of our own galaxy. But what you may not know is René's group also found a second identical image, adjacent to the first. And while this beautiful object surely merits recording in its finest detail, doing so twice might seem a little redundant. A manufacturing defect perhaps? The careless error on the part of some distracted alien clerk?"

"Not at all! Careful examination reveals the two images are in fact, very slightly different. Look closely at this faint star and you will see it lies to the left of this tiny green filament of gas in one picture and to the right in the other. There are similar parallax effects for a large number of other stars. What we are seeing here, boys and girls, are two images of the same object captured from two different points in our galaxy, one from our home planet Earth, and the other from – where?"

"The conclusion seems inescapable – a place of great sentimental significance to the authors of the message. René's group has triangulated the position back to this star, an inconspicuous white dwarf in our southern sky. Not perhaps a very inspiring object today, boys and girls: as a home for intelligent life, this stellar system died five billion years ago, before our own planetary system ever came into being. But if life got going so long ago, imagine what it's like today, ten billion years later!"

"It tells us that intelligent life can be a persistent phenomenon in the universe. That, intelligent life need not inevitably burn itself out, blow itself into incandescent plasma or sink into hedonistic obscurity. Boys and girls, this was their home, their first home. In this planetary system they were born, evolved and learned to cruise the cosmos. Perhaps they are saying they are like us, in some ways. Perhaps even, we *are* them, their cosmic children. Of course we are interested in *you*, they are saying. Who knows? Maybe we will, soon! Read the message boys and girls and find out!"

"A beautiful, once in a lifetime experience. Yet, through your efforts, once a life time experiences are happening every day here at GL4! It is our mission to share these discoveries with the entire world. Long may we do so!" To tumultuous cheers, Ben skilfully manoeuvres René forwards, blushing wildly with the attention and applause.

"As Ben said, what a week, one success following hard on another. Now we need to steady our nerve and prepare for the reality of success. The real challenge now will come with efficient housekeeping, staying up to date as results pour in from around the world. Pulling it all together, coordinating, cross-referencing, verifying and correcting translation errors and misinterpretations. Updating the code and grammar books, review articles and expert comment, and round the clock commentary on breaking news. And last, but not least, second guessing what might lie ahead."

"Of course we can expect enormous help from the outside world – we depend on it, that's what makes us different. Inevitably, there will be no shortage of people and organisations seeking to explain the meaning of it all, from geniuses to crackpots. That is right and proper, democracy in action, a real-time democracy – the first in recorded history. Accurate comment and insight will stand the test of time. Sensationalising, attention seeking, horse-trading and political axe-grinding will fall by the wayside as authentication statistics begin to bite. That is the nature of search engines, it is how they are programmed."

"At the same time we need to be sensitive to fragile new insights, ideas and suggestions, concepts which might lead to new groundbreaking discoveries. In particular we must identify anything that improves our capacity to decode and understand subsequent sections of the message. We have always believed the author's first desire is for us to decode the message, and to that end, *she* has gone to considerable lengths to help us. We expect this help to continue, accelerate even, as we move deeper into the message and fulfil our mission to decode the entire message in just twelve months."

"At the moment we find ourselves in the foyer of a great library, an encyclopaedia of mathematics, science and technology. Insightful text, stunning pictures, all fundamental and important, but no startling revelations on nuclear fusion and time travel. No family outings just yet, boys and girls, to *The Land Time Forgot*. She smiled confidently, glancing at Ben as the room erupted in convivial laughter."

"But soon I think we will need something more than simple text and pictures. Sound perhaps, animation and video. Maybe lectures, movies and documentaries. A handsome young professor who pops up at the click of a button to explain all the new science," she smiled warmly at David, her eyes alive with confidence. "That would be very useful for some of us!" She joked easily now, Ben laughing effusively beside her. "I know David has some fascinating insights on this, so I'll let him explain them to you – properly this time!"

* * *

She had caught him off guard, his mind snared on an earlier remark, so when she called him he was unprepared and momentarily disoriented. She smiled indulgently, holding out her hand with gentle encouragement as he loped awkwardly to her side. "It's fine," she whispered, brushing some imaginary flecks from his new jacket, "just tell them about your ideas."

"Well. I'm not sure I can add anything concrete just yet," he started out uncertainly, turning to René and groping desperately for his rehearsed opening. He had known from the start this was a desperately bad idea and would never have agreed, had not Ben and René both insisted. You need to tell them about your ideas, David, put them out there for people to mull over.

"They're just ideas really, at the moment," he added lamely. "And, as you all know, some ideas are better than others. Maybe an idea works and maybe it doesn't. Or perhaps you need to tweak it a bit, before it … works. Anyway, what I'm saying is, once you get an idea, it's quite straight forward to check it out, see if it works. But where does the idea come from in the first place?"

He paused far too long, as if actually expecting a response, but in reality lost in his thoughts. Ben and René were a little taken aback, realising he had taken their request quite literally.

"Was the idea already in my mind, ahead of time, sitting there in the ideas box, just waiting for the right moment to pop up, like ... like a Googal advert," he asked, laughing uncertainly, "in which case, what happens when your ideas box runs out?"

"Or maybe it's not there ahead of time. Maybe it's put together on the spot. In which case, what is it made from?"

"Sometimes it's all just a simple mistake, an accident, like a copying error. You mishear or mistype something maybe. Say I'm typing a sentence, and maybe I type *globe* instead of *glove*. That's very easily done, *v* and *b* are next to each other on the keyboard and they're quite awkward keys to reach, I'm always doing it. But suppose I don't notice until much later, when I'm reading through. And then to my amazement, the sentence with *globe* not only makes literal sense, but it's actually a great idea too, far better than my intended meaning."

"But where did my brilliant idea come from? My inability to type accurately and whoever's daft idea it was to put *v* next to *b* on the qwerty keyboard – in other words, a complete fluke. The important thing appears to be, to allow a few accidents to happen, but recognize a good accident when you see it, like natural selection in nature."

"Nobody knows how the brain does it, how it gets you linking two unconnected strands of thought at the same time. Perhaps it's always accidental, perhaps not. Nobody understands why some people are good at it and others are ... good at other things. You can try to rationalise famous breakthroughs in history, see how they happen, but people get surprisingly coy about it. Or perhaps they genuinely don't know themselves, can't remember how they first thought of it."

"Sometimes though, you do find something interesting. Sometimes, it all starts with someone getting hooked on a tiny insignificant detail which doesn't quite fit the big picture, a detail which everyone else is happy to discount."

"Why are Jupiter's moons slightly out of position at certain times of the year? Why does Mercury's orbit drift slowly around in space? Why are some substances simultaneously, very poor conductors and insulators of electrical current? Why does light travel at the same speed, even when the light source is moving? Why does Dirac's equation spawn two realities, when only one is needed? Sometimes a little thing can hide a very big thing."

"Why are all the globes the same? Because they carry the same message, that seems clear. So why then are they all in fact, very slightly different? Nobody knows. Is it simply a manufacturing defect? That seems hard to believe."

"And what is this funny little bit of code here and there, which none of us can decode or find a use for? Why is all the maths in base ten? I have ten fingers, so it seems natural to me to use ten counting symbols. But why on earth should they? Ha! They're not even here, *on* earth!" He laughed loudly at his unintentional pun, but then stopped alarmingly as if struck by a sudden thought, leaving his audience hesitant and embarrassed.

"Should we really expect the same chronological sequence of knowledge as our own history of scientific discovery? If our planet were permanently shrouded in cloud like Venus, would we know anything of astronomy? Newton might easily have died from the black plague before figuring out gravity. If Einstein had been given the teaching job he applied for, he might never have found the time and motivation to develop relativity. If Faraday hadn't been a lowly printer's apprentice, he might never have come across the book that set him on the road to electromagnetism. As Einstein said, scientific insight is a delicate flower, easily trampled underfoot."

"Now don't get me wrong, I'm not knocking all our tremendous efforts to decode the message. My questions are not a criticism in any way. But to ignore these ideas now, without a second or third glance, might be a mistake. Of all the senses, our eyesight carries by far the greatest information bandwidth to the brain, something like 50 megabytes per second. So if it's a question of rapidly communicating large amounts of data, why write it all down in one-dimensional binary code? It just seems an absurd way to go about things." He suddenly recalled the point of what he was trying to say, and became hesitant again.

"But there's something else that's been bothering me. I don't know if anyone here has noticed it, but sometimes I have a strange urge, this feeling, a strong emotion that I don't understand." He hesitated, smiling weirdly. A number of his listeners shifted awkwardly, suddenly intent on their shoelaces. Ben and René exchanged uncomfortable glances, but David ploughed on with determination.

"Some kind of unresolved memory, perhaps. Like there's something lurking out there, just beyond the edge of consciousness. I read once that if you place a small voltage at a particular spot in the brain you get a particular urge, or sensation, like a very specific taste or smell or some long forgotten memory. But it's very, very specific and very repeatable, there's nothing vague about it, nothing imaginary – different spot, completely different sensation. Like a memory bank of feelings and emotions. Maybe it's like that. A very specific thought or feeling that seems to pop into my mind from nowhere just at the right moment. Anyway, I'm wondering if anyone else has noticed it?"

He had been rambling for so long his listeners were taken aback by his sudden request for feedback. The room became acutely still lest anyone inadvertently attracted his attention. He stood leaning forwards expectantly, hands wrung tightly together, gazing around the hall with his startled blue eyes. He started appealing again, believing he hadn't expressed himself clearly enough, when he heard Ben speaking.

"Well thanks David, thanks for that, some really useful pointers there to … think about. Now, Peter! Perhaps you would update us on current developments with the code books," Ben asked smoothly, gazing appealingly to his Head of Translation to bring a little reality back to the proceedings.

"Yes, certainly Ben. On the hardware front we've recently implemented an idea of er … David's actually, to simultaneously scan one hundred consecutive tracks with ten banks of compound read heads, the globe spinning rapidly beneath on an electrostatic cushion. High speed circuitry then stitches the one thousand data strings back together in the correct sequence, and fires it down the decoding circuits. The method has greatly boosted our scan speed and represents tremendous progress in just one week. At the same time we are currently designing custom-built microcircuitry for rapid blister decoding."

"On a more personal level, I am anxious to see how the language evolves as we penetrate deeper into the message. At the moment it's all rather crude, just the rudiments needed to do mathematics and science, a primitive vocabulary of nouns and verbs. We're keen to see where adjectives, adverbs and rare tenses appear; stress, nuance, ambiguity – perhaps even humour – constructs indispensible to the higher forms of life such as literature and poetry. How else might such a primitive alien language ever begin to acquire the richness of human thought and expression, a cultural richness derived ultimately from seven thousand diverse human languages in current use around the world?"

"Why would they want to say the same thing in seven thousand different ways?" enquired David sourly, thoroughly irritated at being edged out of the proceedings. Professor Wisehead apparently didn't hear, and continued without pause.

"What is it about human consciousness that gives rise on average to some twenty vowels, thirty consonants and twenty tenses? Is it because we started out communicating through sound? What if we communicated electrically, as some creatures on earth appear to do?"

"Does the physics of communication limit the power of a language? Would a more sophisticated language imply a more sophisticated culture? Can you gauge a civilisation from the sophistication of its language? Is it possible to think without language, or think beyond the limits of language? If the language of the alien message becomes much more sophisticated, will humans be able to understand it beyond a certain point? I believe these questions will prove crucial for understanding the more sophisticated sections of the message."

"Thank you, Professor Wisehead. Finally now, a quick word from …"

But at this point the internal circuit buzzed, and Frances interrupted the meeting. "I'm sorry Ben, I think you should see this. It's running on all the major news channels."

"Sure thing Frances, patch it through. We are in the news again, boys and girls," he glowed, turning to his audience as the giant plasma screen illuminated behind him and the sound came through.

Chapter 21

... just moments after GL4 recorded its one billionth visitor. But tonight, the pre-eminent search engine was the centre of a fierce political storm of international dimensions. The White House is accusing the Googal corporation of inciting racial and political unrest. Public phone systems are at saturation levels and some mobile networks have been suspended. Security forces around the world remain on high alert as governments brace themselves for a torrent of looting and violence.

The international community is said to be appalled at GL4's startling revelation that the alien message carries a warning that all life on planet Earth is about to be extinguished. The White House is strongly denying rumours that NORAD lost contact with an entire squadron of F-22 fighters over the Gulf of Mexico earlier today. The British prime minister admitted to being 'stunned beyond belief' at Googal's reckless and irresponsible behaviour in its latest stunt to boost the corporation's advertising revenue and political profile, and has called for the corporation to be shut down immediately. The whole affair has called into question the integrity of the Googal corporation and its charismatic CEO, Ben Khoeller, who so far remains unavailable for comment.

Abroad, there are reports of looting and rioting on the streets of Bombay, and complete power blackouts in major Turkish cities. China has warned its neighbours against the mobilisation of any military forces within a thousand miles of its borders, a statement which Russia is describing as 'inflammatory and provocative', while the White House has described its decision to mobilise the National Guard as a 'precautionary measure' designed to allay public fear and maintain law and order until the crisis can be defused.

And we've just received breaking news from an official source in London that the extinction message *is* genuine, I repeat, the extinction message *is* genuine, though government officials are stressing that certain aspects of its interpretation remain to be clarified. Meanwhile the British government is urging the general public to remain calm and carry on.

Religious leaders around the world have called for a day of prayer and penitence. The archbishop of Canterbury told his congregation that only prayer and peaceful reflection would save mankind and he implored world leaders to remain calm and act wisely.

The Swiss government, who until now have remained ...

* * *

"OK, boys and girls. This is it. This is what we train for. I'd say we have thirty minutes before they start throwing things at us. For the first ten minutes we are all going to stand still and think clearly. There are enough headless chickens out there, a few more here will help nobody."

"Frances, keynotes please. Jeff, pull together a team of techs and find out everything you can about the extract. Where it originated, when it was posted, who posted it, who verified and authenticated it. Comb the audit trail for secondary links. They'll probably be phoney, but check them anyway. Dig out your hacker's handbook, and pretend you are behind enemy lines once more. Anything else?"

"We need to think inversely on this one Ben, it's pretty much the opposite to what we're good at – advertising. Ask ourselves, how would *we* go about engineering such a stunt. Search for simple mistakes, early dry runs to ... test the water, as it were. Set up a keywords file to scan official traffic for the last 48 hours. It'll be tightly encrypted of course, but I have some vicious LTL software."

"LTL?"

"Less than legal," Jeff conceded with a grin.

"Good. Remember guys, we just need one single breakthrough, after that everything else will unravel. But we need it fast."

"Right, what else? Come on boys and girls, this is your moment. Anything?"

"Yes sir! Once we finger a target we should dispatch our best spyware and keyboard sniffers, both to the target and all its contacts. Search for recent changes in file status. Examine deletion records, check for ghost trails, digital signatures and watermarks. Even trash cans – everyone makes mistakes."

"Ben, if we can get some back-bearings on the power blackout, perhaps we can keyword scan for prior knowledge."

"Just a long shot Ben, look for large financial movements just prior to the event. If someone knew this was coming up, they might be tempted to have a flutter. There are always fortunes to be made in human misery."

"The Googal satellite sir! If the emergency is as great as they're expecting, there should be preliminary troop movements, naval and air force deployments, satellite repositioning sir!"

"Run a consistency check on the timing of announcements, Ben. In a big fast operation, there's bound to be some tiny foul-ups, timing slips, one organisation pre-empting another out of sequence."

"Search for recent changes in the encryption levels of secure traffic. Analyse recent traffic patterns. We could do that quickly sir, without decryption. Recent changes in GPS coverage and precision sir, especially over Switzerland!"

"Anything else?"

"Sir! Keyword-scan emails of service personnel and relatives for tell-tale phrases – leave of absence, cancellation of leave, unit recall …"

"That's the one, I think. Good boy, Justin. Remember, one slip guys, that's all we need. We'll find it eventually, but my guess is they won't give us time. *Hacker's Rules* girls and boys, play foul and mean, beat them at their own filthy game."

"Yes Frances?"

"Appeal for public assistance. We're the underdog, there's lots of sympathy for us out there. Someone will know something – disgruntled employee, a radio ham, a disaffected pilot. And we need to issue an immediate denial, accusing the security services of dirty tricks, even before we find a smoking gun."

"Good girl Frances! Form a team and make a start. Someone monitor the major channels, keep us informed of key developments by plasma screen."

"David … Where the hell is David? René, go and find him. Start developing all the blisters in the vicinity of the extract."

"Anything else? Come on guys, there's always something, a trail of collateral damage, never completely sanitised."

"Internet and email surges in and around Langley and Cheltenham, cross correlated with URL usage on the upload transmissions. And we need to contact the Swiss authorities and local security. Give them our take on this."

"OK, good. Right. Now let's suppose we've found the evidence. What then? Jennifer, draft a ball-crushing response, strenuous and total denial, citing specific evidence of foul play by the big four. Encrypted security flash to each government leader personally, threatening to publish a damning statement if they do not respond immediately. Tell them we have the evidence and we will upload it in plain text the instant we perceive the slightest threat of physical force. Draft it up girl, bite them where it hurts. Come back to me with the first draft, there'll only be time for one."

"Ben, I need to talk to you."

"Not just at the moment, Frances. Ah yes, Frances. Contact the Swiss government. Put them in the picture, tell them we are going live with evidence."

"Right, let's get to it. Everyone do something. Sign up to Frances' list people. Coordinate and report progress. Post all breakthroughs."

* * *

"Frances! What are you doing here? You're supposed to be …"

"Already up and running, Ben. Everyone's doing something. James is running the desk with some of the guys. They're good kids, they know what they're doing. Ben, I have to talk to you, something very important and personal."

"Not a good time, Frances. Oh, and here's René. And David! David, where the hell have you been? Maybe you didn't notice, but we're running a slight crisis here. While you've been sunning your ..."

"Ben, shut up and listen," René interrupted angrily. "Tell him David," she said, gently stroking his hands. "The extract, tell him."

"They've made a mistake, Ben, a simple translation error. The extract is genuine alright, but it's a historical record, not a warning. The extinction has already happened, the Jurassic age sixty-five million years ago – the Chicxulub asteroid impact off the Gulf of Mexico – a key event that changed our planet and the course of evolution. There are images, scientific accounts and assessment reports; pictures of the planet as it was back then, continents, oceans, mountain ranges. Nothing like how it appears now, even to the untrained eye. India is still a bloody island, thousands of miles off the Asiatic coast. There are fabulous images of ancient lifeforms at ground level, dinosaurs and other species I've never seen before. There's the impact itself, the devastation, a fascinating account of how ..."

"David, how the do you know all this? And why isn't it on GL4 already? You know the rule, *Decode-Upload*."

"I don't know where it is, that's the reason I left – to find it."

"Ben!"

"Not now Frances!"

"David, you must have the scan coordinates for chrissakes."

"It's not in the scan records. That's not how I found it."

"What! You can't scan the globes without the system logging the address records. You know that, you built the bloody thing! David, somebody's going to drop a fucking great missile on us any minute ..."

"It wasn't like that Ben. I was ... browsing. It helps me relax, at night. I hold the globe in my fingertips and my mind ... wanders. But it's not dreaming. I see things, real things, connected thoughts and images, video streams. And I hear sound too, in my head. I was trying to tell you, all of you, but you didn't want to know, you thought I was imagining things. I was hoping someone else would tell you, someone you ... trusted. I knew there was someone there – I could feel it, a resonance. I know it's strange and unscientific, that's why nobody wants to admit it."

"I admit it!" Frances shouted in Ben's ear.

"Nobody admits it, David, because it's not there – it's all in your over-active imagination, ego-mania gone wild, delusional stress, whatever. YES, Frances, what is the matter?"

"I admit it, Ben. I sense it too, just like David. I feel a sense, a presence, I have done, ever since the first L4 meeting in your office. You all laughed, but I felt it. Not mathematics or planets or science things. But feelings, deep deep feelings and raw emotion – happiness, awe, sexual excitement. I feel a presence."

"Frances, I don't want to hear this!"

"It's real Ben, trust me."

"OK, right. Frances, you go with David. Find the extract, everything. Don't tell me the details – I don't want to know. Just upload the whole lot. Squeal it up as fast as you can. Forget elegance, we'll tidy it up later – if there is one. Go! René, stay here and help me."

* * *

"We've got it Ben! Service personnel, email to grandparents – cancellation of leave. National Guard, Scott Deanberg, seventeen years old, Washington state, six days ago. Two others coming up – make that five ... eight. Hell, there's hundreds. They all sound mighty pissed off. Patch them through, Ben?"

"Send a few up, Jeff. Then stream the rest to Jennifer, with as much personal detail as you can find – rank, unit, rumour, gossip, fiancé's phone number, bra size, whatever. Don't get squeamish about this Jeff, someone wants to vaporize us. Download snoop viruses to anyone still online. Hell! They're all online, waiting to see us fry! They will have figured it out by now. Cross-correlate everything on Googal causal-maps, email routing, message cascades, the lot. Then take back-bearings to any top dogs with shit under their nails. Well done guys."

"Jennifer?"

"Here boss!"

"How is it?"

"Going up now, Ben. It's not Shakespeare, but it's brutal. I'm appending Jeff's data as we speak."

"Hey, Ben. Get a load of this!"

"Just one second, Jeff."

"OK, Jennifer. Post a copy to my screen and prepare to send in sixty seconds. Hell, cancel that. Jennifer darling, we trust you. Send it now!"

"Yes boss!"

"What have you got Jeff?"

"Everything."

"What do you mean, everything? What everything? Where?"

"Everything we're looking for. All fully decoded and edited in the Queen's English. The Chicxulub impact, pictures, dinosaurs and devastation – fabulous quality. There's even a movie! It's already out there, on GL4! Scientific assessment, data tables, DNA records. Projections and conclusions, summary reports. Someone's beaten us to it! The whole world is reading it. The hit rate is phenomenal."

"Flash just in from China, Ben. Official, private to Ben Khoeller, disclaiming all responsibility for US-UK dirty dealing. Russia likewise."

"Ben – newscast – live."

" ... a rogue British hacker, who penetrated a secure Pentagon network two days ago, was shot dead this morning by police markspersons in his tenement council flat, when he threatened to blow himself up, together with his young family. It is believed the hacker, an unemployed IC1 male in his teens, uploaded a hoax version of the alien extract onto the GL4 website. A neighbour described him as a 'quiet lad' whose ambition was to fly for the RAF."

Chapter 22

She knew it was as countless other kingdoms scattered throughout the cosmos, but it was *her* kingdom. She watched over it patiently as it spun up through the ages, the four inner planets cooling to rocky spheres and rapidly spawning lifeforms; primitive, elementary and barely alive, little more than miniscule watery sacks of chemicals which could grow and divide. And die.

And die they did, in their multitudes, as their geological environments died around them. She knew it would be. Mercury was the first, stillborn almost, in the eons of time. Then Venus, its active interior belching acrid noxious gases into the ever-thickening atmosphere, crushing and stifling its newly emergent lifeforms.

Then life on Mars died, after a long desperate struggle adapting to the ever-thinning atmosphere. Here the fight had been the longest, and the most gruelling, as the precious atmosphere seeped slowly into space and volcanic sourcing of vital gases slowed, then finally halted. Now the planet was silent again, though a vestige of primitive life still clung to rare niches where water, warmth and chemical energy chanced together amidst the frozen landscape. Life would eke out a scant existence here, clinging to the lowest subsistence levels of nature's metabolic pathways, waiting for an impossible break in cosmic fortunes.

Only one rocky planet now remained among her living charges, the blue-green emerald of her kingdom, vibrant in the black sky and bathed in the steady warmth and radiance of its mother star. A modest, long-lived star, spawned from the chemically rich ashes of an ancient supernova whose excessive mass and heady life style destined it to a rapid and cataclysmic end, but in its death throes seeding the cosmic environs with the crucial heavy elements for life.

Abundant in heavy elements, warmth, and awash with that precious watery cradle of life, Earth was always favoured in the cosmic lottery of homes. But her creators knew an easy life did not always grant a long life, and she was sad for her all of her charges. Now she watched patiently with a fierce protectiveness over the blue-green planet.

For thousands of millions of cycles she observed her jewel grow and evolve. She saw the tumultuous birth of its continents, the volcanic upheavals of thick crust spewing chemically rich ash and gas into an atmosphere that would one day support and protect its first tiny lifeforms. She watched the rain of meteors rip through the fledgling atmosphere, delivering metal-rich cargoes to a surface crust depleted of heavy metals, long since submerged to the depths of its molten core.

She saw the long reign of icy comets crash down upon its surface, scarring vast tracts of the arid rockscape, but delivering in abundance that most precious molecule of life. Not since its fiery conception had Earth last savoured the sweet soothing essence of dihydrogen monoxide, the simplest and most chemically adept of all nature's building blocks. Water – oceans of water, now returning by the cubic kilometre as comets, frozen relics of the solar system and tenants of the outermost reaches of her kingdom, and beyond.

She followed the first delicate lifeforms as the tripped blindly over the ever-changing landscape of evolutionary chance. The first tumultuous moment when one lifeform turned on another, savouring the easy acquisition of life's precious chemicals so patiently harvested, a double score tactic in the evolutionary game of hunter rewarded and hunted punished. She watched the quickening pace of evolutionary change as each species made the fateful decision between fight and flight.

She saw the pace quicken again as the first creatures crawled from their watery cradle into the strange gravity-dominated existence of life on land, with its volatile and unpredictable climate. Tentative ventures at first, barely able to leave the comfort and safety of their watery womb, but then more courageous forays, as better adaptations uncovered richer opportunities.

She knew it would be so: nothing for a very long time, possibly forever, then everything in a rush. She needed the patience to watch and vigilance to act. Only once before had she ever interceded, and then but the merest nudge, a lucky break for a newly emerging branch of life. Quick witted and agile, calculating and aware, but struggling under an ancient reign of trampling giants. It was not a light decision; intelligent life might have emerged regardless from the reign of blood and splintering bone.

But already Earth was running out of time, it's sun middle-aged and well along the path to bloating a thousand times into a red giant of stars, engulfing its tiny retinue of rocky planets and incinerating their delicate lifeforms. And the sun was not alone in growing old. The universe too, one day, would die, its nuclear energies spent and exhausted.

The big lumbering creatures who had ruled for a hundred million years scarcely perceived the steady bright yellow beacon in their night sky, much less the tiny point of light which slowly detached itself from the majestic ringed planet.

She watched it track through the cosmic expanse, surf the deep gravitational well of the giant planet, gaining the speed to slingshot inwards, on towards the small red planet, adjusting its destination with the last few decimal points of attainable precision.

Now it was merely a question of time, and precious little time at that, less than a cycle of their seasons. Barely, in one hundred millions cycles, had the lumbering giants shown the slightest curiosity to the world about them, a world teeming with life and the easy existence of might over right, fierceness over curiosity. And now it was too late. Soon they would have other more immediate things to occupy their tiny incurious minds.

Nor did they ever stop to wonder at the small scampering creatures darting between their feet with effortless ease, raiding their nests for eggs and young; fierce, courageous little pillagers, agile and wily, with an uncanny instinct for the inter-species boundary between life and death, between change and conquest. And they would certainly never have guessed that these warm-blooded little scavengers would one day rise to an ascendency of the planet, far more ruthless in their reign of conquest and terror.

Creatures whose agile paws and nimble probing minds would one day learn to manipulate and control, not just every other lifeform on the planet, but the very atoms of which they were made. They would learn to tread the delicate path between fierceness and protectiveness, between curiosity and contentment, between probing the forces of nature and respecting their power. And then, masters of the planet and all its lifeforms, they would stand at the brink of extinction, peering hesitantly into the vast depths of space itself.

For now the pace of life was about to quicken again, or halt completely. It was time to act once more, for she was a caring and dutiful guardian and could not neglect her duties, however painful that might prove.

Chapter 23

Jack sat peering into the eyepiece, gently guiding the telescope until the planet's red disc centred in his field of view, then carefully pressed the tracking button. After all these years, he still felt a childlike thrill at watching another world swing into view across the empty black depths of space. And tonight it was just about as good as it got, here in deepest suburban Kent. He breathed softly, directing his breath away from the eyepiece, as he gazed at the large ochre-red globe with its sparkling white polar ice cap and delicate dark regions crowding the equator.

He scanned the Martian surface for other familiar landmarks. Olympus Mons, the greatest volcano in the solar system, larger than England and three times higher than Mount Everest. Valles Marineris, the greatest abyss in the solar system, great enough to swallow the Grand Canyon two hundred times over. He knew them all.

His expensive camera accessories would pull up a thousand times more detail, which he would pore over at leisure in the weeks to come when viewing conditions deteriorated. And when he exhausted all that, he would play with the new image-enhancing software. But this most perfect of nights belonged to raw human emotion, to awe and beauty, to other worlds and distant dreams. Only reluctantly on such a night, would he head home for a few hours of strangled sleep, before dragging himself off to work.

"Hey Jack! You dozed off again? I'm freezing my rocks off over here. Any more coffee?"

"Yes, I'll be there in a moment." If anything, the conditions had improved slightly, so there was little point delaying further. Besides, the moon would be rising soon and its glare would ruin the image. He gazed at the planet once more and gently pressed the record button. Backing off carefully, he stood up, gently easing himself upright and slowly straightening his back. The cold night air seeped through his clothes as he inhaled deeply for the first time in an hour.

Slowly he looked around the silent church yard to where his friend sat, huddled over the eyepiece of his favoured Schmidt-Cassegrain, its short stubby barrel almost vertical. Still rubbing the small of his back, he wandered over to his car parked beside the ancient yew tree and crumbling cemetery wall.

"I take it you disabled the boot light?" his friend shouted, only half-jokingly.

"Yes, I did. But I can flash the headlights for you if you've lost something." He heard George swearing loudly as he rose to the bait.

"You bleeding dare, mate. I'm trying to do some real science over here – bloody amateurs!"

Jack smiled to himself as he fumbled for his flask and two small china cups. It was an odd friendship he reflected, pouring the steaming black coffee. Odd but old, going back to their first school days together. He closed the boot carefully and carried the cups over to his friend. In junior school they had shared a passion for stars and planets, swapping pictures and books and wild schoolboy theories of what lay buried on the far side of the moon. And once a month they waited impatiently for Patrick Moore to reveal fascinating insights from the grownup world of astronomy.

After school they had gone their separate ways for a while, George drifting in and out of jobs and hopeless relationships, while Jack moved slowly through a modest career in teaching.

George was an enigma, brilliant at school, but distracted and easily bored. To Jack it seemed unfair his friend could do so little and come top of the class so consistently. It was still unfair, thirty years later, but now it had reversed. Now he was sad his friend could do such brilliant things and attract so little reward. George though, didn't give a damn, at worst branding some official incompetence with his favourite epithet. Bloody amateurs!

"Here, drink it while it's hot."

"Caw, thanks mate, it's been a long night. Bloody brilliant viewing though. You don't get many like this. Make hay before the sun shines! What about you, still gawping at that bloody old rust bowl?" he scoffed gently. "About time you found yourself something serious to do, what with all that expensive equipment of yours."

Jack sipped his coffee quietly, savouring its stark bitterness and the hot rivulets warming his chilled insides. He stretched his back again and slowly tilted his head to the region of sky that George was photographing. He needn't have bothered. He already knew where his friend's attention would be focussed this most perfect of nights.

"I don't suppose you know where I can find the Andromeda galaxy, do you?"

"Ha bloody ha! Just make damn sure you don't kick the tripod, bigfoot. It'd be a crying shame to spill these last zillion photons, seeing as they've spent two million years travelling here just to appear in my picture. Imagine that, setting off when your ancestors were still falling out the branches. Destiny is what I call it. This one's a real corker."

If George said it was a good, it had to be special. He was a good observer, several of his photos appearing in *Amateur Astronomer* over the years. He wondered again about his friend, what exactly made him tick. He did just two things: earn a living driving taxis and spend it all on telescopes. He had no interest in women, or men come to that, as far as Jack knew. He didn't smoke, and only ate and drank when he had to. And read. He read voraciously on anything astronomical.

"Got much more to do?"

"Nope. Besides, the moon will be up soon. That'll put pay to any serious work. I might just try for sunset over Copernicus before I turn in. What about you? You lot still on holiday? Bloody teachers."

"Double 10H, last thing. Highlight of my week."

"About time you got yourself a real job then, wasn't it? *Those that can, do. Those that can't, teach!* That's what my old man used to say."

"Yes, very helpful. Thanks mate. Perhaps one day we'll teach *those that can*, not to foul things up quite so completely as their parents. I take it your father wasn't a ... oh damn!"

"Woops! Left the camera running, have we? Bloody amateurs!"

He was halfway back to his telescope before he pulled up abruptly, laughing to himself. There was no need to rush. He was recording by video, thirty frames a second, straight onto the digital hard drive. He had only to upload the data and delete as many frames as he wished. No overexposure, no loss of quality, no damage. No expense either, if you discount a few milliamp-hours of battery power. The wonders of digital technology. He peered carefully into the eyepiece to check the alignment, marvelling once more at the amazing conditions and feeling a sharp pang conscience for quitting now. But it had been a long night and he had an even longer day ahead. Gently, he pressed the stop button and started dismantling his equipment.

"Are you about tonight, George?" he called softly.

"Nope, wheels of industry old chap. Some of us have to work for a living. Anyway, there's a warm front edging in lunchtime."

"OK, give me a ring when you're out next. Take care, George. And good luck with the picture."

"Not a question of luck, matey. Bloody amateurs!"

Jack got into his car, slamming the door just a fraction too hard. He was a bit beyond humour now, and suspected George was too. He had been a fool to stay up so long, 10H would run him ragged. TFIF he said to himself, incorrectly but with feeling.

* * *

Seven-thirty the same evening George was just leaving for work when the phone rang.

"George?"

"Yes."

"It's Jack. Can you come over?"

"What, now? I'm just off to work. Friday night an' all. Some of us have to work for a living. What's the problem?"

"There's something wrong with your program. Either that or the universe has just exploded."

"Oh Christ. Don't you have any marking to do?"

"Come on, George. It won't take long, then you can climb back on your wheel. I'm on my last legs anyway."

"Alright, fifteen minutes. But you owe me one."

Jack put the phone down, a slow smile spreading across his face. There was nothing wrong with the software. And there was nothing wrong with the individual frames. But there was definitely something wrong with the sequence of frames. And Jack wanted his lifelong friend to be there when they figured it out. For as George never tired of telling him, he owed him one.

Jack handed his friend a steaming black coffee as he stomped straight through the front doorway and into the tiny office.

"Christ, it's like a bloody sauna in here Jack. No wonder you can't think straight. Open the window before we both pass out. Where's the data file," he said, sitting down at the keyboard and launching the image processing program.

"Right in front of you," Jack said, pointing to the top item of a list. "I've called it George1."

"The hell did you call it that for?"

"Well, it's your program. I thought you might as well get all the credit when it failed."

"Thanks, pal. Right, here goes." He brought the first frame up on the screen and zoomed in on a faint star. "Well that looks OK, pretty good in fact, four definite pixels and a few faint side lobes." He flicked to the next image and that too looked clean, as did the next twenty. He fast forwarded through the frames, staring intently at the star for loss of definition.

"Christ almighty Jack, how many are there?"

"About twenty minutes worth. It was recording when I was called away on butler duty. Then I was hijacked by another riveting lecture on the Andromeda galaxy."

"Oh great. Thirty frames a second, that's ... thirty-six thousand. We'll be here all night."

"How was the blessed Andromeda, by the way."

"Bloody tops, matey. Here," George said, fishing out a memory stick from his top pocket and tossing it over his shoulder. He chuckled softly as he heard his friend scrambling to catch it. "Thought you might appreciate a bit of real astronomy."

George fast forwarded to the end of the video file and examined the last twenty images. "Well, I can't see anything obviously wrong with the frames – very good definition in fact." He launched the stacking program and sat back while it processed the image data.

"So how does it work, your program?" Jack asked, knowing he had five clear minutes before the final composite image appeared.

"RTFM," George said, gulping down the hot coffee.

"What's that supposed to mean?"

"Read The Effing Manual."

"That's RTEM, surely? Come on George, nobody reads computer manuals. Not unless they're intent on murder."

George let out a longsuffering sigh. "Imagine each of your images – all thirty-six thousand of them – on one long continuous spool of film, just like the good old days."

"You mean that dreary old stuff you use for the blessed Andromeda?"

"Now chop it up," continued George, ignoring him, "and put all thirty-six thousand images on top of one another. Bingo! You now have one composite image with thirty-six thousand times as much definition. That's the theory, at any rate. Of course, it's not quite so straightforward in practice. You have to line all the images up perfectly for one thing, or you'll just end up with thirty-six thousand times as much mess. And sooner or later the background light fogs everything out. But basically, that's it."

The final image started painting itself across the screen, showing the deep orange Martian disk with its sparkling white polar ice cap.

"Hmm. Decent bit of colour contrast and saturation. Let's take a closer look." George zoomed in on a background star, working the keyboard and mouse simultaneously in a blur of motion.

"Christ Almighty, Jack! The definition is terrible! Truly bloody awful," he exclaimed, as an elongated strip of pixels painted itself diagonally across the screen. They're all over the shop. What the hell were you doing for twenty minutes, scratching your balls?

"Well now, that's just it, I reckon. The pixels are not all over the place. They're just not all in one place, which is where they should be if your program was working correctly."

"There's nothing wrong with my program, old son. Must be your equipment. Not been cleaning the mirror with Windolene again, have we?"

"Come off it George, that was twenty years ago," snapped Jack, incensed at his friend's incessant teasing of his simple gaff.

"Well, maybe you've found yourself a comet. Did you check the NASA database?"

"It's not a comet, George, all the stars are showing up as short parallel streaks of light, like one of those grotty holiday snaps where someone jolts the camera. But this isn't a single image, is it George? It's thirty-six thousand images, each one crystal clear. You said so yourself."

Jack knew he had said enough to goad his friend into a frenzy of activity. If George left for work now, he'd stew all night over a bug somewhere in his program. Jack left him simmering at the keyboard, muttering obscenities under his breath, and slipped quietly out of the room.

"Well, you were wrong about one thing," George announced triumphantly, as Jack returned with two bottles of beer and a coffee. "What's that for?" George said warningly, eyeing his favourite brew. "I'm working, remember?"

"The beer's for me," Jack replied, handing him the coffee. "What was I wrong about?"

"The streaks aren't all parallel, for one thing. And they're not all the same length, either."

"So what does that mean?"

George leant back expansively in his chair, gently tapping his fingers together in front of him. "It means we've got ourselves an interesting problem."

* * *

"Under perfect seeing conditions, each one of your thirty-six thousand frames would be identical. But conditions are never perfect. The biggest problem is turbulence, blobs of warm air rising up through the field of view, each one acting like a big distorting lens. Same sort of thing you see over a bonfire. Every part of the image gets enlarged, contracted, twisted or skewed this way and that, making the point image of a star jump about all over the shop. It's why stars appear to twinkle; they don't twinkle when you get outside the atmosphere, like the Hubble telescope."

"The Stacking program tries to undo the distortion by applying an equal and opposite amount of distortion to each frame, which it figures out by measuring how far certain reference stars get shifted. In the final picture, the images of each reference star are all perfectly aligned and everything else in between should pretty much end up where it should be."

"So what happened," asked Jack reasonably.

"One of the sixteen stars chosen as reference points, wasn't a star. It was moving. Not a problem, we'll just choose a different reference star ... there you go," he said, in another blur of motion as he re-launched the stacking program. "I reckon you've got yourself a damn good picture there. Right matey, I'm off, someone's got to keep the wheels ..."

"So you're saying one of the reference stars your program happened to choose, was moving."

"Right in one Jack. So, not a star."

"Not a star *and* moving."

"Bloody fast too, I'd say. Probably not a comet though – no sign of a tail. Maybe an asteroid."

"I checked the database, George. There's nothing listed anywhere near this part of the sky."

"Perhaps you made a mistake, typed the coordinates in the wrong way round or something."

"George. I didn't make a mistake. I've checked and rechecked."

"I know, Jack," George said, smiling and easing up slightly on his friend. "That is why it's an interesting problem."

"So what do we do now?" asked Jack, feeling they had come full circle.

"We recheck the minor planets database," said George, holding up a cautionary hand as his friend began to erupt. "Then we check to see if it's still there and moving. Then, if nobody else has reported it in the meantime, you get to name your asteroid. I'll let you call it George1 if you like!"

"Perhaps we can try for another fix tonight?"

"Not a snow ball's chance in hell. Don't you ever check the infra-reds? Eight-eighths cloud cover and persistent rain later. I suppose we could get a rough idea of the orbit from your frames, after all, there are thirty-six thousand of them. Certainly enough to find it again when this pea-souper has moved on. OK, let's get to work. Better give me have one of those beers."

"But I do have earlier images of Mars! Hundreds of them," exclaimed Jack, excitedly.

"I dare say you do. Thirty years worth, I shouldn't wonder. It's what comes from being a boring bloody physics teacher and gawping at Mars all your life. But it's not Mars we're talking about here, is it? Mars just happens to be cruising past this bit of the sky. It's this little baby we're interested in," George said, scrolling a box around a sharp streak in the new composite picture painting itself across the screen.

They stared intently at the spectacular image. The planet hung suspended like an iridescent orange pearl in the deep empty blackness of space. But the two men had eyes only for the faint streak of light grazing its north-eastern limb.

"Oh Christ!" exclaimed George suddenly, staring intently as he zoomed in on the streak. "It's curved!" The two men stared at the faint track of light.

"What does that mean?"

"It's curved man! It's not just some damned line of sight coincidence. It's in hyperbolic orbit. A death defying slingshot orbit past Mars!

"Congratulations my friend," said George in quiet awe. "I'd say you've got yourself the image of a lifetime."

"*We*," Jack said, smiling at his friend. "We've got the image of a lifetime."

"How fast would you say it's going?" asked Jack, after a moments quiet reflection. "It's moved what, half a second of arc in twenty minutes? That's ..."

No, it's not as simple as that. We're seeing the motion obliquely for one thing, and all that's relative to Mars. My guess is it's doing at least 50 km/s to be booted like that.

"But that can't be right!" said Jack. "That would make it interstellar, from another part of the galaxy!"

"Well it could be of course, but not necessarily. It might just have wondered too close to Jupiter and got its arse kicked. Or Saturn, maybe. And now it's just narrowly missed clobbering Mars. This baby is living dangerously!" said George thoughtfully.

"Hang on a minute," said George, after another meditative silence. "There's something not right here. Too many coincidences."

"How is that?"

"Well, it's definitely moving, right? And it's definitely big, right? Otherwise your equipment would never have picked it up, no offence like. So why didn't WISE find it?"

"Who?"

"WISE, Wide-field Infrared Survey Explorer – NASA's answer to Armageddon. The asteroid hunting satellite for chrissakes! Don't you ever read any of your magazines," George exclaimed, slapping a pristine pile of *Amateur Astronomers*. "WISE scans the entire sky right down to magnitude 23, looking for anything that moves. When it finds something it recalculates the orbit and updates the database. All in seconds."

"So it should have been there when I checked," Jack said, now totally confused.

"It should, yes. But maybe the camera was down, malfunctioning, out of coolant, undergoing software upgrade, any one of a million things. Who knows, maybe someone pressed the wrong button. Bloody amateurs!"

"Perhaps they're waiting for independent confirmation?"

"No. This baby's been cruising for years, they'd have seen it ages ago and verified it umpteen times by now. Something that big and fast would be incredible news, it's exactly what the NEO was set up for in the first place. Big, fast and planet hopping. Oh my God!"

"What on earth is that supposed to mean?" Jack said, thoroughly irritated at being two steps behind all night.

"It means trouble, my old friend. That's the only possible explanation, the curious case of the dog not barking at night – Sherlock Holmes. This dog should be barking the place down."

"George, please. Plain English."

"NASA have seen it, Jack. They are tracking it. But they're not telling us. Right – things to do! We need that orbit. When was your last image of Mars taken?"

"Wednesday, forty-three hours ago."

"It might just be there. If it is, that will definitely confirm how fast it's going. Then we'll try to work out an orbit."

* * *

It was 4am before the pair were through. "That's it then," Jack said, struggling to keep his eyes open. "They have found it ..."

"And it's bad news, too bad for human consumption. Armageddon, only for real this time. My God."

"What should we do?"

"Get some fresh air, I reckon. Nothing else we can do. A nice weekend break, somewhere warm and sunny, while we can."

"Are you crazy? Besides, I've got a school trip next Monday, remember?"

"I do remember, old pal. And now, I'm part of it."

"Don't be daft, you can't do that. It's all booked up. Plane tickets, bus tour, everything. Anyway, you have to be CRB cleared for that sort of thing."

"For God's sake Jack, I have to drive the little sods to school every day, don't I? And today, by sheer good fortune, I'm your minibus driver. You need to get out there a few days early. The local bus company's gone tits up, you have to check the veggie meals for nuts or something, make sure the toilet paper's soft enough, that kind of thing. Where are we going, by the way?"

"CERN, Genève. A guided tour of the European particle accelerator. Then on to Lausanne for a spot of culture and practise a few French verbs."

"And a fine university too, not that it will make much difference by Monday."

"George, I can't agree to anything that will endanger the kids, much as I'd like to sometimes."

"Don't worry, Jack. Culture will be the last thing on anyone's mind by Monday. Governments will be busy protecting their citizens with all sorts of restrictions once Joe Public finds out what's coming. Look at the god awful mess they made of it last time. Bloody amateurs!"

"Do you think it's as bad as that? Maybe we've got it all wrong."

"No, they must have known about it for months, possibly a year. Someone would have spotted it, sooner or later, By not saying anything now they'd just look totally incompetent. No

Jack, there can't be any other reason for keeping it secret. And you can't keep that sort of thing quiet without a lot of fancy footwork."

"Better not tell anyone, Jack. Not the milk man, not your mum, no one. No emails, no phone calls, nothing. In fact, best forget about it yourself, matey, you're such a hopeless liar. Pack a few warm clothes, a good sleeping bag and something to eat. Oh, and take all your school trip stuff, we better look the part. Nothing astronomical though. I'll sort the coffee," he said, grimacing inwardly at thought of the instant stuff Jack drank. "I don't want to stop once we're out there. I'll let my boss know I have a spot of moonlighting, slip him a few readies. Let me book the ferry, OK matey? Pick you up at say, eight? That's two hours Jack, think you can manage it?"

"Are you kidding? I get more done between lessons!"

"Do you really old pal? Blimey. Every day's a learning day! See you later then. Take care, Jack."

* * *

As George left, he worried again about his friend, whether he quite realised what he was getting into. George was a cynic when it came to politics and science. Big science meant big money and big money meant doing as you were told, which in times of public unrest included keeping your mouth shut. That just left the amateurs, thought George. And only a pair of complete bloody amateurs could conceivably get themselves lost up a remote Swiss mountain on route to Genève.

He thought again of his friend's attempts to access the NASA database. We need some backup, he said to himself, belt and braces. Post is too slow, email and phone too dangerous. A hazy headline floated up from his subconscious, *Burglar nabbed by email*. A newspaper article he'd read years ago. By the time he pulled into his driveway he had recalled the details. The burglary was recorded live on the computer's video-cam then promptly emailed before the computer could be disabled and stolen! His mind focussed on the details. It might just work.

Chapter 24

The room was the size and shape of a CONEX freight container, dark, subdued and purposeful. At one end, two fresh faced officers in sage green flightsuits with colourful shoulder patches, sat impassively before a bank of control panels and displays. Two hours ago they had lunched pleasantly with their young families before returning to work, an air force base in central Nevada. With any luck, they would be home in time to mow the lawn and light a barbecue. gloom. Calm, impassive clips of information passed between them, then on via encrypted radio to a handful of intensely trained professionals scattered across the world. A clipboard detailing standing orders for the day, dangled from a nearby nail.

Pilot, Sensors. Target eight miles.
Pilot copies.
Pilot, Signals. Expect to be cleared hot on target.
Pilot copies. Pre-launch checklist:
Peer reference code.
Entered.
Code weapon.
Coded.
Weapon status.
Weapon ready.
Pre launch checks complete.
Pilot, Signals. Clear to engage target
Pilot copies. Clear to engage ComCenter
Launch checklist:
MPS autotrack.
Established.
Laser.
Laser selecting.
Go ahead. Arm your laser.

Laser armed.
Master arm missile, go to fire laser.
Lasing.
Within range.
3, 2, 1, rifle.
3, 2, 1, impact!
Excellent job guys. Let's go home.
Pilot, Control. We have second target. White minibus. Three miles north-west.
Control, Pilot. Sir, target 1 destroyed as ordered. I have no orders for target 2.
Pilot, Control. Second target, pilot. Flash Priority. Authorisation follows. White minibus. Two civilians. Licence plate Foxtrot …
Control, Pilot. Sir! I have express orders. No casualties. No collateral damage.
Pilot, Control. New orders pilot. Highest authority. Status is critical.
Pilot, Sensors. I have white minibus. Range 2 miles. Licence plate Foxtrot …
Pilot copies.
Pilot, Sensors. Target appears stationary on mountain road. No cover.
Pilot, Control. Stand by for orders.

* * *

They were clear of the tree line now, snaking up a mountain road in the deep gloom.

"God I'm tired, Jack. How much further?"

His friend peered at the map with his torch. "About 4km by road, almost there. What a truly desolate place to build a research centre! Remind me again George, why are we driving up a remote hillside at the dead of night – without lights."

"Saving the planet, Jack. Doing our bit for global warming," George snapped, close to exhaustion now. He had driven continuously from Zeebrugge with just one stop to refuel at a small village, where he was careful to pay cash. Tiredness and stress were sapping his concentration as his mind lurched wildly between paranoia and hysteria. As if to test him, a silent blue flash lit up the skyline, followed by a sharp crump a few seconds later, as a volley of thunderous echoes rolled down the valley.

"Christ! What the hell was that," he said, braking sharply and jumping out.

"Avalanche control, I expect George. They work at night sometimes, it's safer for tourists. Or maybe Swiss Army training. Who knows? Come on George, I'm knackered, let's just get there. You're getting paranoid, old man. First it's British customs, searching and apparently bugging the bus, now you've got the Swiss authorities bombing us. They're just doing their jobs," Jack moaned wearily, as he climbed out stiffly looking for a convenient tree.

* * *

Control, Pilot. We have target 2. What are my orders sir?
Pilot, Control. Destroy minibus ... and occupants. Take it out. Execute the order, pilot!
Control, Pilot. Pilot copies. Vaporize minibus and occupants.
Pilot, Sensors. We have two personnel outside vehicle. One staring uphill. Second is uh ... urinating sir. This is gonna hurt, buddy.
Pilot, Signals. Clear to engage target 2.
Pilot copies.
Go ahead. Arm your laser.
Laser armed.
Master arm missile, go to fire laser.
Lasing.
Within range.
3, 2 ... what the fuck!
Pilot, Control. Report status ... Pilot!
Control, Pilot. Weapon malfunction. Loss of contact, sir. Loss of ... everything.
Defensives?
No defensives detected sir.
Target status?
Target status is unknown.
Backup?
None in range sir.

Pilot, Control. Secure all facilities. Full debrief. Sensors report to me immediately.
Yes sir.

The two young officers remained inert, transfixed by the white flecks of cosmic microwave radiation now dancing silently across the dull grey screen.

* * *

Ben was sleeping soundly when the explosion rocked his bedroom. He snatched up the phone and punched a few numbers.
"Ben here. What was that?"
"Explosion sir, over by the satellite dishes. No perimeter alarms tripped."
"Any injuries?"
"Unlikely, but we're checking. It's a steep isolated part of the hillside, shouldn't be anyone near there. I've sent a team out to look. Nothing too close, just scan and report. Swiss Army and bomb squad already on their way sir. Incoming helicopters."
"OK. Johnston isn't it, gate security?"
"Yes sir!"
"OK Johnston, well done. Offer them every assistance. Keep me posted."
"Yes sir!"
Ben put the phone down and pulled on his clothes. "I'll have to get over there honey. Stay here until I ring."
"Be careful, Ben."
Jeff was already waiting outside when Ben arrived at his office, panting for breath. "Hi Jeff, good to see you. Are you alright?"
"Yeah, fine. We under attack?"
"Not sure. Sabotage, possibly. We had an anonymous tip off last week. Check the high resolution infra-reds will you Jeff, plus anything else pointing towards the satellite dishes. Organise a team to search for anything suspicious."
"Sure. I'll check out the satellite images too."
"Good idea," said Ben, reaching for the phone.

"Hi Frances. Yeah, me. It looks like we've lost the satellite link. I'm going out for a closer look. I'll be on my mobile. Will you organise the medical services? Check everyone is safe and accounted for. Send someone round to René's parents and the locals, for reassurance. They may even have seen something, anything odd the last few days. And monitor the news channels."

"OK Ben, I'm dressed now. There in three."

"Good girl, thanks."

"Ben, Inspector Migrane is here," Jeff called through the office door.

"Hello Ben. Good to see you."

"You too Karl, that was damn quick. What do you think?"

"Possible sabotage, we're checking. Unlikely, I'd say, given the isolation and security. The Swiss Army doesn't miss much up here. The entire mountain is bristling with sensors and there's a considerable ground force active round the clock. We think it's more likely to be a missile, probably delivered by stealth."

"Anything at all on radar?"

"Nothing obvious. They are checking for ghost trails. The Swiss Air Force is overflying and we have helicopter camera crews scanning the area. There was second explosion further down the valley. They found a minibus. It is being examined."

"Should we evacuate?"

"You should consider it. The bunker is ready, and the bolthole nearly finished, just a few items left on the snagging list. But personally, I'd say it's a timely reminder to the world at large, big boys flexing their muscles. We are the obvious target, but there are many others. Too many to go after, so set an example. What happens if you don't toe the line – strange phrase that. I've requested an additional squad to patrol onsite, help boost morale."

"Thanks, that was thoughtful."

"We are sorry they got through. How long will you down."

"GL4? No time at all. We've been on fibre optic all week, testing the new link. Streaming direct to Bern, or any other satellite provider we choose. We installed it the moment they cut the tunnel. No, GL4's not the problem Karl, it's the effect on morale. They're just kids really, and a long way from home, most of them. We had better evacuate, but I'm going to miss this place,

I've grown very fond of it up here. I could even retire here one day."

"You might be in for a surprise Ben. Some of these kids look pretty hardnosed to me."

Chapter 25

"Ben, there's a couple of English guys out here under Swiss escort. They're badly shaken up, but asking to see you. They were driving up here in a minibus when they say they were attacked."

"Thank you, Frances. Ask security to take care of them would you, inspector Migrane will be down shortly," he added, acknowledging the inspector's nod.

"Ben, one of them has an urgent message, wants me to read it to you. He said it was too sensitive to email. It's only a few lines."

"OK, do that Frances."

A large asteroid, approximately 50 km in diameter, recently observed in a grazing orbit past Mars, is now crossing the inner Solar System at 60 km/sec, ETA to Earth orbit 87 days. NASA's WISE satellite is reported to be functioning normally, but is currently denying all knowledge of this TORINO SCALE OBJECT.

George McGuthrie and Jack Cousins
Amateur astronomers, Kent, England.

"OK, I'll be down in two minutes. Look after them Frances, refreshments and a medic – and a guard. Ask René and David to drop by right away. Then make arrangements for a full staff meeting at 10am, but don't announce anything yet. And Frances, thanks for everything you're doing out there."

"Yes boss!"

"Jeff, can we control the Googal Sky satellite from here?"

"Sure, we have all the codes and frequencies. But it's streaming live images of L4."

"We'll just have to show recent footage for a while. I want to take a good long look at this object," Ben said, handing him some scribbled coordinates. "It should be somewhere near Mars."

"What are we looking for exactly?"

"Armageddon, apparently."

"Jesus Ben, you kidding me?"

"No, Jeff. Get onto it right away. Forget the infra-reds for now. I want to know how big it is, how fast it's travelling and where it's going. And have someone run a background check on these two. Everything you can pull up in ten minutes, then join us in here."

* * *

"Why do you think NASA is denying all knowledge of this object?" Ben asked, after the pair had recounted their harrowing trip.

"Strictly speaking, they're not denying it, just omitting to mention its existence in their database," George explained. "In reality, they should be shouting it from the rooftops, it's exactly what the NEO was set up to do in the first place. They must have known about it for months, perhaps even a year. Most of the professional observatories would have found it by now, in any case. It's the fact nobody is saying anything at all that's so very ominous."

"I don't get it, why should that be so ominous?"

"High speed objects like this can't remain in the solar system for very long, the Sun hasn't enough gravity to hold on to them indefinitely. So it's either a rare interstellar object just passing through, or a local asteroid that's been kicked inwards by one of the major planets. And now it's just narrowly missed colliding with Mars. Two grazing flybys in one orbit, that is so very unlikely, statistically."

"I can't see why," Ben persisted.

"OK, think of snooker. It would be like trying to pot the black by first ricocheting the white off two reds at opposite ends of the table. It would just never happen in real life. The slightest tiniest disturbance – a fly landing on the cushion or a jumbo taking off in Cape Town – would be enough to nudge the white slightly off-track and eventually miss the black. You can calculate mathematically that it's utterly improbable."

"Or utterly probable," David said slowly, "if it's being guided."

"Are you seriously suggesting this asteroid is inhabited by intelligent life?" Ben asked, incredulously.

"Why not? Think about it. Everything we've ever said about L4 and the globes has turned out to be wrong, sooner or later. Suddenly, after billions of years of nothing, there are things going out there we know nothing about. We've been looking at all of this from the wrong perspective, assuming all these events are natural, inanimately driven. But what if there really is a live intelligence behind this? We'd see things differently then, wouldn't we? A highly improbable orbit then becomes a highly ominous orbit."

"We'll know soon enough," said Ben, studying an email from Jeff. "They're calculating the orbit right now. And Jeff's dug up some earlier surveys, going back several months."

"It's such a shame about your Mars picture, Jack," said René sympathetically. She felt very sorry for the quiet man, who seemed quite overwhelmed by events – and his boisterous companion. "I suppose there is no way we could steal a copy now, is there?"

"There certainly is," George interrupted loudly, checking his watch. "It might even be here by now, on GL4 website. But if it is, it means my house has been trashed. Yours too Jack, I'm afraid. Hell of a relaxing break, eh matey!"

Jack glanced up angrily at his friend.

"Don't look at me like that," said George, grinning. I had to do something, in case we were … delayed. Well, I couldn't just leave behind the image of a lifetime!

"It's here all right," said Ben, staring in astonishment at his screen. "It's absolutely amazing, beautiful. I never imagined you guys attained such high definition," Ben said, genuinely impressed.

"We'd never have got it published in England, so I decided to send it to you, let you worry about it. Reckon you to be one of the good guys in all this."

At this point Jeff and his assistant burst into the office. "We've got it Ben, 55 km diameter and screaming along at 65 km/sec. Closest approach to Earth, fifteen million miles, that's nine weeks time."

Ben looked questioningly at George.

"I said it was an Earth crossing object, not that it would collide with Earth. Well I had to get your attention somehow!"

"But that's not the issue, Ben," interrupted Jeff. "It's on a direct collision course for Venus! And we've tracked the orbit back in time. Fifteen months ago it passed very close to Saturn. Before that we can't say, just yet. We're looking through earlier surveys right now."

There was an eerie silence as the implications of these revelations sank in. Early dread gave way to relief. But slowly, the relief evaporated, as a numb bewilderment settled over the company in Ben's office.

* * *

"That clinches it then," said David, after a long pause. "It's alive!"

"But how can you say that, Schatz?"

"Because of the orbit, René – a high speed slingshot track in from Saturn, grazing Mars inch perfect for a few last minute adjustments, then slamming straight into Venus three months later. That's just so bloody unlikely, it has to be deliberate. It's being steered, and very very precisely. That explains the numbed silence from the superpowers. They're completely bewildered, scared witless I shouldn't wonder. I mean, think about it. It's something utterly beyond their control – unthinkable for a politician. What are they going to tell their seven billion citizens of Earth?"

"But if it's intelligent, why smash itself into Venus," Ben asked reasonably.

"Curious, isn't it Ben? How we never ask the *why* question until we think something is alive and conscious. Someone should write a book about it. I don't know why, Ben, we'll just have to wait and see. But we should be publishing this right now, whether or not it has anything to do with the message. We need help from all the amateurs out there – help with tracking its motion, looking for any slight changes in orbit, rotation, temperature and anything else they can measure. Surface features too perhaps, anything that might help explain its purpose, the *why*. Between us we might come up with something, I very much doubt the superpowers will feel inclined to help."

"Right, Jeff, let's upload the story straight away. I want every stargazer around the world in on this. Get together with Jennifer and draft a sensational appeal for help. But this time, we'll tell them they're one step ahead of the professionals – it's no use being first if you're not allowed to tell everyone. Then we'll keep them ahead. But what we desperately need onboard right now is a couple of keen amateurs to coordinate it all, organise observing schedules, advise on latest equipment and techniques, correlate and publish all their results, along with all their beautiful pictures. I don't suppose you two could hang around a few months and help out?"

"Absolutely love to," George said quickly, as Jack opened his mouth.

Ben glanced at his watch. "Right then, full staff meeting for ten-thirty, lots to discuss. Frances here will you fix up with food and accommodation. We lunch at one, if you feel up to it. Meanwhile, I'll organise an observatory and some equipment – the best money can buy. Give me a list of what you need and it will be here by tonight. Welcome aboard fellas."

"And hey," Ben yelled, as they filed out the door. "We're all good guys here!"

* * *

This morning GL4 stunned the international community by publishing news of a gigantic rock approaching planet Earth from deepest space. But the pre-eminent website was quick to stress that the asteroid, which is larger than the state of Rhode Island and travelling 45 miles *every* second, poses no actual threat to life on Earth, though calculations confirm it will impact devastatingly with the planet Venus on December 10 next.

Major governments around the world were quick to claim prior knowledge of the object, which NASA has named NERO.

"We've been tracking the Near Earth Risk Object for over a year now, analysing its potential threat to mankind, as part of NASA's ongoing program to protect our planet from rogue asteroids," NASA spokeswoman, Nancy Greenspink explained. "Certain aspects of NERO's orbit meant we were obliged to act with global responsibility before publishing this news."

The White House has accused GL4 of inciting global unrest, in yet another attempt to boost the corporation's flagging advertising revenue and global profile. In a separate statement, apparently confirming their worsening relations with Googal, the White House has admitted that the US Air Force last night attacked the Flaubert Institute, a GL4 infoplex high in the Swiss Alps. A Pentagon spokesperson disclosed that a single SID [Smart Invisible Drone] last night flew unopposed through Swiss airspace to 'surgically decommission' GL4's satellite communications centre.

Sources in Switzerland are alleging the attack was disguised to appear the work of terrorist extremists, pointing out the US-UK coalition were forced into admitting responsibility only after the drone was unaccountably lost in Swiss airspace. Pentagon officials blamed a 'minor hardware malfunction' for the billion dollar loss, though some local newspapers are boasting hi-tech Swiss countermeasures may have played a significant role. Nobody was injured in the attack, although two British campers were said to be badly startled when the drone crashed out of control in front of their minibus.

The attack has heightened speculation that the coalition is now preparing to use routine force against any nation or organisation refusing to abide by the terms of the CGS treaty. The United Nations has yet to ratify the precise terms of the Charter for Global Security, which obliges 'in times of global crisis the world acts in unified force against all threats to global security.'

Meanwhile, a major row has erupted within the American arms industry over the unauthorised disclosure of the SINNOT findings, the board of enquiry set up to investigate the downed SID. In a secret annex, defence contractors have variously blamed birdstrike, hardware malfunction and even unidentified Swiss countermeasures to account for the unexpected loss of the pilotless aircraft. But fears that the Swiss may have identified a weakness in the command encryption system were dismissed as 'beyond the realm of scientific credulity'.

The Swiss government has neither confirmed nor denied the American speculation, and continues to protest vehemently at the illegal intrusion of Swiss airspace. Meanwhile staff at GL4 are said to be 'apprehensive' over recent hardening of international opinion to their venture, urging their charismatic leader Ben Khoeller to show greater global responsibility.

Asked whether Ben Khoeller's forced acceptance of two independent observers on the GL4 team, will help avoid future misunderstandings, Jennifer Comely, spokeswoman for GL4, said 'BK's invitation underlines Googal's continuing commitment to deliver a global information service second to none. We operate a policy of open global democracy here at GL4. Every human being on the planet can contribute and have their say. There aren't too many governments around the world who can say that, but they're all very welcome to come here and see how it's done.'

In an extraordinary move to demonstrate its hardening resolve, the White House has released unprecedented footage of the attack carried out by SID, the pilotless vehicle whose flight and attack mission is supervised remotely by a US flight crew somewhere in Nevada. The thirty second clip features SID's stealth evasion of Swiss defences and the clinical dialogue between flight controllers and battlefield command as the attack unfolds. The sequence ends with copybook congratulations from battlefield command: 'Excellent job guys. Let's go home.'

The footage also makes reference to a previously undisclosed attack which was aborted at the last moment due to 'Personnels On Target', demonstrating the coalition's supreme confidence to strike with 'stealth, precision and zero collateral'. Informed sources close to the White House are saying that the release of top secret footage demonstrates the coalition's iron resolve to enforce the terms of the CGS charter. 'From today nobody nowhere can hide from legally sanctioned countermeasures defending peace and global security.'

Finally on a lighter note, scientists around the world are gearing up for the long-awaited cosmic fireworks extravaganza. NERO is bang on course to smash into Venus in 72 days time and telescope sales around the world are said to be at an all time high.

'Everything will happen so incredibly quickly,' gushed a well-known astronomer. 'NERO will punch right through the Venusian atmosphere in just two seconds. The planet simply won't know what's hit it. The devastation will be utterly stupendous. It will be the devil of a job recording everything at that speed. Everyone in high-energy science is invited to the party. Nobody will ever witness anything like this again.'

Chapter 26

"OK you guys. Ready to roll?"

"Ready," George said quickly.

"Hello folks, I'm Gavin Brooks for GK News, here at GL4 headquarters, high in the Swiss Alps, where there have been some pretty amazing developments in the NERO story."

"So George, is it true? You've found strange markings on NERO? Like alien symbols or perhaps a flag?"

"No, nothing like that Gavin. But it does seem the object can change its shape abruptly."

"Change into what?"

"We're not sure at the moment."

"Are we talking tiny changes here George? Like a bit of dust blowing up here and there?"

"Hell, no. Huge changes Gavin, sometimes a hundred kilometres across – larger than the object itself. Sometimes we see straight edges. Sometimes the entire form appears to flicker. Here, take a look at this video clip from Sunday. Is your camera equipped for UHD-stereo Gavin, like GL4?"

"Why do you think nobody else has reported these effects, George? NASA has described your results as 'fanciful'. They've proved mathematically you can't possibly see this degree of detail with the kind of equipment you are using."

"Have they really? Well, well."

"NASA found no evidence of straight edges, and Hubble is by far the best telescope being used to study NERO."

"Our results are based on millions of separate images taken 24/7, from different perspectives all around the world. And the straight lines are very ephemeral, a few seconds at most. At the moment, Hubble is only looking at NERO six times a day – it's missing them, bloody amateurs!"

"NASA says you see straight lines because you want to, like the discredited canals on Mars. Jack, explain to us how your equipment is supposed to work."

"We use standard observing equipment, combined with some sophisticated image processing. Basically, we upload images from amateur observers all around the world, integrate the time signal and subtract out the random noise. That's the power of statistics you see, if the noise is completely random you can ..."

"Could all the image massaging be throwing up something weird, like an optical illusion – lens glare for example? More to do with bad observing technique than anything else."

"We don't see straight lines most of the time Gavin, only now and then. If it was a software problem, it would show up all the time. Also, we ..."

"How many anoraks do you have out there Jack, working for you?"

"To date we have received data from more than 100,000 dedicated enthusiasts worldwide. Most have demanding professional daytime jobs. They dedicate all their spare time to observing NERO and making their results freely available, while your viewers are expected to pay professionals to keep their results secret! I think our amateurs deserve your gratitude Gavin, not your scorn."

"Do you really think amateurs can make a serious contribution these days Jack?"

"Absolutely, and it's increasing all the time. GL4 hosts a telescope upgrade scheme. Whenever a user outgrows their equipment, they can trade it in for the next grade, absolutely free of charge. Nothing goes to waste. We have enthusiasts signing up all the time, eager to get started. The combined viewing power of our network greatly exceeds anything the professionals can muster. In fact, the interferometer baseline ..."

"You also think the rotation is all wrong, don't you George?"

"We have detected small anomalies in NERO's rotation, that is true."

"Something else NASA disputes."

"Yes, probably for the same reason. They're not looking hard enough."

"But all that's about to change now, isn't it George? Global One, NASA's powerful new satellite is approaching NERO as we speak. It will map surface features down to the size of a dollar bill. Won't that put you and your anoraks out of business?"

"Global One is approaching NERO with a closing speed of 72 km/sec on a tight flyby orbit. It will fly past NERO in less than a second. There is a limit to what you can see at that speed, even with the best equipment. If the straight lines aren't there when it arrives, it won't see them. But we'll be here, Gavin. GL4 and its global network of amateur astronomers will be observing NERO round the clock."

"Global One will also undertake various geophysical and chemical investigations. What do you think they'll find Jack?"

"Yes, that promises to be very exciting. Hopefully they'll be able to measure the mass and its internal distribution, which may go some way to explaining the strange rotation. They may even find clues to the origin of NERO. Is it just a rogue asteroid or something from another stellar system?"

"A battle cruiser from an alien galaxy?"

"That's not what I ..."

"Any plans of returning to teaching, Jack? We gather you rather abandoned your students,"

"Well, I wouldn't put it quite like that. Mrs Jennings, the retired head of Physics, is a very experienced teacher and graciously stepped in for me, virtually overnight. We still get emails from the kids saying we're doing a great job, bringing the subject to life. They've even formed a NERO observers group to ..."

"OK guys, it's a wrap. George, Jack – awesome work guys, thanks for talking to us here on GK News. Back to you, Melissa, *love* the new hair."

* * *

The two men relaxed after their exhausting scramble up the final scree slope and gazed back appreciatively down the steeply sided valley. The institute lay bathed in bright sunlight some three kilometres in the distance. A kilometre beyond that the ground fell away sharply into the vast Engadine basin.

"It was formed during the last ice age by a tributary glacier feeding the massive Engadine ice sheet. Over time, the ice sheet gouged away the foot of the valley forming a steep cliff. It's one of Europe's finest examples of a hanging valley. Its key feature is the almost perfect horseshoe profile, landlocked on three sides by a high mountain ridge and a single narrow entrance."

"Is that an advantage, defensively?"

"A severe disadvantage normally."

"But in this case Karl?"

"Crudely speaking, we should be able to detect anything fast and low, more or less everything you can see from here."

"Even stealth?"

"Especially stealth."

"How does it work?"

"I'm sorry, I don't really know the details."

"Anything to do with all the recent spraying?"

"Just greening the environment Ben, local wildlife measures."

"How much warning can we expect?"

"It depends on their approach, but no, not much warning I'm afraid. A matter of seconds, thirty at the most. But we believe they will want to avoid casualties. Just take out the institute."

"Is there really no defence at all?"

"They're working on something Ben, it's still largely untested. We need a few days to install it, possibly tonight if the weather deteriorates sufficiently." The two men gazed out over the ridge. The air was crystal clear but heavy storm clouds were massing to the south-west.

"Well, sooner them than me. It looks like being a filthy night, even for up here."

"That's what they're praying for, I gather."

They climbed to their feet and set off back down the treacherous slope. "The bunker is ready, on continuous standby, manned and defended round the clock. The army will see you there safely."

"I take it you're not really a police inspector, Karl. Swiss Secret Service?"

"The institute is expendable Ben, the staff are not. If necessary, we'll rebuild it."

"Do you know what I'm going to do, when all this is over?"

"Relax, I hope."

"Damned right I am. I'm going to buy myself a hang glider and hike up here each morning, then glide all the way down, do a few lazy circuits over the institute – what's left of it – then out over the cliff and down to the village for lunch. Then drive home and go to bed. With Frances, hopefully."

"Sounds a very good plan – for about a week," Karl said, smiling sympathetically. "How are things between you two, any ... Lieber Gott! Is that René Schante down there?"

"You must have damn good eyes Karl, I can't tell from here. I wouldn't have thought so, not by herself. They're pretty inseparable outside. Something to do with their first walk."

"I'm not surprised, they're a good-looking couple."

"No, not like that – I don't think. She started to tell me once but ... fell asleep."

"Must be the effect you have on them, Ben. I wish I could make my wife fall asleep."

"We were having dinner at the Schante's place, do you remember, the first night here in the valley – you had to leave early. It seems a lifetime ago. Have all the locals been evacuated?"

"All safely down in the village," Karl replied, smiling warmly as the girl sauntered up to them.

"René, my dear. How are you? And how is your cute little Englishman? Still fattening him up with our honest Swiss food?"

"Inspector Migrane! It's really lovely to see you again. David, he's well. He's ... David, you know. Busy. I came out for some fresh air. You can't imagine, inspector, what it's like being cooped up 24/7 working for the mad dictator," she whispered conspiratorially, but gazing thoughtfully at Ben.

"Some snaps for the family album, my dear?" the inspector asked, nodding casually towards the camera swinging from her belt.

"Wild flowers mainly. Plus the odd alien of course, whenever I find one. Not much today so far, only one decent specimen. Flowers, I mean. Here inspector, take a look at this."

"*Leontopodium alpinium?*"

"Yes!" she smiled in surprise. "Fairly rare here, but lately the whole valley seems to be thriving, especially the last few days."

"Must be all the warm rain," said the inspector, mumbling faintly to himself. She left him gazing through her photos while she chatted quietly to Ben.

"I'm glad I bumped into you Ben, up here I mean, away from ... work. I didn't know you enjoyed hill walking."

"We all need fresh air René, now and then. Come on, girl. Out with it. What's the matter?"

"It's David. I'm worried sick about him. He can't seem to relax properly anymore, it's like some part of him is always somewhere else."

"Well, he was always been a bit like that, René. That's just David, it's what we all love about him. I gather he perfected the keyword search index for blister images. Everyone seems to be using it."

"For a while he was like a big kid again, deliriously happy – like the old days."

"And what about you, René? How are you coping?"

"I'm well, really Ben, never felt better. I don't have problems switching off, always sleep like a baby. No conscience I suppose! We've developed the new process for unpacking thousands of blister images simultaneously. Another of his throwaway ideas, you know what he's like, forgets things as soon as he thinks of them these days. Only this time Justin was there to chase it up. He seems to be spending a lot time with us lately. I think maybe he has a crush on me? Honestly Ben, these youngsters! Where on earth do you find them?"

"Justin? He just walked in one afternoon, hotfoot from GCHQ. Quite literally, trekked all the way up from the village and asked for a job. Said the air smelt sweeter up here."

"Well, Justin developed it, David's idea I mean, made it all work. Together with the keyword search, it's revolutionised the way we merge the text and video streams. Now we illustrate the message in glorious interactive 3D imaging and video."

"I've still not found my handsome little professor, you know Pop-up-Prof, the one to explain all the science to me." She gazed sadly at him, her big brown eyes swimming with tears. "We're losing him Ben, I can feel it, a little more each day. It's the damned globe, he sits up all night with it. He says it relaxes him. Only he can't live without it. He's burning up, can't concentrate on anything anymore. And he speaks strangely, as if I'm out there with him, wherever it is he goes at night. He asks me strange questions about things I've never heard of, I mean things he *knows* I've never heard of."

"Low energy transfer orbits, energy sponge states, projection electromagnetics, quantum entanglement, super-luminal acknowledgment, Higgs tunnelling ..."

"The Axiom of Choice, for god's sake! I'd never heard of it Ben, we had to look it up. Something to do with free will and limitations of the mathematics of infinity. I still don't understand it. But what on earth does *he* want with it?"

"I'm frightened, Ben. I record it all, just in case. I hate to, it's like being unfaithful. But maybe it's important, for the future I mean. It's strange how right he's been about so many things, even when the rest of us thought he was ... well, cracking up." She blew her nose fiercely.

"We'll keep an eye on him René, I promise. See if we can't distract him more, get the pair of you out here in the fresh air. I think we could probably all do with a bit of a break, a big party or works outing or something. I'll ask Frances to organise something special."

"And you, Ben? I must say you're looking pretty relaxed lately. Frances too, I think," she added meaningfully.

"Yes, I suppose I so," he replied with a nervy smile. "We'll have that party René. What do you say, inspector? Do you think we could all manage a good night out somewhere?"

Chapter 27

As NERO approached its final week as a solid coherent body, mankind waited with mixed feelings for the impending cosmic calamity. For once politicians were surprisingly reticent in their comments, religious leaders and philosophers wary, uncertain of their ground. Only the general public, egged on by a frantic news industry, seemed genuinely prepared to enjoy the spectacle of a lifetime. Christmas, it seemed, was coming early this year.

News crews worked themselves into a fury, desperate for every fresh new angle on the approaching cataclysm and thoroughly frustrated by their inability to advance, delay or otherwise influence the schedule of events. So intense was the coverage that members of the human race destined to reside on the wrong side of the planet at Time Zero, were inclined to feel discriminated against, somehow cheated in life. But the news companies, with generous support from their sponsors, were quick to assure every-one that blind-side coverage would more than adequately make up for any sense of loss, with some shows offering live counselling sessions for registered sufferers of cosmic rejection syndrome.

In the scientific community, astronomers and planetary scientists worked around the clock to perfect their equipment and observing schedules, spending long hours setting down in irrefutable print, detailed theoretical predictions on the approaching devastation and its aftermath. It seemed quite ironic to them that of all the planets, Venus, with its surface permanently shrouded by impenetrable cloud, should have been singled out for interplanetary demolition. What a spectacle the unobscured surfaces of Mercury or Mars would have offered!

But gradually it became apparent that the dense Venusian atmosphere would have its scientific merits. Vast amounts of rock would be blasted back into space along suborbital trajectories, providing a spectacular side show as it returned minutes later to bombard the planet's entire surface with widespread destruction. Nowhere on Venus would escape the pulverising bombardment of incandescent rock. In addition, the dense white clouds would beautifully record the stupendous turbulence and shock waves emanating from the point of impact. In fact, computer studies revealed the dense Venusian atmosphere would be a thousand times more effective in propagating the deadly shock waves right around the planet. No, scientifically speaking, if there had to be a target, Venus was ideal.

Few scientists concerned themselves with the *why* question. Why Venus? Why now? The few that came close to questioning the improbability of recent events, merely shook their heads with a resigned 'there but for the grace of God'. Tame scientists were wheeled out at regular intervals to assure the public of absolutely no danger to Earth. Then again, in hasty retraction, when more considered studies revealed that some impact debris would undoubtedly reach escape velocities and eventually find its way to Earth. But the risk from secondary impact was declared minimal, and much emphasis was made of the glorious spectacle the resulting meteor showers would bring mankind, a fitting memorial to the day when Venus drew the short straw in cosmic roulette.

The GDS lobby were quick to point out it could all so easily have been the Earth facing annihilation. The two planets were almost identical in size and had the roles been reversed, we would already be dead, NERO having crossed Earth's orbit some weeks ago. Moreover an object the size and speed of NERO would be impossible to stop or even deflect using current technology. It was only a matter of time before a similar fate befell planet Earth. Surely it made sense now to develop a defensive capability. Was this not in fact, a timely warning for all mankind? Should not the public at large be assured a military option was available and could be developed to safeguard the long-term survival of the species?

It was a curious kind of role reversal, but the military got their way, and were sensible enough not to gloat when large slices of GNP were quietly earmarked for the military. Besides, there were other considerations why a military option might, in due course, prove useful.

There were from the very beginning of course, rumours of international consortiums heavily engaged in large-scale military projects; component modules for a versatile space platform, designed, constructed, tested and launched as manageable subunits for assembling in space. Undoubtedly, such rumours had a basis, undertakings of such magnitude cannot be completely hidden from the public gaze. Only their ultimate purpose remained unknown, or rather ambiguous. Ostensibly to study NERO and foster scientific cooperation in space, the platforms were 'Design Function Compliant', should some unforeseen contingency arise. It was a matter of economic good sense, pure and simple.

Or perhaps the superpowers had discovered some fabulous new technology further along the message and were now intent on exploiting their commercial advantage. Lord knows, their economies were in dire straits, with confidence in Global Economic Theory now at an all time low. Or maybe the world's wisest and wiliest nations were prudently building a superbomb, lest the day ever came when the rest of humanity begged – or possibly bartered – for their assistance.

Slowly, all such rumours petered out and then scotched completely, the day the big four announced all their efforts had culminated in the launch of three highly advanced space platforms to reconnoitre NERO and observe its impact on Venus. Global One had already admirably fulfilled its mission. Global Two and Three were now successfully parked in high reconnaissance orbits above the Venusian surface, patiently counting down to Time Zero and sending back invaluable data on NERO's approach.

The mission attracted massive sponsorship from the science, media and defence sectors, and for the first time in history, a substantial profit from a space venture seemed on the cards. The entire event was to be shown live on all major channels around the world at ultra-premium viewing rates. A spokesperson for the franchise marketing the venture boasted "GL4 is not the only outfit round here looking out for planet Earth. Having shattered an international agreement to announce NERO's approach in a calm and responsible manner, GL4 will definitely *not* be invited to the cosmic fireworks, or the champagne celebrations afterwards," she added with a smile. The politicians could almost be heard slapping each other on the back.

In the end, it seemed virtually everyone was happy. Even if the Global Economic Theory looked decidedly shaky at the moment, life on Earth still marched to the reassuring economic realities of supply and demand, at least as far as human desire and expectation was concerned. Leading economists breathed a mutual sigh of relief. They had found, virtually without looking, an economic windfall to tide humanity over yet another mysterious failure in GET. Now there would be time for a little financial bloodletting on the global money markets before the next inexplicable meltdown.

Only one small faction remained deeply frustrated. The diehards of the Armageddon brigade had wrung their hands when NERO was waved through Earthspace unchallenged on route to Venus. A deflecting attack now would have had proved a massive morale boost, vouchsafing the industry for decades. They despaired at the missed opportunity, wrought by that fatal combination of weak government and a distracted populous, though they would be as shocked as any to discover how soon their services would be recalled.

* * *

It was the ever vigilant network of amateur astronomers and their meddlesome GL4 foster parents who first raised the alarm. NERO it seemed, unlike every other object in the known universe, was not content to follow Sir Isaac Newton's laws of motion, or even Albert Einstein's refinements of them. What originally appeared a precisely aimed volley for the centre of the Venusian disk, was now drifting off target, a little more each day. At first, the professionals were tempted to dismiss the findings as inept science, but mindful perhaps of recent embarrassments they were cautious enough this time to check for themselves.

It seemed the amateurs were right, on this occasion, though some of their extrapolations were undoubtedly exaggerated. The target point was on the move. Since no convincing scientific explanation was forthcoming, it became open season as to what lay behind this fresh mystery and by how much the final target point might eventually drift. Certainly not enough at current rates to miss the planet entirely. The whole affair seemed one more anomaly to test the patience of the scientific community, anomalies which had steadily mounted since L4's original appearance.

For the world's political leaders the news actually came as light relief, clear evidence that the cosmic phenomenon was not after all a wilful act of vandalism on the part of some adolescent alien. NERO was not carefully aimed at the centre of Venus, it was not carefully aimed at anything, merely a freak accident in the cosmic lottery of time.

One enterprising young presenter even hosted a game show offering the ultimate infinite prize money for successfully predicting the exact point of impact. Since later entries obviously carried an unfair advantage, the prize value was arranged to decrease inversely to time of impact. Carefully adjusted parameters in the formula ensured nobody could physically submit an entry before its value had fallen to manageable levels. As predicted, premium-rate phone lines were saturated within seconds of the announcement, decreasing still further the chance of a sizable payout.

The tempo of human mystification increased further one week out from impact, still forty million kilometres from the planet, when the target point began to drift by more significant amounts each day. At one point it was feared NERO might miss the planet entirely, a scenario now regarded unacceptable, causing several scientists to withdraw from the endeavour in a state of severe shock. Having spent a sizable portion of their five year budget, the latest news came as an act of personal betrayal by Sir Isaac, albeit some four centuries earlier. And if Newtonian mechanics was beginning to totter, what else might be at risk? Everyone in science was quietly mystified by what was happening.

The discovery was leapt upon by the news companies, desperate to fill the final week with unremitting tension and speculation. Here at last seemed endless opportunity for controversy. Massive squandering of scientific and public resources, political ineptness and public unrest, all jostled for outraged scrutiny. Curiously enough, only journalistic hysteria failed to feature prominently in their scathing coverage.

It quickly became apparent that nobody had really considered what would happen if NERO actually missed its target. Conventional scientific opinion had it that the object would slingshot out of the solar system. Certainly now, that seemed the fervent hope of most politicians, sick to death at one of nature's itinerant rocks mocking their every effort to organise and run a modern society.

Everything depended on *by how much* it missed, apparently. Curiously, the smaller the miss, the greater the subsequent uncertainty. With small factors now assuming huge significance, it was realised NERO's mass was an important factor. The strangely inconclusive attempt by Global One to measure this quantity was then recalled with great consternation, accompanied by loud gasps of media incredulity. Official bodies were harangued over the failure, which resulted, it was said at the time, from someone pressing the wrong button.

After intense public lobbying it was revealed that Global One had in fact, performed perfectly, but that the observed mass was deemed embarrassingly large for public consumption. NERO weighed in at nearly 10^{20} kilograms, a figure deliberately meaningless to everyone except a planetary scientist. Eventually it was admitted this value was around a thousand times greater than what one might expect for an ordinary lump of rock the size and shape of NERO. And while its mass did not begin to compare with Venus itself – or the Earth for that matter – it did represent a terrifyingly large amount of material to be flying around the inner solar system at speeds of more than eighty kilometres per second, a speed which, one helpful GL4 observer pointed out, could manage the Washington – London hop in 52 seconds.

As yet another curiosity, it was calculated that NERO's anomalously high mass would result in a surface gravity almost identical with Earth's. Media speculation was rife. Could this really be yet one more meaningless fluke? What possible implications might it have?

Just twelve hours out from Venus, it finally became apparent that NERO was heading not for the planet itself, nor for a complete miss either. Almost inconceivably, NERO was flying a tangential entry course for the thin layer of Venusian atmosphere, a feat which seemed incredible given NERO was nearly half that width itself.

The scientific implications now changed yet again, as scientists struggled desperately to salvage their observing schedules and adapt their theories of interplanetary demolition with just twelve hours to go. It seemed unthinkable to them that, having spent six months meticulously adjusting and refining their theories, they should now be asked to start from scratch on a completely different problem. They were certainly not impressed by the numerous frantic appeals from their political paymasters on the possible implications for planet Earth.

Massively intricate calculations were performed for various scenarios, depending on exactly how NERO penetrated the atmosphere, at what orientation, how it might subsequently rotate or disintegrate, precisely what effects NERO's irregular shape and internal composition might have, and a thousand and one other imponderables. GL4's speculative reports on the object's ability to change shape only fuelled the controversy, as government experts were called upon to make snap judgements and calming predictions.

The most comprehensive calculations, assuming no more anomalous behaviour, concluded that on entering the atmosphere, NERO would either deflect downwards and impact the surface, or bounce outwards back into space. That such conclusions required calculation at all, came as a profound shock to the general public, who felt it merely a matter of common sense and wondered if the government scientists had finally lost the plot.

In fact, the scientists had a point. Of course, one of two mutually exclusive possibilities was inevitable, eventually. But *which*? That was much harder to calculate. Rather than alarm the public with indecision, it was felt prudent to leave the matter open, and emphasize that neither possibility posed the slightest risk to Earth. Privately, the politicians were furious with their scientists, and beginning to despair entirely of their long-term value.

Cautionary voices were gently muffled for fear of arousing greater public anxiety. The navigational precision required to target the wafer thin atmospheric layer was surely far more demanding than to strike the planet itself. If it was all highly unlikely before, how much more unlikely must it be now? But since when, in course of human affairs, was talking good sense ever a sufficient criteria to be heard? Or necessary, come to that. Cautionary voices were lost in the background roar of authoritative platitudes. The political message was clear. Get back to the bottle washing and let the experts worry about the future. It was precisely this prospect that was beginning to terrify the general public.

In the end, and against their better judgement, the scientists grudgingly submitted a definite prediction. If the object didn't disintegrate more or less immediately, few experts could entertain a path deflection of more than twenty degrees. Simple trigonometry then implied that if NERO emerged at all, it would be within thirty seconds of injection, say one minute for absolute certainty. The politicians had their prediction. The scientists had their noose.

At Time Zero, NERO duly plunged into the thick Venusian atmosphere and promptly vanished from human scrutiny for the first time in eighteen months. For most inhabitants of Earth the end came as blessed relief, exhausted from months of relentless media pounding and only too happy now to heave a collective sigh of relief. Very soon, the whole saga would be over for good. NERO would crash or bounce. Who on earth really cared which?

Chapter 28

The next shock came almost immediately, when NERO churlishly declined both government options. Satellite images showed vast trails of massive atmospheric disruption in the wake of the careering asteroid, but the object itself failed to crash or re-emerge at the appointed venue. The news companies were beside themselves with mirth at the incredible spectacle of stunned bewilderment in official circles.

Government scientists were recalled for a rapid rethink, and reluctantly agreed the object might just conceivably – for a short while longer – neither crash nor bounce, but stressed the situation would resolve itself *very shortly*. How very shortly? Suddenly, confident words became confident arm waving, as panels of experts played for time, hedging their bets and squirming uncomfortably on the world stage.

Politicians on the other hand, scarcely cared one way or another, the longer NERO took to decide the better, as far as they were concerned. Certainly, they need not be troubled in the meantime. It wasn't until both amateur and professional observers alike began reporting some rather peculiar disturbances that politics once more took up its reluctant cudgel with the wayward rock.

Almost inconceivably, NERO appeared to be flying the knife edge of probability zero, a scenario poised exactly between crashing and bouncing. Within minutes of NERO's insertion, GL4's team of amateur astronomers were reporting high speed jets of incandescent gas streaming off the planet. As the gas expanded rapidly in the vacuum of space, the fierce solar wind ripped apart its atoms, causing the resulting plasma to fluoresce brightly in a myriad of kaleidoscopic colours.

Buffeted now by the sun's magnetic field, waves of ghostly luminescence spread through the clouds at incredible speeds, causing the whole spectacle to shimmer eerily across the depths of space, a phenomenon which GL4 observers were quick to dub the *Venusian Lights*, one leading one devout observer to tearfully describe the scene as the gently waving hand of God.

And while government scientists were quick to confirm their predictions of massive atmospheric turbulence, many were privately stunned by the enormous degree of ejection. In vain did the franchise companies explain their satellites were actually too close to the action to capture a perspective view of the phenomenon. In contrast, GL4 was able to devote an entire web channel to the unexpected bonus material, attracting billions of viewers within seconds.

Viewers still limp with exhaustion from the relentless media pounding, soon found themselves relaxing before one of nature's most soothing and ethereal spectacles, played out free of charge on their cosmic doorstep, much to the despair of the franchise companies who could only watch their viewing figures plummet disastrously, along with their advertising revenue.

As for NERO itself, official opinion steadfastly maintained the entire phenomenon represented one more gigantic fluke, an improbable combination of NERO's irregular shape and angle of insertion into the swirling Venusian atmosphere. Very soon the object would have to re-emerge or crash.

In the meantime, perhaps the whole world was witnessing the celestial birth of another planetary ring system, rather like the glorious Saturn. Many stunning pictures of Saturn were hastily screened alongside computer animations of Venus in ringlets, all accompanied by the soothing strains of Gustav Holst to help dispel the rather gloomy air of official confusion.

* * *

Meanwhile, to their embarrassment, GL4 was suffering the burden of too much information. Ben first heard about it in a snatched phone call from Jack, though when he arrived in person, everything appeared quite normal – at least as normal as things ever appeared at his institute. The usual crowd had gathered for

George's coffee break and a small group were still clumped in one corner following a heated exchange. George in particular, was in caustic mood, firing scathing questions at David's *why* philosophy on interpreting cosmic events, while René hovered about anxiously with mounting concern.

"No George, Venus is just a side show."

"A side show! So what's the main event, David?"

"Earth of course."

"Earth! How do you figure that out?" George asked incredulously, shaking his head in disbelief.

"Venus is being astro-engineered – made habitable. Mars too, probably."

"Habitable – who for? Aliens?"

"No, not aliens. Not initially."

"What's that supposed to mean? Come on David, how does it happen?" George demanded, glancing up at the agitated René, fussing over David and shaking her head warningly at George. But George was oblivious to her sympathies, intent on dismantling David's daydream theories, or DDTs as he called them lately.

"So where are they, then, these aliens? Are they here already, on Earth? Or are they in NERO? Where are they heading?"

It was never a good idea to ask David four consecutive questions at once, but in the present circumstances it proved farcical. David was no longer communicating in human terms, while George was still groping around for the right question.

"Everywhere really, George. But no, not Earth. Yes, in a sense. Everywhere." The confusion caused by this response rather strained the group's concentration, which David sensed to some degree, causing him to backtrack and only add to the confusion.

"It's a prediction, George, nothing is definite. A probability calculation of species survival in the face of short term threat – a precautionary measure. Perhaps humankind survives regardless, mutates and adapts. But genetics is slow and modern day threats rapid, there may not be time to mutate. Species come and go, sometimes very quickly. So they're advancing the schedule a bit, improving the odds."

"Who is? What bloody schedule? How are they advancing it? Are they taking us over, is that what you mean, like some endangered herd of highland cattle? For God's sake David, get a grip!"

"George!" pleaded René.

"So what's NERO doing now?" snapped George, unable to back off.

"Gliding."

"Gliding! George squeaked almost incoherently. "It's a fucking rock for chrissakes!"

"It's generating an aerofoil field, intensely resonant EM pulses that simulate solid control surfaces, infinitely and instantly deformable. Projection Pulse Electromagnetics – you saw it in action yourself a few weeks ago, some kind of system test probably or midcourse correction."

"Here feel this," David said, suddenly jumping up at the startled George and offering to demonstrate the virtual control panel on his globe. But George seemed unwilling to trust his own senses now, almost exploding after a few sceptical prods when David admitted the sensitivity took a little getting used to.

"But it's all happening on *Venus*," George repeated, refusing to be drawn any further from his original point. "How is Venus a sideshow?"

"Venus is almost finished."

"And then what?"

"Then they come here." It wasn't at all the answer George was expecting.

"To do what, David? Fix the fucking economy?"

"OK guys," Ben said, calmly taking over. "That will do for now. Let's try checking some of this out. David, I'd like talk to you. Now, in my office please. Boys and Girls, if you'll excuse us?"

* * *

The unprecedented bewilderment in official circles soon led to a remarkable discovery by the media industry. Frustrated by the dwindling enthusiasm on the part of official experts to furnish instant commentary on the dizzying pace of events, television producers turned in despair to interviewing their viewers, live over their video-cam links. Though originally conceived as a light-hearted stop gap, it soon became apparent that herein lay a rich vein of entertainment gold. Suddenly, everything was on tap, instantly available and free of charge, from banal lunacy and humorous comment, to poignant political insight and unfettered scientific debate.

The only problem of course, was filtering the input in real-time so as to generate an editorially acceptable output. The first attempt was an unmitigated disaster, rapidly degenerating into a chaotic pantomime so complete, one viewer ended up interrogating the shell-shocked presenter. But then a strange thing happened. After an agonising ten minutes of anarchy, with program editors fighting desperately behind the scenes to control the flailing beast, it suddenly became apparent that things were settling down to a new equilibrium. Informed comment was getting through, pertinent questions were being asked – and answered. And entertaining television was being made. There was no need for a tight editorial rein, it was far better on the editorial nerves – and viewing figures – to let the whole thing flow.

After all, what in the present circumstances, was there to lose? Nobody of any consequence had the slightest clue what was happening, so who was to say if the programme content was right or wrong, balanced or biased? What did biased mean anyway, in the present circumstances? It was simply personal opinion that was being reported, that much at least the show had made clear from the outset. There was no verifiable right or wrong in the current hiatus, no historical precedent from which to dispense lofty political or philosophical judgement. Journalistically, tomorrow was another day, and in all probability, a very different day.

And if politicians and philosophers wanted to argue this a lapse in journalistic standards, that too was fine. They could join the live debate as a contributory viewer or visit the studio and voice their opinion amidst an acknowledged panel of experts. The only problem was, well, nobody was listening to acknowledged experts at the moment.

And it really didn't help matters much that astute program presenters now began bandying about terms like increased democratic participation, enhanced representation and real-time democracy. Public opinion seemed surprisingly robust in getting to the heart of the matter, and in many cases, far more reliably than orthodox political debate.

As program formats evolved rapidly in the changing political climate, producers came to rely heavily on GL4's growing database of amateur enthusiasts to furnish facts, hypotheses and informed opinion. With over 500,000 online contributors across 24 different time zones, and real-time audio translation in 3000 languages, the GL4 network rapidly became the pre-eminent global studio for news and scientific debate.

* * *

After four hours and nineteen complete circuits through the Venusian atmosphere, it became finally apparent to just about everyone, that NERO was somehow cruising just below the cloud tops, and in the process venting vast quantities of the planet's atmosphere into space, much like rapidly peeling a potato. Parts of planet's surface were becoming visible for first time in geological history.

And while some presenters still tried for the light-hearted angle – *Aliens in a spin* – the general public were quick to home in on the *why* question, so carefully avoided by official experts. None of the recent cosmic events could any longer, be considered natural or accidental. There remained one irresistible – if unpalatable – explanation to every cosmic disturbance since L4's original appearance.

Suddenly, and with little official dissemination of the facts, it became apparent to the seven billion human inhabitants of the planet, that another intelligent species had arrived in the solar system and was manipulating events and processes on an interplanetary scale.

New scenarios suddenly became apparent. Was Venus being prepared for habitation by an alien species? Were the aliens using the thick Venusian atmosphere as a velocity brake, in preparation for a landing and colonisation of the planet? How would they view long-term cohabitation of the inner solar system with planet Earth?

Official experts were not convinced. Atmospheric carbon dioxide on Venus was, they insisted, still far too high for anything more than a primitive form of bacterial life. Besides, not a trace of water was to be found on the planet. If Venus was their final destination, the aliens had badly miscalculated.

Chapter 29

"It's starting, David," she yelled again, just as he joined her on the sofa.

"Hells bells, René. They're only kids."

"So were we, once. And not so long ago," she said softly, gazing into his tired eyes and absently smoothing one of his shaggy locks. "Where did it all go David?" she asked sadly.

"Search me. I wish I knew." He cuddled up to her reassuring softness, gently nestling his head on her shoulder and secretly deciding to fall asleep. A sixteen year old boy with a surprisingly deep mellow voice, was introducing the show.

"Ladies and gentleman. Or more precisely, girls and boys. For it's girls and boys we are talking to today. This is a historic occasion, a two hour in-depth documentary-debate screened by all the major channels, and of course, beamed live in fabulous UHD-stereo by GL4 with real-time audio translation by our sponsors VirtualVoice."

"Documentary-debate! There's a contradiction in terms. Who's kidding who? Come on darling, let's go to bed."

"You go Schatz, I'll be along soon. I want to see Ben collect his degree."

"*Honorary* degree, you mean. Anyway, he's obviously recording it all for you."

"Don't be so mean, David. We owe him this, we all do. It means an awful lot to him. He's just a big kid in some ways, anxious for your praise and admiration." The spotted youth was just getting into his stride.

"That's what I'm saying! What does he want a degree for? He runs the world's biggest information service – knowledge, advertising, education and the message. What a scary combination! If things ever …"

"Crikey! Who the hell is that?"

An attractive blonde bimbo, seventeen looking twenty-five with breasts to die for, had taken up the discussion. Big moist eyes and a dumb-blonde persona, until the moment she opened her mouth.

" ... decoding breakthrough. We're way through the freshman's introduction; we find vast tracts of mathematics, science and technology opening up, more than the sum total of human knowledge. All the code looks accessible, wherever we sample. Understanding the new results is still chronological of course, as with any learning process, but we can skip ahead. We find tantalising glimpses of the future, only today. Whole tracts on the Theory of Infinitesimals, stuff we thought a complete cul-de-sac. Totally new methods of mathematical proof ..."

"Not more maths, surely to god. When are we ..."

"Shut up David, I want to hear this."

" ... entire tomes on the Proof by Contradiction and its combinatorial extensions. The Riemann Hypothesis is proved as a trivial corollary of a powerful new theorem. There are five line proofs of Fermat's Last Theorem and the Four Colour Theorem, and huge tracts on the theory of Non-cooperative Games, with tantalising results for the socio-political arena."

"Who is she? How can anybody concentrate with those things hanging out?"

"David, she's a kid. They're all kids now, haven't you noticed? That's what this program is all about, kids educating themselves and taking over. That's what Ben has done – Ben and the message and us. We don't know half of what's going on out there. We ought to get out more David, travel and see the world. David I want a baby!"

It was unfortunate timing for such an abrupt demand, for the bimbo had turned her attention to science, and David was now blind to all mammalian accessories.

" ... and in biochemistry there are entire workshop manuals for the assembly line synthesis of proteins and enzymes, meta-sequences for growing large-scale organs and carbon-based memory structures of vast size. There are enzyme techniques for cultivating perfect diamonds in UV carbonated water, nanotronic circuit synthesis using messenger RNA analogues, and specialist logic circuits designed by natural selection processes."

"New families of elementary particles are listed with exotic processes at energies vastly exceeding CERN's current limit. There are pseudo-stable states of matter, energy sponge states and projection pulse electromagnetics – far beyond anything currently available. We've seen Feynman-Higgs diagrams for quantum tunnelling in dark states of matter, amazing new materials with fabulous strength to weight ratios and high temperature superconducting ceramics. It endless!"

"Whoops! And here is the man himself, bang on cue!" scoffed David.

"David, stop this," said René, as Ben Khoeller's calm face appeared filling the entire screen, smiling confidently and bestowing mutual empathy on all.

"Bloody hell. They've made him up to look twenty-five. This is so absurd!"

" ... not really, Gwyneth," Ben said, gazing steadily into her eyes. "I just sign the cheques these days. I have teams of brilliant youngsters working for me. It's them you should be congratulating."

"Did you ever think Ben, just a few years ago, Googal would be handing out university degrees today?"

"Well it's the Googal-Wikipedia consortium actually. We just distribute the study programs and oversee the tutorweb. The kids do all the hard work; all the studying, assembling knowledge-trees and running the critical peer-assessment groups. Each group tutors a younger group in exchange for EduCredits. It's a self-sustaining process, fabulously efficient, virtually cost free and immensely satisfying for everyone."

"And yes, Gwyneth, this is a proud day for me – for everyone. You listen to people, you take on board their brilliant ideas, and do your best to turn it all into reality. It's wonderful to see all these young people teaching themselves at their own pace and in their own style. Not just on the Googal Ed site of course, but everywhere. It's what education is all about."

"Do you ever regret not finishing university yourself, Ben?"

"I only managed a few months, Martin. I didn't fit in, too impatient. I always wanted to get straight to the answer, I was never really interested in the reasoning or understanding. But that is precisely what's so marvellous about modern education. Students can jump about wherever they want. Develop at their own pace, take their own directions, backfilling the gaps whenever they choose. They can tackle the subject matter when they feel ready for it, not just when the teaching system is ready for them."

"In the past, education only really served the tiny proportion of students fortunate enough to fit the established teaching mould. Now we mould the teaching to fit each and every student. Everybody is different, always has been. That's what makes human beings so wonderful and special, it's what makes human society tick. Everyone is needed, everyone is good at something. Everyone can find a niche somewhere and excel. But now we can tailor the teaching to fit the student. Today, everyone can have a university education. Even me!"

"Looking forward to the ceremony, Ben?"

"You bet Martin, although I'm only here for an honorary degree. But I understand congratulations are in store for Gwyneth!"

The camera cuts abruptly to a furiously blushing Gwyneth, as Ben continues in his smooth tones.

"Self-taught orphan, youngest Googal doctorate to be nominated for a Nobel prize in physics, now off to Bern to head up a brand new research facility in dark energy physics."

"How did ..." she managed weakly, as the camera zooms in on Gwyneth wiping a stray tear, then cuts quickly back to Ben.

"I run the world's biggest information service, it's my job to know. Just as it's my job now to present Gwyneth with startup funding for the brand new orphan centre she's setting up here in Bern. Congratulations Gwyneth!" The camera catches Ben beaming broadly as he hands Gwyneth a huge colourful Googal cheque.

"Why are you so interested in modern youth, Ben? Do you regret wasting your own?"

"Youth is our one truly sustainable asset Martin, and education its passport to a better future. Human insight is a delicate flower, easily trampled underfoot in the daily struggle to survive. It has been my good fortune to find the time and resources to help foster this asset, for our children's future and that of all Earthkind."

"Because one day Martin, and perhaps quite soon, we will need to move on, leave this planet and venture out to other planets and beyond. Make new homes on new worlds. And perhaps, in time, found a new species. Still human, but more so."

"Why do you think Ben, world governments were so quick to contract out of universal education?"

"They had virtually no choice, Martin. Kids were voting with their feet, leaving orthodox schooling in their droves, educating themselves over the internet. Once they saw their elder siblings self-teaching, they wanted it for themselves. We had to set up web services for secondary education virtually overnight. Now we find ourselves doing the same in the junior and primary sectors. They're teaching their younger siblings, while they teach themselves. It's a self-sustaining process. By simply acknowledging reality, politicians were able to salvage some of the initiative and explain it as innovative cost-cutting."

"But there's more to it than that. The old guard of nationalist politics can't get their heads around the fact that the future belongs to kids, and it belongs to them today, not some ever receding horizon of the future. They still think they can corral our youngsters, pen them in and release them only when they are tired and broken, like themselves. So they emphasise tradition, an outdated cycle of learning and a grudging handover of power. They desperately hope the alien message will provide the technological means to prolong this stranglehold over youthful drive and imagination. At GL4 we passionately hope the politicians are wrong, our children's future is too great a responsibility to leave to the middle aged."

"How do you see the latest moves against NERO, Ben? Do you think the coalition is still secretly planning to destroy it?"

"I very much doubt the USUK coalition has ever considered NERO a credible threat, in the sense of alien invasion or anything like that. The threat they see, is that NERO may form the next critical link in the chain of humankind becoming a cosmic species. It's only a threat to them because they don't control it – they're not in the loop."

"In what way, Ben?"

"Well, just take the question of real estate. Compared with Earth, NERO is tiny. But it's volume, not area, that figures in modern society – cubic feet, not square feet. And in terms of cubic, NERO's interior has space for over a thousand New Yorks. That's a fabulous amount of real estate to suddenly turn up on our cosmic doorstep. It represents an enormous opportunity for human expansion and growth. Not since the opening up of trade routes by the British and Dutch, or the American prairies by the pilgrim fathers, has such a golden opportunity presented itself to humankind."

"But it takes a willingness to take risks, to explore and tame the unknown, and it requires great changes in the way society is run. World government is nervous, they see it as the first step to losing power, of being left behind in an ageing world with only the old and weary to toil for them. They shouldn't see it like that. They should welcome the opportunity with open arms, help our youngsters grasp the new opportunities and wish them godspeed, not stand in their way and wreck things for the entire species."

"So do you really believe USUK is planning to destroy NERO, if – as your website is now predicting – NERO starts heading for Earth?"

Ben paused dramatically. "Yes I do, Gwyneth. We have no proof, just lots of indicative evidence: the disappearance of huge capital sums into non-responding domestic budgets; large unexplained trends in the recruitment of young scientists; and large numbers of unscheduled shuttle launches over the past months. And just last week, the first evidence of a massive thermonuclear explosion on the far side of the moon."

"We have received several unattributed reports of a superbomb which can be fabricated and tested in manageable subunits, launched and assembled in orbit to form a giant planet-bursting device. We believe the USUK coalition might well be planning to use it against NERO in the very near future, with or without United Nations' ratification."

The camera zooms into to Ben's face, now serious and anxious. "That is why, boys and girls, you must vote now on the GL4 website, all of you, no matter how young you are. It's *your* future that's being decided here, not ours. And it's being decided without your say, without you ever casting a single vote. Go to the GL4 website and vote now, along with all your little brothers and sisters and young friends around the world. Tell them all to vote. There are three billion of you out there. You must have your say. And don't forget, each of you will receive one hundred EduCredits the moment you vote."

"Thank you Ben, and good luck."

"Thank you. And best wishes guys, and all you youngsters out there – don't forget to vote!" he said, waving goodbye and smiling gushingly into camera, shamelessly endearing himself to three billion children.

"God almighty, René. Did you know about this?"

"Some of it, yes. Of course! Well the web, David, for heaven's sake! Don't you ever stream global news and opinion?" She sighed in frustration at his blank expression. "But I never realised the bigger picture. It all sounds very serious. I think Ben is taking a huge risk."

"It sounds like we all are," said David glumly.

* * *

Ben's appearance served only to sharpen the public's appetite for better information and debate, and since official sources remained terse and highly predictable on the subject, the news companies were forced to rely still more heavily on the GL4 network.

It wasn't long before the public found itself considering a scenario far more unsettling than the bacterial colonisation of Venus. For if the aliens were capable of controlling their braking manoeuvres so precisely, was there not yet another, more ominous, possibility? From nowhere at all the word *astrobraking* appeared on everyone's lips, the use of a planet's atmosphere to decelerate a high-velocity inbound object for orbital ejection onto another planet. Another planet such as Earth. After all, where better to shed a large momentum excess than in the dense atmosphere of a handy neighbouring planet?

But why in the cosmic scheme of things, go to all that trouble, if Earth was the final destination? Could it be that NERO was actually speeding to Earth by stealth, taking in a useful diversionary feint around Venus first? Suddenly it seemed, there was little time to assess the new scenario, much less act against it.

For now it was realised NERO could eject from Venus along a Hoffman transfer orbit direct to planet Earth, arriving in just under six weeks. Hasty calculations confirmed the current planetary configuration to be the one of the most favourable, the fastest transit departing Venusian orbit in just under two hours time. It became imperative to monitor NERO's braking manoeuvres and measure its emergent velocity, if indeed the object did emerge.

Unfortunately, just at the moment Global Two was fully engaged in the task, a powerful jet of incandescent gas unexpectedly vaporized the probe. Still more unfortunately – for news of the event took a full nine minutes to reach the Earth and then another full nine minutes to alert Global Three – mission control could only watch with mounting unease and disbelief as a second incinerating cloud rose swiftly towards Global Three as it calmly recorded its own cremation.

The simultaneous and dramatic loss of both probes hardly affected public opinion however, for shortly afterwards the world's superpowers, acting in pre-arranged concert, moved rapidly to a state of Undeclared Global War. Publicly voiced fears and opinions fell silent, replaced by the calm measured tones of government certitude. Finally it seemed, the moment had arrived for concerted global action, by men of concerted global destiny.

Chapter 30

"Hello Ben, come in. I didn't expect you quite so soon, I've only just sent the email."

"After yesterday, I thought it would be prudent to consult my favourite astrologers, learn my future – if I still have one!" Ben said, smiling broadly.

"Astrologers! You should know Ben, there are some things it's best not to joke about."

"Where's Jack?"

"Last seen spending shedloads of your money again – telescope time at the Chinese, Australian and Chilean observatories. He's even pitching incognito for Hubble. The man has no fear these days."

"Good, that's what it's there for. So what's the big flap, George?"

"Another unexpected development, incoming comets. Lots of them," George added with emphasis, tossing a heap of spectacular images on the table. "We thought you'd like to know right away."

"How many?"

"Patrick's found twenty-three in last four days, fairly large ones at that, with new sightings coming in daily."

"Patrick?"

"After Patrick Moore," George smiled. "Affectionate name for our network of amateur astronomers, 320,000 at the last count. And here's the big spender himself, and René too! Must be coffee time."

"Hello guys, David will be along in a moment. Gosh that smells so good, George!" she said smiling, snaking an arm over his shoulder as he fussed about with his coffee machine.

"We might as well be comfortable. I'll call the gang and you can tell us all about your new cosmic chums. Any chance of favouring us with some of your Peruvian brews?" Ben enquired, eyeing George's shiny new coffee machine.

"Every chance," said George. "We also provide sugar and cream if you want to totally ruin it."

"So what's with all the comets, Jack?" Ben asked, when everyone had settled. "Bored with NERO already?"

"There are just too many of them. It's rare to see more than two or three at any one time. I've just got another batch of pictures through. That's forty-seven now."

"What about their orbits?" asked René, gazing dreamily at the beautiful pictures.

"Ah yes, dear lady. Exactly!" smiled Jack. "Seventeen are on a near collision course for Venus. Four others are heading for Mars. The other two are heading initially for Jupiter, but will slingshot on to Venus. None are coming remotely close to Earth. We're still waiting for data on the remainder."

"OK," said Ben. "So let's ask the *why* question, before David gets here! If there is an alien intelligence behind this, why comets? Why Mars and Venus? And why now?"

"And why *near* collisions?" said René.

"Aquarius apparently," said George, mysteriously. "Don't look at me like that René, it's David's loopy idea. The aliens again. They've just finished Venus, re-engineering the planet and sorting out its atmosphere, now they're shipping its oceans. Same with Mars too, he reckons."

"Good god! How many comets do you need for that?" asked an astonished Ben.

"We can work it out!" said Jack, one step ahead of his friend for once. "Earth and Venus are a similar size. The Earth's surface is roughly 500,000,000 square kilometres and there's enough water to cover it approximately two kilometres deep, so that's a billion cubic kilometres of water. Let's say the comets are all thirty kilometre ice cubes, so that's roughly 25,000 cubic kilometres each. Divide the big one by the small one and you get … 40,000 comets! That's just for Venus of course. Mars would need much less, about a quarter as much, say 10,000."

"Are there that many comets?" asked Ben incredulously.

"Good God yes! Trillions in the Ort cloud, out beyond Pluto."

"So how do they get them in here."

"God only knows," replied Jack.

"Then perhaps you should ask him," George suggested sarcastically.

"*Him*?" René mused.

"Her," George replied quickly, "that's if they still bother with sex at that level."

"But that's the *how* question," said Ben. "Where is he, by the way René?"

"He went to see Frances about the GL4 schedule today. I mean *scheduling* for heaven's sake! I'm surprised he even knows what it means. Anyway, we better save him a good strong coffee, he seemed quite agitated."

"Ben," Jeff said suddenly, surreptitiously surfing. "NASA news statement."

* * *

In a startling new development around 4am Eastern Standard Time, a Whitehouse spokeswoman announced the imminent approach of over a two thousand comets heading for the inner solar system, with new objects being sighted at the rate of almost one hundred daily. All the comets appear to be approaching along widely different orbits. NASA stressed it had been closely monitoring the situation for the last three weeks, since the first object was sighted. No further information was available and no comment made on whether the new phenomenon is in any way connected to other recent cosmic disturbances. But informed sources suggest the administration clearly views the latest development as yet another major threat to global security.

* * *

"We need Patrick on the case," said Ben, "to locate the comets and see where they're heading. If it's true they are for the oceans of Mars and Venus we need to publish the fact very quickly, before USUK has a chance to suggest something more sinister."

"What does it matter," George said gloomily. "There's nothing we could do about it anyway. We can't protect ourselves against a single comet, never mind tens of thousands. If they're coming for us, that's it – curtains! If not, it's a null-problem. We should just sit tight and observe."

"I doubt if anyone in government will view it quite like that George," said Ben carefully, "certainly not the superpowers. And even if they did, they'd still want to make political capital out of it. No George, this needs uploading straight away. If we have the orbits for the first twenty-three, perhaps we can build a case on that, and simply predict the rest will follow suit. How do you suppose they'll arrive, just come crashing down? It all sounds a bit destructive."

"And none too efficient, either. Probably blast most of ice back into space as superheated steam."

"How would *we* go about it Jack, if we could?" asked René.

"Two of the comets heading for Venus are due to arrive at virtually the same time, though along wildly different trajectories. The data is not sufficiently accurate to say much more at the moment."

"Well then, that has to be it!" said George, excitedly. "That's exactly what we'd do, if we could, arrange for pair-wise collision of comets, zero net momentum, right in front of the orbiting Venus. Perhaps just enough energy to vaporize the comets, but quickly refreezing as a vast cloud of ice crystals, only to be sucked up by the planet's gravity as it ploughs through the cloud. It's the monsoon season for Venus – Mars too, maybe. It's beautiful! But my god, think of the calculations involved! Makes you feel small, doesn't it?"

"We'll have to publish this as a prediction for testing. If we can show that all the comets will pair up just in front of Mars or Venus that would prove the alien's intentions are honourable. Perhaps deter USUK from doing something rash."

"Am I right in thinking the brighter comets are closer, and more likely to arrive first?" said René. "That might reduce the combinatorics a bit. If you take me through the orbit program George, we could get this out on the distributed processing platform, perhaps have a million computers working on it by lunchtime."

"Meanwhile the rest of us ought to re-evaluate some of the other aspects again," said Ben. "Like what kind of lifeforms they might have in mind for Mars and Venus now there's water on the way, and how would they view cohabiting the solar system with planet Earth? See if there's any data or guidance in the message on planetary engineering or colonisation. Case studies, reviews and conclusions, that sort of thing. Where the hell is David, this is exactly his kind of baby. OK boys and girls, we better get started. Great coffee George, thanks. What an amazing day, and it's not even eleven o'clock!"

At that moment the pale shrunken figure of Frances appeared around the door looking for Ben.

"Ben, it's started. Personal from the White House. They're on their way. We have thirty minutes to evacuate, then they level the place."

Chapter 31

Historically, it would be become known as the *Battle of the Ghosts*. Modern historians are fond of citing it a pivotal point in the war. For war, it was quickly realised, was what the world had effectively embarked upon. Not the conventional type of conflict, more an unseen struggle between undeclared adversaries, largely unaware of each other's intentions.

In stark contrast, the opening salvos were to be exchanged in the full glare of public scrutiny, each move and countermove streamed live around the world as battle waged. Here on a remote Swiss hilltop, Armageddon had arrived on Earth for humankind to live and relive in glorious stereoscopic slow-motion with red-button interactive replay.

With remarkable Swiss efficiency, a small posse of soldiers arrived to escort everyone to the water treatment facility built into the hillside. Sentries scanned their badges, visually identifying each member of staff and ushering them brusquely through a heavily reinforced blast door. From there they were whisked off in small groups by waiting rail pods to a fully refurbished Cold War bunker, buried deep in the heart of the Swiss mountainside.

After a quick medical checkup they were assembled in a small hall, surrounded by teams of technicians in grey battle fatigues busily attending racks of electronic equipment and radar displays. After a few minutes, Inspector Migrane appeared before them.

"Ladies and gentleman, friends. We are profoundly sorry it has come to this. Every one of us hoped hostilities might be avoided, but it seems not to be. I wish to assure you that you will all be perfectly safe here for the duration. You need to know that GL4 is still live and functioning as normal, and will continue to operate whatever happens above us. The Swiss Army is heavily engaged in defending your gallant and noble enterprise and we ask that you return to your vital work as soon as possible. It is a critical moment and any delay now could be disastrous for everyone. We have a full suite of rooms, facilities and all the necessary equipment for to continue your work from here. Ben will explain the details in a moment. Unfortunately I must leave you now, but I will be in constant touch. Please do not hesitate to contact me if you need anything at all. Good luck."

As he left he murmured a few words to Ben, whose eyes lifted involuntarily in René's direction. It was a badly shaken Ben who stepped forward to addressed his devotees.

"Boys and girls, we need to get back to work as soon as possible. Five miles away our hosts are risking their lives defending our brave venture and we must not let them do so in vain. We must keep the world informed of what is happening, both at Kristalberg and in deepest space. Now, more than ever, we must be vigilant to the slightest hint of what might come next. Make no mistake, we are fighting not just for our own survival here, but for that of the entire free world. We cannot fail them."

"Frances has posted a plan of the bunker with designated work areas. You will find all the necessary equipment already installed for this very contingency. Well done boys and girls, now let's get to it."

As his staff dispersed, a tearful Ben gently caught René's elbow and took her quietly aside. As it turned out, the GL4 staff were virtually the only human beings on the planet not to witness the entire battle live, as with little more ado they settled into their new quarters and got back to work.

* * *

Eighteen nautical miles from target the drones broke tactical formation, each following a speed and course computed to arrive on the target within milliseconds of each other from strategically selected points of the compass. Onboard computer control systems piloted the drones to within twenty metres of the rapidly varying terrain, well below the radar skirt of any defensive force, with weapon control systems already primed to detect and tactically neutralise any defensive radar within seconds of illumination. Any radar not coherently deflected skywards by their mirror like surfaces would be instantly quenched by the microwave-absorbing bioskin.

It was to a text book attack. The ultimate presentation in weapons procurement, battlefield management and global diplomacy, all rolled into one seamless seductive package. Primetime viewing for the global community, from wavering third world powers to hard line political extremists to bored Swedish housewives. Computer planned and scheduled, deployed and executed with micro precision from the far side of the world, the systems were so state of the art, each drone quite exceeded the cost of the institute they had come to destroy.

The time for fiscal logic having long since expired, the coalition's mission was now too important to budget. Global politics itself was at stake and common sense had deserted the battlefield. The political and financial dividends would come later, when the world realised its utter vulnerability to the new pilotless platforms. Only four such drones were ever rumoured to exist, but the valleys below Kristalberg that morning boasted eight units, all cruising undetectably just above the tree tops.

When the prototype Ghost radar system was covertly installed one filthy night on the mountainside high above the institute, no one could have predicted its pivotal role in the fate of the world a week later. Perversely, the Ghost system searched for the *absence* of a radar echo, a ghostly silhouette flitting across a brightly illuminated backdrop. As such its range was severely limited to the opposite hillside. Its three radar antennas arrays were necessarily sited in highly exposed positions, chronically vulnerable to the most primitive radar seeking weapons.

The Swiss had done their best to camouflage their units, encasing them in tough plastic skins, carefully tailored replicas of the rocks they now impersonated. The arrays now sat inert, never once breaking electronic silence in idle chat or synchronising banter, waiting for the moment everyone hoped would never arrive.

As the drones whisked over the final contour, flooding the terrain with their electronic emission, the Ghosts arrays powered up, scanning the surrounding landscape ten thousand times a second with their maser powered pencil beams. Caesium clock crystals synchronised each Ghost array to peek out in a manner so precisely coordinated as to deceive any detector into computing a false location, much as individual orchestral pieces are perceived around a high fidelity sound system. As each decoy position was attacked, the electronic sleight of hand obligingly shut down for a millisecond, only to start up again from another remote site, also chosen for its expendability.

Meanwhile, the three radar data streams, travelling at the speed of light, fired down fibre optic cables to powerful computers housed within the nuclear bunker, where sophisticated software scanned successive frames for the fleeting silhouettes. High speed discriminator circuits eliminated spurious effects like electronic noise and slowly-moving foreground objects. The Swiss could ill afford to engage any adventurous red kites dropping in for early lunch.

With the static background signal electronically removed, any high speed foreground object betrayed its presence as clearly as a black fly skimming a white wall. Sophisticated tracking software then vectored each drone's position as a small blue arrow on the battlefield control screen. Eight pale blue arrows now eerily converged in radial formation on the institute.

Within a second of cresting the final line of sight contour, the eight drones had tactically conferred to a 99.99% assured destruction battleplan of their assigned targets, scarcely blinking electronically when a hundred yards ahead the ground lit up in a blaze of magnesium flares, launched vertically in a desperately futile attempt to distract their attentions. Nor did the drones flinch when the flares turned beneath them with suicidal g-force and come screaming after them, guided now by the peek-and-poke Ghost radars antennas. Nor when, against all odds, the puny rockets caught up, slipstreaming beneath each wing, their entire fuel reserves already spent and a puny 5% payload remaining, a mere 80 grams of Hexogen the size and shape of a golf ball.

But 80 grams of ultrahigh explosive can wreak significant damage, particularly to an object travelling 70 centimetres every millisecond. For one millisecond is what it takes for the drone's attitude control unit to respond to a badly deforming control surface. And it doesn't help much if at that instant, another 80 grams of Hexogen detonates beneath the other wing, and another 80 grams in front of the main sensor pod, knocking out the flight control sensors. With the drone flying blind and unstable, and the remaining flares rapidly catching up, eager for their brief explosive embrace, it is only a matter of milliseconds before the drone disintegrates catastrophically in the fierce air turbulence and crashes impotently into the steep hillside.

To the human onlooker, very little of the high speed drama is apparent, each drone appearing to engulf itself in a blaze of light and fall heavily to the ground like an angry insect. Nor was it apparent to billions of viewers who gawped at their screens in disbelief, as a myriad of random flashes lit up the Swiss hillside as the drones fell lamely from the sky in virtual formation.

Only later, when the Ghost images were processed and painstakingly repainted from false perspectives, and then slowed a thousand times, were excruciatingly clear images available for all, chronicling the loss of twenty-five billion dollars worth of elite coalition hardware in a matter of milliseconds. Never before in the field of human conflict, had so much been lost to so little before so many.

Yet still the battle was not over. For reasons never adequately explained by either side, a single drone flew unopposed through the hail of stinger bees, as the Swiss defences were rapidly christened. The final drone sped on unchallenged towards the institute and at the optimum instant, launched its spread of smart warheads towards each of its reassigned targets, for it was already electronically aware it was fighting alone.

Chapter 32

Weeks passed, and the GL4 website remained live and intact, coordinating data and world opinion on all aspects of the extraordinary events. Comment poured in on the sophisticated Swiss defence of the Flaubert Institute and the pointlessly savage attack by the USUK forces. Many tributes were paid to the brave Swiss Army, gallantly defending both the lives of their foreign guests and the democratic right of all humankind to free and immediate access to global information.

The astonishing effectiveness of the Swiss Ghost radar was the talk of defence departments around the world, rife with speculation on how, with a few homemade flares, the Swiss had humbled the most sophisticated efforts of the coalition forces. Nor were the Swiss slow to exploit the many discreet enquiries from around the world for flight data and re-engineered components of the drone wreckage.

There was even speculation, strenuously denied, that the Swiss had permitted the single drone's penetration as a purposeful scenario control, to publicly promote the effectiveness of their Ghost defence system, the cost of rebuilding the institute written off as a short-term high-yield investment by their burgeoning defence industry.

But life goes on, and it was the GL4 star gazers who provided the most critical data as they patiently correlated the orbits of tens of thousands of inbound comets. In a massive effort powered by René's distribution platform, nearly ten million supporters surrendered their computer's processing time and resources to calculating with unprecedented precision the orbits and destination of nearly sixty thousand inbound comets. It was a gigantic effort, with results instantly updated on GL4, as the whole world waited with bated breath each day for the *Exception*, a single errant comet which spelt the end for all Earthkind.

Some watersheds do not happen overnight, but accumulate gradually, more as a dam of silent evidence and public opinion. As millions then billions of minds assessed the data and judged for themselves, humankind found within itself a growing self-awareness as a single cohesive species, and the courage to demand due political recognition of the fact.

Meanwhile the superpowers maintained a stony silence on the matter, other than reiterating that sixty thousand inbound comets posed an unmistakable threat in anyone's language and one which only a massive global taskforce could conceivably address. The UN Security Council met in continuous closed session as one by one, world governments fell in line with the superpowers' call for unity and action. Only the Swiss held out for reasoned, calm and democratic behaviour.

After their pyrrhic victory with the Ghosts, the USUK coalition trod more lightly over world opinion and were mindful now to court the support of national leaders. If they entertained further thought of military action they wisely it kept to themselves, making every effort to foster an atmosphere of political trust and cooperation, sweetened as necessary with discreet financial arrangements, for in truth they were only talking to their own kind and the only real discussion was price.

Inevitably, the superpowers won their Charter for Global Security, after which the Global Operation Defence Squadron was a formality. And while the world's press, cynical and weary of the heavy handed treatment of global opinion, carped impotently from the sidelines of GOD squads and Charters for Global Senility, coalition leaders maintained a tight-lipped smile, quietly biding their time and talking up prospects of a new world order for peace and genuine prosperity for all. For the moment it seemed, banal normality had returned to the world's political stage.

One surprising innovation, which rapidly became a widespread and popular leisure activity, was the discovery by GL4's stargazers of the Virtual Observatory. By logging onto the GL4 observatory, users could surf the myriad of planets and stars catalogued in the globe's compendious image bank, from the comfort and safety of their laptop. Virtual trips to the moon and planets and weekend expeditions to the galactic centre quickly became a popular pastime for the general public.

Surfers reported they could see, hear and to some extent even feel their surroundings with astonishing realism. So convincing was the simulation that some authorities felt obliged to launch a series of public awareness campaigns. GL4 in particular was asked to preface each virtual tour with a liability waiver, informing by means of a large white banner and funereal black lettering the warning PERCEPTUAL OVERLOAD CAN KILL, a notion so preposterous that GL4 readily agreed, with huge success.

Soon it was discovered entirely new phenomena could be studied interactively, using the helpfully provided scientific tools and instrument panel. Learned works by unknown amateurs began flooding the scientific literature, detailing their astonishing discoveries with reams of careful measurements, summarising graphs and closely argued conclusions.

The initiative was fiercely criticised by professional scientists, incensed at hordes of GL4 amateurs trampling over their hallowed fields of learning. The old guard in particular argued bitterly that none of it was *real* science. But the young bloods were quick to defend their contributions, arguing the Virtual Observatory was simply yet one more amazing new tool for studying the cosmos. New techniques were always, by tradition, suspect in science. Are the observations real or an artefact of the new technology? Are the conclusions falsifiable? It was simply a matter for critical investigation, as it had always been down through the ages, from the invention of the telescope four centuries earlier to the modern anti-proton scannerscope of today.

GL4 authors simply prefaced their work with a qualifier, strangely echoing an earlier era of Riemannian mathematics. 'If the GL4 Portal is real, the following phenomenon has been observed in …' Soon, the qualification dwindled to a terse acronym, then disappeared entirely, as the powerful new tool was taken up by hard-pressed professionals finding themselves increasingly edged out from startling new fields of discovery.

Philosophical diehards raised the spectre of covert alien censorship, subtly perverting the course of human knowledge.

Mankind they declared, would rue the day it abdicated responsibility in the search for scientific truth. Young enthusiasts merely enquired sweetly of the last occasion philosophy felt inclined to test its wordy pronouncements with mundane observation and measurement.

Besides, what was so new about cosmic censorship? At worst, it was just one more censor, one which, so far, seemed hell-bent on supplying as much data as anyone could reasonably handle. How was it so different to renting time on the Hubble or CERN? Apart from being free of course, and available to all. Philosophers shook their heads wisely. No such thing as a free lunch, they warned, determined as ever to have the last word.

And so it was only a question of time before some intrepid stargazer decided to pay NERO a virtual visit. It was while pulling out of a high-gee inverted fin-rattling dive that she sighted it, for Pollyanna was more a frustrated galactic fighter pilot than a dedicated observer of the skies. As she rocketed low and inverted over enemy defences, she caught fleeting sight of a beautiful pink oval, rushing past high and to starboard. She checked her headlong plummet with an accurate split-arsed turn, then doubled back low over her bomb run, only to discover the oval was now flashing red and green. She backed off in one smooth manoeuvre, parking just beyond the anti-proton cannon range to monitor and report the aliens' cunning new tactic.

But after almost five seconds of complete inactivity (for in truth, Pollyanna was barely nine years old and had not yet had breakfast) she decided to jet out. Time was pressing. She desperately needed to rejoin her squadron of junior cadets now fighting for their young lives in a last ditch attempt to repel the alien invaders and save the blue-green planet.

She trimmed her jet flares and was about to rejoin the fray, when to her amazement she saw the entire oval begin to slide open. She carefully searched the sinister black interior for signs of stars which would indicate the enemy had perfected the dreaded star gate, a breakthrough they'd undoubtedly use to swamp Earth's defences with millions of laser firing glob pods, the most fearsome gunship in the aliens' arsenal. Her fingers tensed purposefully, readying themselves over the fire control panel.

For a further three seconds she agonised on how best to proceed. She was about to approach cautiously when, with a loud gasp, she slipped from her kitchen stool, nearly dropping her mother's laptop. The black interior was lighting up. Powerful violet-white panels flickered on, brightly illuminating thousands of levels down through the interior. As light continued to power on into the distance, Pollyanna began to feel acutely disoriented from staring down the bright precipitous shaft, right through the alien ship and possibly out the other side.

With a caution never previously admitted in her long flying career, she edged carefully towards the opening, continually cautioning herself it was all simulation. At any moment she could hit the *pause* button, slam the lid shut and drink her cool reviving cola, though she already knew she would never abandon her young warriors. Slowly she edged in, scanning the walls for clues and the first sign of an alien ambush.

Should she decide an up and down now, in the event she needed to manoeuvre instinctively? She prudently decided down was under her bottom and stared into the distance. Ahead she could see a large arrow, flashing alternately red and green and wondered once more if this was some generic form of alien signal. Proceed with caution, she decided. She did.

Distance was becoming a problem as she realised she had no sense of scale. Almost immediately her young courage faltered. She stopped the craft and turned about to check her progress. A black fist clamped fiercely over her young heart when she saw the massive oval door drawing shut. She closed her eyes and breathed deeply, squeezing the bridge of her nose as she'd seen her mother do in a downtown traffic jam. After a few seconds she opened them again. The door had closed. She calmly turned her craft around and headed deep into the alien interior.

She must have travelled ten miles she computed, and was just beginning to feel a little of her old self again, when she saw something that almost made her wet her pants. Ahead, maybe two hundred yards, from what she preferred to call the roof, hung a huge alien signboard of some description. She edged cautiously up to it and was already drifting gently past, intent once more on the terrain ahead, when she stopped abruptly and re-examined the sign.

It wasn't that the symbols were unclear or even that she failed to grasp their meaning. It was precisely because she found herself acting implicitly on its message, that she stamped so violently on her retros. She stared long and hard at the holographic signboard, which indicated with crystal clarity that she might now consider turning left for London, right for Washington, up for Moscow, down for Beijing, or proceed ahead for All Other Directions. A sixth arrow, Return To Earth, pointed back the way she had come. It was de-activated.

It was at this point she freely admits her courage failed her. Or, as she preferred to rationalize later, it was perhaps more the case that as a hard-headed tactician, she had already computed the strategic value of turning back. Head for base and report, eat her Coco Pops and return with reinforcements. First though, she had to test the exit route with the same careful professionalism.

Her return was uneventful, save for a heart stopping eternity while she waited for the large oval door to open. The moment relived vivid memories of a grainy movie she had watched once with Granpaps, recalling the heart chilling words 'Open the pod bay door, Hal.' But Hal, if that really was the doorman's name, was either asleep or AWOL.

She told herself sagely, in the seconds that stretched to consume her entire childhood, that waiting was probably an integral part of adult life. 'Opening an exterior space door is a major undertaking, not something to be entered into or undertaken lightly,' she intoned quietly to herself, quoting from her imaginary space cadet manual. She sat patiently, trying to recall just how long she had waited outside, and realising she hadn't the faintest idea.

Dark thoughts raced through her mind. Had she checked the oxygen supply before gallantly jetting out to defend her brave young charges? What was her current fuel status, weapons readiness, hull integrity and solar flare activity? Under what circumstances might she consider breaking radio silence? What were the latest military protocols on being taken prisoner?

Eventually to her immense relief, and she admits, to a loud accompanying yelp, she saw the door begin to move. She waited calmly until it was almost fully open, then headed slowly out into the star studded blackness of space.

A sudden overwhelming urge to stand on her jets and scream mach 500 for home seized her, but at the last moment and with commendable presence of mind, she parked her craft and turned carefully to observe NERO once more. Pollyanna smiled her gentlest of smiles as she saw the shaft door begin to close. Then she turned, and with an exuberant return of girlish delight, squealed full pelt for home, thinking she might just land out at JFK for the sheer hell of it and buy her mum a Manhattan. Whatever that was.

* * *

When Pollyanna's discovery hit GL4 it caused an overnight sensation, the website recording a billion hits in just two hours, as news of her incredible experience spread exponentially down the personal contacts tree. With each contact linking on average to eight others, it took barely eleven waves of messaging to alert the entire world to Pollyanna's amazing adventure.

Her naive and unedited recording of the entire experience immediately endeared her to billions of fans, as even her hesitation and fear was evident in the video replay. Suddenly it seemed, the entire world wanted to explore NERO and travelogue its cities and byways. If the young Pollyanna, with her flushed cheeks and flailing pigtails, was disappointed at not exploring deeper into NERO's interior, she gave no sign of it, showing genuine delight and a beguiling patience with the endless media attention, all the while offering sound professional advice to her young followers for safely exploring the new world for themselves. To this day GL4 still carries the historic footage, now famously entitled 'Freaking Jeanie' after one of her rare but audible expletives.

Strangely, few major surprises awaited the waves of intrepid young explorers who quickly returned to explore and map the New World. For a New World was what it seemed to them, in cheerful defiance of the sour faced professionals who insisted NERO could at best be categorised only a minor planetoid. But with the cubic capacity to swallow the world's major centres of population and industrial heartlands, no one took any notice, and

NERO leapt to global status overnight, one headline famously announcing "Aliens speak the Queen's English!"

Chapter 33

The foreign minister for the Eastern Democratic Republic of African Free Confederated States had spoken for a full fifteen minutes in her gushing faltering English, but barely had anyone listened beyond the first sentence. It was the price to pay for unanimous support of resolution 8223. That of course, and the newly acquired squadron of obsolete F111's. The prime minister's eyes glazed over as he glanced surreptitiously at his watch and noted with grim satisfaction the American president doing likewise.

A text surfaced silently on his private display. *The Eagle Has Landed And The Cuckoo Is Hatched.* The prime minister flinched, more at the grammar than the content, which in truth he had been expecting for more than an hour. He allowed himself a brief moment of reflective doubt, but there was no going back. There never had been really, not since the first fateful moment he had thrown in his lot with the American decision to build the superbomb. In the event, even that had proved a compromise. After running out of time and spending an absolute fortune, they had settled on proven technology. Now the device had been safely delivered and it was simply a matter of waiting.

In a strange way it was reminiscent of all the thrillers he'd read as a boy, in which the murderer feels obliged to carefully explain why the victim must die. He wondered if it was ever quite like that in reality. Surely the victim would be despatched at the earliest opportunity; in an unpredictable world it made sense to eliminate uncertainty as quickly as possible. He tried to recall the reason why the fuse was so long and whose responsibility the decision had been. It irked him that his normally perfect memory now failed him, as it had on a number of occasions lately. Something to do with the relentless pressure of leadership no doubt. That, and events cascading unpredictably, one after another.

At least now they had finally acted. A decision had been taken and the bomb deployed. Nobody could change the course of history now. Somehow the simplification of choice pleased him. He suddenly recalled the technicalities for the one hour delay.

It was decided that if at all possible, the superbomb should detonate near the centre of the object for maximum effect. The craft would be carefully making its way there now, patiently following the central shaft. He wondered at the irony of the aliens naming the central city Hong Kong, and whether there would be any comeback from the Chinese. He doubted it. The four super powers were in it together, fully committed to ridding themselves of the alien menace once and for all. Well, for a thousand years at least, someone else would have to deal with it after that. They had done their bit, safeguarded the purity of the human species from alien influence. He mused on how history might judge him: judicious and calm, standing at the brink, wisely counselling the fate of mankind.

Though enormous, and several orders of magnitude greater than anything previously detonated, the superbomb was still puny relative to the size of its target and NERO would probably survive intact. The real superbomb was still decades away, despite the frantic technological effort and funding it had consumed. In the end, they had run out of time and switched midstream to a vastly scaled up conventional device, a massive cluster of hydrogen bombs clad in a thick dense blanket of highly radioactive isotopes. On detonation, the incandescent radioactivity would spread supersonically throughout the interior, irreversibly contaminating every surface.

The exact cocktail of radioactive pollutants had to be painstakingly computed so as to sustain a ferocious level of radioactivity for a thousand years. Apparently, this was no easy task as the popular press had supposed, when the spectre of dirty bombs was first raised in the public arena. But then, public opinion was always easier to sway than scientific fact. Not for the first time in his career, the prime minister despaired at the unreasonable immutability of scientific law. He carefully checked his watch.

The foreign minister was still at it, which had to be something of a record. Not for the foreign minister of course, who was obviously quite capable of speaking for weeks, but for the council to permit her. But then it was important the debate continue right up to the eleventh hour. Under the circumstances, eleven seemed a strange number for such a historic moment.

The device was already primed. It had been of course, the moment the huge bay door had sealed behind the Space Delivery Platform, as the yanks with their insatiable appetite for redundant syllables insisted on calling it. Once primed, the bomb would detonate in one hour, or sooner if tampered with. And once primed, nobody, not even God Almighty, could stop it. Remarkable measures had been taken to prevent any one – or thing – from interfering with detonation. Countdown circuits with quadruple redundancy were fused in situ on priming, and all communication circuits vaporized. Even NORAD was locked out of the abort process, on the faint possibility that the president might suffer a severe mental seizure and change of heart. The decision did not sit lightly with either party, who from time immemorial had jealously guarded their right to press a big red button on occasion. But in the end, scientific caution prevailed, amid fears the encryption protocols might conceivably be compromised if the aliens possessed a quantum computer. He wondered if they had already discovered their desperate plight and were now agonising over the final fifteen minutes of indecision. In an odd way he felt a strong sense of affinity for them.

He started, as a faint shadow passed over his desktop, momentarily fearing he had fallen asleep. Not that it mattered of course, the debate was being conducted in the utmost secrecy. Still, one could never be absolutely certain these days. He glanced up to check the foreign minister's progress.

* * *

She was still going strong, in contrast to a good number of delegates who were now sound asleep, the more experienced bolt upright in their stress relieving chairs displaying fixed expressions of concerned judicial debate. As usual, one or two delegates were examining the heavens in a desperate plea for inspiration or possibly even divine intervention.

Certainly something seemed to be attracting their attention, as the prime minister found himself glancing upwards in sympathy. It took a moment for his eyes to adjust properly, so dark and indeterminate was the scene. And when his eyes focussed, it took another moment for his mind to place the object. Even then, a numbing shockwave of disbelief flooded his brain as he fought desperately to control the impossible confusion of thoughts.

For just five metres above the foreign minister's head hovered a life-sized apparition of the coalition's space delivery platform. As the seconds crawled by and his brain grudgingly admitted further detail, he noticed the image was slowly rotating around the vertical axis. Surface features too were becoming more evident, as if a magician were slowly conjuring them into existence. As reason gradually returned to his oxygen starved brain he felt a sudden insane stab of anger that the Americans should pull such a stunt without prior consultation or warning.

He glanced over at the American desk only to find the president staring insanely back. The prime minister shook his head fractionally and returned his gaze to the image. Even the foreign minister was silent now, gawping upwards with a look of maligned distrust. The vast assembly hall froze in one heart stopping moment, as every head craned upwards, each delegate privately accepting for the first time in their professional career to having not the slightest idea of what was happening.

Inevitably, someone directly beneath the apparition upset a bottle of sparkling water and the resulting shock wave precipitated the assembly hall into a frenzy of legs towards the nearest emergency exit, in what delegates hoped might not appear undue haste. Only the coalition delegates remained glued to their seats, gripped with courageous indecision.

The hologram, if that's what it was, had rotated still further now, bringing the cockpit module into sight, though the glare reflecting off the thick glass windscreen made it quite impossible to see inside. As if reading their thoughts, the craft rotated a little further until it faced the small knot of delegates clustered around the American desk, and stopped. Two dumbfounded faces stared out motionlessly from behind the glass.

"They are watching us," breathed the prime minister.

"Of course not," snapped the president derisively. "An apparition. A clever stunt."

"Hell of a stunt," murmured the prime minister. The president reached slowly for his tumbler and with great deliberation and sense of occasion hurled it at the cockpit, unfortunately missing by quite a wide margin and frightening an elderly security guard.

"Passed right through. A hologram," snapped the president.

Unfortunately, an enthusiastic aide, who was not quite so quick-witted but of surer aim, scored a direct hit on the windscreen, shattering his tumbler into a shower of tiny fragments which cascaded to the ground. The two occupants gazed dumbstruck at each other.

"What do these fuckers think they're doing," yelled the president almost incoherently, just as the two occupants stood to attention and saluted, courageously attempting to stand bolt upright and retain eye contact.

"I imagine they think you are attempting to attract their attention," intoned the prime minister drily, now quite carried away with the sheer banality of it all.

"Get NORAD on a secure line," snapped the president.

"But ..."

"Do it man! Tell them to abort the countdown!"

"Sir, the weapon is primed. There is no abort. And NORAD is in lockdown ..."

The president squinted briefly in concentration. "Right. Let's get out of here. Better come with us, prime minister."

The prime minister looked at him incredulously. "You don't understand, do you? It's over."

"Never say over, prime minister. That's what's makes us a great nation. Always will. We'll find a way."

"And the other ten million New Yorkers?"

"Helicopter standing by on the roof, mister president. We need you out of here and secured."

The president glared once more at the cockpit. The two pilots were motionless, saluting their president.

"Patching you through to NORAD now, mister president."

"I'll take it in-flight," snapped the president, as the delegation broke into a run, heading in tactical formation for the stairs.

* * *

The prime minister watched the two astronauts salute their departing leaders. *They were never told*, he thought. *And now they have no idea they've returned it.* He sat down heavily and studied his watch. After a moment, Tompkins appeared in the door way, spoke briefly to the guard and walked over towards him.

"Hello prime minister, I saw you were still here. The entire event is being streamed live on GL4. They seem as completely gobsmacked as the rest of us. I asked the guard to patch it through."

The display lit up in various windows, mostly recording the frantic scenes outside. The one static scene showed Tompkins and the prime minister sitting alone in the vast assembly hall, apparently staring at camera. The presenter seemed beside herself, unable to decide on which scene to commentate, and desperately trying to recollect from which state she was reporting.

Another window showed the scene within NORAD command centre, if the caption was to be believed. A large digital display read 00:04:28 and was counting down by the second. Fresh faced young officers in crisp fatigues moved smartly between the racks of displays and communication equipment. The prime minister checked his watch.

"NORAD is broadcasting live for fuck's sake ... has everyone gone completely insane? Good Lord. Whoever said they lacked a sense of humour."

Yet another window showed the scenes of abject panic outside the UN building, with traffic brought to a standstill by ranks of ambulances, fire squads and platoons of FBI marksmen, decked head to toe in high visibility siege armour and arranged about in grim formations. Squads of police officers stood by authoritatively, bravely attempting to calm the fleeing waves of delegates as they scattered in every direction, randomly penetrating the ranks of their protectors with diplomatic immunity, and all the while screaming directives and invectives with equal abandon at their mobile phones and anyone else who crossed their path.

"What do you think Tompkins?"

"I think we're done for, sir."

"I'm inclined to agree. Come on, let's put these poor sods out of their misery," the prime minister sighed wearily, waving at the still saluting pilots to disembark. "I can't see how things can get much worse."

At that moment an elderly security guard approached them, respectfully holding out a small object. "The remote, sir. In case you required the sound."

"Very decent of you. Thanks," Tompkins replied, without a trace of irony.

* * *

" ... meanwhile the Pentagon is strenuously denying accusations that *Ambassador Earth* is literally a flying superbomb, apparently unaware that the craft's specifications, blueprints and procurement video have been plastered over the internet for the last hour. Earlier claims that the craft was a sophisticated communications centre, were dramatically discredited when ..."

"We must tell them, prime minister."

"Tell who?"

"Them. The Aliens. Whoever directed it here."

"Do you think they don't already know?"

"Tell them what they've done – what we've done. Ask them to stop the countdown. Perhaps if they can redirect it here, they can redirect it somewhere else. The Moon maybe."

"Yes, perhaps. But why would they want to? We sent it to destroy them. It's our problem. My God, ten million human beings. The cream of the world's diplomats and political leaders. No one will escape in time."

"The president perhaps."

"The president perhaps, yes. How will he live with himself, knowing he devastated New York and made it uninhabitable for a thousand years? How will any of us?"

The two astronauts joined them. "What is happening sir?"

"You unknowingly freighted a massive nuclear bomb into NERO. It has been returned to sender – unopened. We have about two minutes. Will you sit with us commander, perhaps it will save the world."

"Do you know," the prime minister intoned sadly into the enveloping silence, "it is a strange and wonderful thing that with so little time, there is so little to say. A little music would be helpful." They sat silently, lost in private thoughts.

"Oh God, Tompkins. What is that?"

"It sounds like the Moonlight Sonata, prime minister. I always found it quite funereal, myself."

"Very personal thing, humour," sighed the prime minister finally.

Chapter 34

The UN catastrophe and its political fallout, coincided with NERO's arrival at Solar L1, the principal Lagrangian point a million miles out from Earth towards the Sun. Solar L1 is the major nexus of keyhole orbits and gateway to the interplanetary superhighway, along which a spacecraft can cruise on low energy transfer orbits to virtually any point of the solar system for as little 25m/s – the kick from a modest serve in tennis.

The superbomb did not detonate at the designated time, or at any subsequent time. To this day *Ambassador Earth* and its payload hovers motionlessly above the floor of the general assembly hall. Early attempts to examine and disarm the mechanism were abandoned when volunteer engineers came up against impenetrable new technology maintaining the craft in stasis position. Even the shattered remains of the crystal glass tumblers remain where they fell, now permanently entombed in acrylic for school children to ogle in wide-eyed amazement.

Giant plasma screens recount with crystal fidelity and acute political discomfort, every world drama leading up to the arrival of NERO. The UN building itself is now a global museum, dedicated to human tolerance and species diversity, after the world's politicians and diplomats felt unable to function at their best beneath the *Shadow*.

That honour now returns once more to Genève, which hosts a new world governing body, the Global Peace Senate. The former British prime minister, its First Secretary General, creditably undertook the challenge of hauling the politics of global division and coercion out of the political stone age, though whether the political charabanc ever reaches the twenty-first century remains to be seen. The previous era of *Might is Right* lasted a hundred million years.

The vast majority of New Yorkers refused to abandon their city, scornfully despising the fleeing cream of humanity, and subsequently resisting all notion of its return. They live with pride beneath the *Shadow* as a living memorial to tolerance and peace. The city itself has become a cultural centre for global humanities, a Mecca for the coming of age in political pubescence.

Ben's mission remains incomplete. The message was not completely translated, for the simple reason that it was not completely written, and may never be. The discovery that the message is actually part of a self-evolving program, continually sampling its cognitive environment and updating itself, came as a complete shock to many.

A large number of David's *why* questions remain to be answered. No aliens have ever been seen, either within NERO or anywhere else, and the sensation that many observers describe as a presence is now scientifically discounted, officially at least.

A general consensus on the alien phenomenon has yet to emerge. A commonly expressed view echoes David's sentiments, that a key role of the alien intervention is to offer humankind a timely assist in its hazardous transition to cosmic status, a breathing space perhaps to develop the social responsibilities commensurate with its advancing technology.

However, a minority faction holds a more sombre view. They interpret NERO's presence as the first tangible sign of *Cosmic Migration*, the mass exodus of advanced civilisations towards the less inhabited backwaters of the galaxy, bringing in their wake all the civilising benefits of sustained economic growth, law and order, education, defence and galactic taxation. They argue quite convincingly that not all intelligent lifeforms are expected to show 'species tolerance' and that mankind may well yet have occasion to welcome the long arm of the galactic law, should hordes of malevolent species turn up one day in their cosmic backyard.

It has to be said mankind's acceptance into polite galactic society, and its undisputed civilising effects on human behaviour, have yet to attract universal political appeal. Certainly nothing like the enthusiasm generated for colonial development, national expansionism and global economic enslavery witnessed in the industrial era leading up to NERO's arrival. On the other hand, few humans see NERO as the son of God in any shape or form, or that its ultimate purpose requires a complete act of faith.

Whatever its long-term purpose, only time will tell if NERO proves a sentimental hope on the part of its creators, a triumph of hope perhaps, over a more common and tragic experience. For better or worse, humankind's destiny still rests entirely with itself, though the big fish in the small pond innocence has gone forever.

Ben became the first president of the New World when it was discovered NERO did not respond well to the original appointee. He lives and works with his wife Frances and three young children in Hong Kong NERO, administering the colonisation and development of the New Worlds.

After a short spell of rehabilitation, René returned to her cottage in the Alps. She lives there contentedly, writing children's books for a modest living, sketching wild flowers and going for long enchanting walks with her teenage daughter.

Politicians still dream of their return from superfluous exile, but while full and free democratic access to their every word and deed continues, their dreams are likely to remain just that, having yet to enthusiastically embrace the levels of surveillance and personal intrusion previously enjoyed by their subjects.

Like much of the alien phenomena, NERO remains a work in progress. To date it is a huge powerhouse and energy resource, rich in rare minerals, heavy metals and new world technologies, a technological infoplex for the booming space industry now serving Earth and the New World colonies. The interplanetary superhighways are open for business, courtesy of NERO Logistics. Thriving communities have been established on Mars, Venus and three major asteroids, though conditions on the New Worlds still pose enormous challenges as Earthkinds adapt to ever greater extremes of survival.

NERO's signboards to the more distant planets and star systems remain inactive, their corridors coming to an abrupt halt after a few hundred metres. Perhaps humankind is not yet quite ready. When, or perhaps what will activate them, remains to be seen. As is the case obviously for the arrivals lounge.

Meantimes, everyone is welcome aboard Pollyanna's voyage of discovery, to acquaint themselves with the cosmic myriad of planetary systems, their diverse inhabitants and fascinating cultures.

Epilogue

He was sat back to the wall, his legs dangling lazily over the edge. She stared hard, then eased down gently beside him, slowly understanding her dream. She sighed deeply, reaching up to smooth his unruly locks.

"You came," he said softly.
"How is this possible?"
He smiled his old smile.
"*Why?*" she smiled.
"We must travel."
"Are you real?"
"A particle facsimile."
"Am I dreaming?"
"A little, in one dimension of your time."
"Travel, where?"
"Wherever we wish – I will pilot."
"Now I know I'm dreaming!"
"A good instructor. Young, flailing pigtails, very patient."
"How long do we …"
"It is relative, René. Perhaps a week. A gift – one of two."
"And then … ?"
"You will see," he smiled. "It is good. Don't be afraid."

Lightning Source UK Ltd.
Milton Keynes UK
UKOW031937040113

204453UK00006B/263/P